Nanibala's Belief

September 4, 2015
Mamie,
I've enjoyed
meeting you again
after all these years.
Enjoy the read!
Constance Mukherjee
(Patricia R. LaGrange)

CONSTANCE MUKHERJEE

BALBOA.
PRESS
A DIVISION OF HAY HOUSE

Balboa Press books may be ordered through booksellers or by contacting:

Balboa Press
A Division of Hay House
1663 Liberty Drive
Bloomington, IN 47403
www.balboapress.com
1 (877) 407-4847

Because of the dynamic nature of the Internet, any web addresses or links contained in this book may have changed since publication and may no longer be valid. The views expressed in this work are solely those of the author and do not necessarily reflect the views of the publisher, and the publisher hereby disclaims any responsibility for them.

The author of this book does not dispense medical advice or prescribe the use of any technique as a form of treatment for physical, emotional, or medical problems without the advice of a physician, either directly or indirectly. The intent of the author is only to offer information of a general nature to help you in your quest for emotional and spiritual well-being. In the event you use any of the information in this book for yourself, which is your constitutional right, the author and the publisher assume no responsibility for your actions.

Any people depicted in stock imagery provided by Thinkstock are models, and such images are being used for illustrative purposes only.
Certain stock imagery © Thinkstock.

Print information available on the last page.

ISBN: 978-1-5043-2786-2 (sc)
ISBN: 978-1-5043-2787-9 (e)

Balboa Press rev. date: 05/13/2015

CONTENTS

Thank you to my husband, Ajit, for his support and undying love.
Thank you to our son, Misha, for bringing me joy.
Thank you to our lovely dog, Madison, for inspiring me to find these stories.

The goal of all life is spiritual wisdom.

-Bhagavad Gita

Acknowledgement

I am forever grateful for the guidance, support and friendship
of my writer's workshop group.

Pat Caloia

Melody Deal

Alice Huston

Shel Weinstein

***

Thank you to Anne Allen, a soulful photographer,
who took all of the photos in this book.
Bonjourimage.com

***

Thank you to Ranu Mukherjee, a talented artist and kindred spirit,
who designed and painted the original cover art for Nanibala's Belief.
RanuMukherjee.com

INDIA meets INDIANA

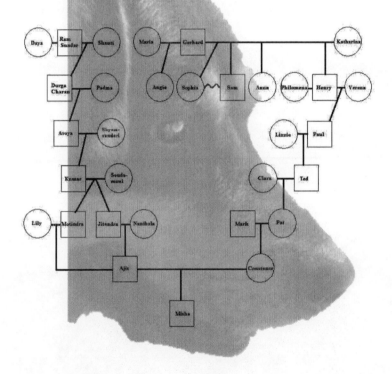

India meets Indiana

PROLOGUE

NOT THE BEGINNING

California 2036

In a quiet corner of the blue cottage by the sea, a young woman turned to the epigraph page of the yellowed manuscript. She read, *The goal of all life is spiritual wisdom. —The Bhagavad Gita.* A powerful energy emanated from the depth of her soul as she mouthed the words, exhaling a whisper on the phrase "spiritual wisdom." Pria peered through her window toward the sky melting into the vast Pacific waters. The marine layer which weighed down the shore began to lift.

Unfurling her legs, Pria rose from the wing backed chair. She grabbed the pink jacket to shield her body from the onshore flow of salty ocean winds. Gathering her thick dark mane into a ponytail, she bounded down the weathered outside steps heading toward the shoreline. Without warning, a breaching whale broke the surface of the calm ocean with volcanic force. The animal pointed its snout to the sky, revealing its individual white markings. The whale retreated back into the water with barely a sound.

Pria laughed aloud with joy at the startling sight. She soon spotted four additional whales swimming near her vantage point on the shore. The huge mammals seemed dangerously close to the beach, but didn't hurry to swim out to the deeper sea. Nor did they seem rushed to resume the journey north to their eventual destination near the Arctic Circle.

A wet-suited surfer swam to the whales, leaving his board behind. As he played in their midst, his dark head became a dot in the ocean, disappearing, then reappearing, between the crests of the waves. He returned toward the shore, making the transition to land with long slow strides. The surfer gave the appearance of a primordial amphibian evolving into a human being.

Pria whispered a grateful goodbye as the whales moved into the lagoon beyond. One ethereal blow in the middle of the circular bay rose slightly above the grey water line. Small in the vast ocean, gentle and translucent in its spray, and fleeting in time, the spout almost seemed a dream. The magnificent creatures had bid her farewell.

Still enchanted by the wonder of the whales, Pria returned to the warmth of the cottage. She wrapped herself in a long waffle-weave robe, tying the belt in a loose knot. She prepared hot herbal tea sweetened with honey, accompanied by three crisp lemon biscuits. The manuscript lay on the side table where she'd left it. Pria sat, sipping her tea, pondering the epigraph in a new light. *The goal of all life is spiritual wisdom.* All life. She had previously skipped over the word all, concentrating instead on the goal of life... spiritual wisdom. She wondered if the whales found wisdom more easily than humans.

Pria positioned the tea cup on its saucer, evoking the auditory memory of the clink of Grandmother's favorite mug on the tiled patio table. Her grandparents lived in their casita built on a corner of her parent's property, under tall thin Cyprus trees her grandfather called Dehradun pines. As a teenager, she had often visited her grandparents after school. She pictured her grandmother sitting on the patio one such day.

***

Light streamed through the tangle of paper thin scarlet bougainvillea intertwined in the arbor trellis. Rays of sunshine spotlighted Grandmother's curly golden hair, drawing bees from the nearby sweet smelling roses to investigate the sparkle. Between sips of tea, Grandma gazed at the blue sky as if looking for answers. That was the day Grandfather died.

Pria felt devastated by the loss. She had never experienced the death of a loved one. Even the family dog had been part of her life since she and her two brothers emerged one after another on a crisp fall morning.

With Grandmother holding tight to an urn containing her husband's ashes, Pria, her brothers, and parents rode a small boat toward the islands. The family huddled around their matriarch as she poured his remains over the side into the sea. They stood mesmerized by the ashes scattering to the winds and disappearing into the ocean waters. A small wave tipped the boat, causing

Pria to collapse on the floor, more out of grief than loss of balance. Pria and Grandmother sat on a bench. Grandma hugged the innocent girl to her chest.

"Don't be sad, Pria. Your grandfather lived a good life while on this earth."

"I just want him to pinch my cheeks again."

Grandmother tightened her arms around Pria, rocking her to the rhythm of the ride. Nearer to shore, she gently shook her grieving granddaughter and pointed toward the middle of the ocean. A defined diagonal line extended across the water from near the rocky shore toward the islands. On one side of the dividing line, the water sheened a dark grey-blue, blending into the ocean. In contrast, the shore side shone like a fine cut Indian turquoise gem.

"Pria, the sharply divided colors of the ocean can be compared to existence. Life on one side, death on the other. The two appear to be different, separated; yet under the surface, only one big ocean exists. We are destined to live a spiritual life on a physical plane."

"I don't understand, Grandma."

"Nobody really does, honey."

***

The next week Grandma invited her granddaughter for a drive up the coast.

"Where are we going, Grandma?"

"To a special place that may help us accept Grandpa's passing," Grandma said.

"What place?"

"You will know soon enough. For now, let's enjoy the journey."

The highway turned inland near Point Mugu, toward the slate-blue mountains shrouded in morning mist. Perfect raised rows of strawberries stretched forever across the Oxnard plain. Like an old hippie, Grandmother belted out the Beatle's classic *Strawberry Fields Forever*. But she quieted when passing the condo where she and Grandfather had lived for many years, before moving to Los Angeles to help with the triplets.

Pria and her grandmother watched the scenery unfold, each lost in her own world. North of Santa Barbara, they parked off the main road and walked along the narrow dirt path. They passed a tree bent to the ground in an arc, reminding Grandmother of elaborate Japanese garden bridges crossing small streams. The sun highlighted a tree blooming in yellow mystery flowers, prompting a brief pause of admiration. Further along the path, Pria found a tree with three equal size forks stemming from near the base. She christened it the triplet tree.

The peeling paint on a wooden information sign rendered it impossible to read. A charmingly grumpy old man, a docent it turned out, pointed them toward the grove. He explained that most of the butterflies had previously departed for their final destination. Soon the path became defined on one side with wooden fences, which led them toward a vantage point overlooking a narrow, but relatively steep canyon. The last of the monarchs hung in clusters high above in a eucalyptus tree. Grandma and Pria observed a few fluttering around near the top of the canopy.

"I wanted to bring you here, Pria, to see the home of the monarch. The insect starts out as an egg containing a tiny gold and black striped caterpillar. In the course of becoming an adult, it sheds its outgrown skin several times." Grandma gazed into the canyon.

"We studied monarchs in biology class, Grandma, but I've never seen them in their natural habitat."

"It's magical, isn't it? The caterpillar self-attaches to a branch and wraps itself in a green cocoon where it undergoes metamorphosis. When the cocoon is shed, the caterpillar has transformed into an adult butterfly. It's a powerful symbol of rebirth."

Grandmother and Pria began to hike beside the fenced ridge path encircling the home of the monarchs. They craned their necks skyward, gazing toward the upper branches of the rough barked trees. Grandmother stopped to rest her neck and straighten her posture. She happened to look down and cautioned her granddaughter.

"Pria, watch your step. A butterfly is lying spread-winged on the path."

"Is it alive?"

"It may simply be resting in preparation for its next flight."

They followed the trail through the grove to the brown grassy hillside. Grandmother stopped to turn around.

"Take a look at the canyon. From here it looks unassuming, insignificant."

Pria glanced back. "You'd never know the butterflies live there."

They continued on. Grandmother bore left at the fork.

"Are you sure this is the right way?" asked Pria.

"I'm following my instinct."

"What if we get lost?"

"I'm not too worried. We'll eventually find our way."

They meandered to the edge of the sea. The sun dipped behind the clouds, changing Grandmother's mood from one of observation to reflection. A small round break in the clouds allowed a peek of the clear sky above. A shaft of sunlight threaded through the hole, forming a patch of brightly lit sapphire water in the midst of the vast grey ocean. The hole widened, enveloping Pria and Grandmother in streaming rays of the sun.

Grandmother spoke softly. "Your grandfather was special, Pria. Sometimes when he stood in front of the sink washing dinner dishes, he sang long intricate Indian ragas. He'd close his eyes during a high pitched run of notes, and I'd stop whatever I was doing to listen."

She took Pria's hand. "Following his long morning shower, he'd use his index finger to write the symbol *Om* on the foggy bathroom window. I will miss the mystery of him."

Pria said, "You really loved him, didn't you, Grandma?"

Tears welled up in Grandmother's eyes. "You're an old soul, Pria. Yes, I loved him very much. I like to think that Grandpa's essence is still alive in another form, like the stages of the butterfly."

Out of nowhere a lone monarch appeared, flitting circles around them. "Life is indeed full of possibilities," said Grandmother.

***

Years passed. Again, Pria faced the loss of balance in her life. Three college friends asked her to a holiday lunch celebration, but a final exam prevented her from joining them. The girls hit a patch of ice, and slid into oblivion. Pria moved back home to recover from the shock, having completed all but a few classes needed for her degree.

That winter, Pria spent much time in the comfort of the casita. One day, Grandmother cupped Pria's strained face, peering into her reddened eyes.

"I don't understand why they died and I lived," Pria said.

7

The old woman walked to the natural cherry wood china cabinet in the corner of her casita. "Perhaps you have more to learn on this earth."

She reached up to switch on the cabinet lighting, and stood looking through the glass doors. "I like to study these heirlooms from my family in Indiana, or those from your grandfather's forebears in India. I feel the ancestors speaking to me...and through me."

"I've always been fascinated by your treasures, Grandma."

"Did you know that I wrote about the ancestors who owned these keepsakes?"

"Dad mentioned something about it, but I don't know the details."

Grandmother tugged on the tiny doorknobs, rattling the glass doors and mementos displayed on the shelves. She bent down, reaching into the bottom of the cabinet. "I've been waiting to share this with you, Pria."

She retrieved a light grey file box tied with a blue satin ribbon. "I've owned this box since 2008, when I took my first writing class at Indiana University. It contains the manuscript of a novel I wrote about the ancestors." Grandma hugged the box to her chest. "Let's go out to the terrace."

Grandma set the box on the colorful patio table. She gently pinched the free end of the bow between her thumb and index finger, then slowly pulled through the air until the knot untied. The shiny satin ribbon waved in the breeze before she placed it into her sweater pocket. Grandmother lightly juggled the lid with both hands, releasing it from the box.

A half-size manila envelope lay on top of the manuscript. Pria slid a multi-folded piece of yellowed paper out of the envelope and began to unfurl the many layers, being careful not to tear the fragile sheet. Grandma watched Pria spread it out on the patio table to reveal a four foot length torn from a blank newspaper roll. On it, a timeline of the family's history, dating back to the early 1800's, was detailed in Grandmother's hand.

"I drew this when I first conceived of my book," said Grandma.

Pria barely glanced at the timeline before loose papers fluttering in the grey box captured her attention.

"These are drafts I couldn't bear to throw away," Grandma said. She laid the notes and timeline to the side, weighting them with a heart stone she kept near the potted succulents on the table. Then she stared into the box. "Looking at this manuscript takes me to my sacred space."

Pria touched Grandmother's arm. "I'm honored you're sharing this with me. Thank you."

"I'm the one who needs to thank *you*. I take more joy in sharing my manuscript with you than you will ever understand." She slid her arm around Pria's waist and kissed her on the cheek.

"What prompted you to write the book, Grandma?"

Grandmother sat down and motioned for Pria to sit in the patio chair beside her.

"Your grandfather's Hindu mother, Nanibala, sparked the idea. She believed if a pet comes to you in an unusual way, it is a reincarnation of an ancestor. She instilled the same belief in your grandfather.

"Your father, Misha, adopted our dog, Maddie, from the pound a few days before her scheduled euthanization. Misha moved to LA for work and couldn't keep her, so we inherited her. Your grandfather thought Maddie met the criteria of coming to us in an unusual way and consequently believed she was an ancestor."

"Did you believe it too, Grandma? That Maddie was an ancestor?"

"I didn't have faith in the belief like your grandfather, but remained open to the idea. Each person must decide for themselves. Our being alive in itself I found, and still find, astonishing, so I didn't rule out too many possibilities.

"Maddie displayed a wide variety of personality traits, easily allowing me to understand how she could have been a person. Grandfather and I would often sit around the kitchen table, talk about Maddie's virtues and vices, and theorize which ancestor shared those same traits. Was Maddie formerly a male or female, from India or Indiana?

"One night a vivid dream stirred me in my sleep. An old wooden ship anchored out in the middle of the ocean. A long diagonal line of blond women stood in the water with arms outstretched, holding hands, spanning the distance from ship to shore. The women passed something from the ship down the row to one another until the item reached the coast.

"In the dream, I lived on the shore in a blue and white bungalow with my family. Two similar type homes stood to the left of mine. Each of the houses contained an identical small unscreened window facing the shore. I stuck my head out the window to watch the scene, as did someone in both of the other homes. The last woman in the chain of blond women glanced at the other onlookers framed by their windows, but she stretched to me, choosing me to receive their gift. She handed me a piece of white cake adorned with golden yellow icing."

"That's kind of funny that they gave you cake," said Pria.

Grandmother let out a thoughtful giggle. "I know. But dreams are full of symbols, and sweets meant love to me. When the last woman in the line of women ancestors handed me that beautiful piece of cake, I felt joy, and never gave a thought to eating the cake. The ancestors chose me to receive their love."

"Following that dream, I felt compelled to write the stories of the ancestors. Imagining myself in a tunnel lined with multiple doors, I opened each to view the lives of the men and women who preceded us. The ancestor's true nature and the defining moments of their lives were revealed to me. The work became a mystical intersection of India and Indiana, a fusion of east and west. In the end, it evolved into more."

Grandmother looked into Pria's brown eyes.

"I am entrusting you with my manuscript, Pria. You can stay at the cottage and read the stories of your ancestors who owned the precious heirlooms. Whatever it is you learn, that is what you need to know."

Pria reached under the patio table to retrieve a loose page of text which had escaped from the file box unnoticed. "Do you mind if I read this now, Grandma?"

Glancing at the page, Grandmother said, "One of my favorite passages. Maybe you could read it aloud to me."

Grandmother slipped her hand into her sweater pocket and rubbed the soft satin ribbon between her thumb and index finger. A faraway look in her eyes and contented smile softened her face as she relaxed in the chair, listening to her granddaughter's soothing voice.

In the thin blue veil of the netherworld, I existed in stillness without need or want. Upon leaving the earth, my soul released from the body I'd inhabited. I eased lightly into the time of transition between lives, as if I'd taken flight on the wings of a butterfly. I came to rest in the place of stillness, merging with the collective soul of the universe, until I felt a stirring. The time had come for my energy to return to the physical plane once again. Mimicking the slow unfolding of lotus petals on a mist covered pond at the break of dawn, I opened my essence to find where I belonged.

I propelled forward toward the ether between the metaphysical and physical worlds, the astral plane outside of time and space. Instead of a black void, a kaleidoscope of mirrored reflections unfolded upon the screen of the heavens. Colors changed seamlessly into various shapes and sizes to reveal glimpses of thousands of my past lifetimes... my soul tree. The task at hand was to choose a new life in which I could apply previously learned lessons. More importantly, I needed to incarnate into a being that would allow the learning necessary to balance my karma. "Enjoy life" I said to myself just before the whoosh of transformation, the light speed travel of my free soul being sucked into a body on earth. The blue stillness fell away.

Urbashi

ONE

truthful

India 1814

My name is Ram Sundar.

I am the twenty-ninth generation of our line of descent.

In the refuge of the cool morning air, I stood in the doorway observing my wife at her dressing table. A thick dark braid clung to the curve of her delicate back, ending with the point touching the chair on which she sat. Daya's lovely face was reflected in her hand mirror. She dabbed rose water on one side of her nose, then the other, large brown eyes peering at perceived imperfections. My wife reminded me of our green clay statue of *Urbashi*, the goddess of beauty, preening at herself in a mirror.

Daya inhaled an audible quick breath. Her face contorted and left hand grabbed the underside of her belly. The mirror slipped out of her hand, but didn't break when it hit the table. The cat scampered away.

"Daya...?"

"Ram, it is time. Get my mother."

The fastest servant boy ran to the village to retrieve Daya's mother, the local midwife. I sat with Daya until her mother arrived and banished me from the room. Moans and whimpers from our upstairs bedroom seeped under the door and out the window.

Hoping to soothe Daya as she labored, I wandered outside and positioned myself in the fork of the climbing tree nearest to our bedroom. My voice flowed from one classic raga melody into another, inspired by the aura of a new life soon to be born on this earth. I sang on the wind well into the evening, interrupted only by nourishment handed to me by the tallest of the servants.

15

Without having heard the cry of the newborn, I descended from my perch in darkness, disappointed and weary.

I felt helpless, lying in the guest room bed, unable to comfort my crying wife. The next day when the sun shone high in the sky, the servant boy shook me awake from my nap on the patio. Before stepping into the room to greet my firstborn, I heard my wife speak to her mother.

"She's not even pretty."

Upon entering, I kissed my wife and our sweet little daughter sleeping peacefully in her mother's arms. Daya probably sensed my disenchantment, not because my daughter wore the wrinkled face of a newborn. As with all Hindus, I wanted a son.

***

Daya quickly became with child again. Fifteen months after our first daughter came to us, the midwife shooed me out. Listening through the door, I once more heard my wife sob to her mother. Despair filled her voice.

"Momi, I am ashamed. I did not give my husband a son."

I stepped into the room, focusing on the baby at the foot of the bed. A newborn girl laid on her back, blue and lifeless. Bruises on the stillborn child's neck remained where the cord squeezed the life from her.

"I'm sorry," Daya said, closing her eyes.

Late in the afternoon, wearing a pristine white doti, I carried my jute bound daughter to the Hindu priest's home in the village. We simultaneously bowed Namaste, honoring each other's light and peace. He chanted an incantation over the tiny bundle I'd laid on the table, blessing the child for her return to the heavens.

I asked the priest to read my palm. He instructed me to sit across from him. First, he studied the back of my hands and knuckles of each finger. He turned my hands over and followed the lines on each of my palms, then the sides of my fists. I told him my birthdate, time of birth, and day of the week of my birth, and provided the same information about Daya. His lips moved silently as he used his index finger to perform astrological calculations mid-air.

"What do you want to know?" he said.

"Will Daya conceive a son?"

"No. But you *will* have a son, born of a different woman."

We bid each other farewell, once more bowing Namaste. I cradled the bundle in my arms while walking to the cremation ghat. My second daughter went up in flames, the intense heat of the fire causing the welling in my eyes to flow into tears. Not only did I sob for the poor child, denied her first breath, but also for Daya's pain and my own. I cried for the past, knowing the changes to come would inevitably alter my life with my wife.

The small hot fire burned out rapidly. While waiting for the embers to turn white, I gave the vendor a rupee for a marigold garland. Once the ashes were cooled sufficiently, the ghat workers searched for the navel, which had not been consumed by fire. They presented me with the charred navel and my child's ashes in a small clay bowl. I negotiated the uneven steps leading into the river, and waded in waist high. Holding the bowl high above the water in one hand, with the other I removed the garland from my neck and gently laid the wreath on the surface. Into the center of the ring of flowers, I poured my baby's remains.

Oars of the boats on the river caused the garland to rise and fall, ebb and flow. The flowers and scattered ashes intermingled with the cremated remains of others. They rode the gentle downstream flow to join the waters of Mother Ganges, and eventually the Bay of Bengal and the oceans of the earth. I bowed to my daughter, the river, and the setting sun. My heavy wet dhoti clung to me as I waded out of the water, as did my spirit which had been weighted down by the events of the day.

***

Returning home in the afterglow of sunset, the task ahead loomed large. I loved Daya and wanted to live a harmonious life with her. She should understand we needed a male heir to inherit our worldly possessions. If we were parents to only a daughter, my property would be passed on to my brother or his sons. More important, we needed a son to support us in our old age. When the time came, he would circle my funeral pyre, barefoot and bareheaded, before scattering my ashes in the Ganges.

Daya lay sleeping in the bed where she gave birth to our stillborn daughter. I could not bring myself to tell her of the priest's words and decided to wait until

17

the mourning period of eleven days passed. On the morning of the twelfth day, Daya left her bed and sat at the dressing table.

She picked up her hairbrush. The gold bangle on Daya's arm slipped from her wrist toward her elbow, but the smaller red and white marriage bangles remained in place. Without changing focus on the task at hand, she dropped her right arm to her side, and shook the precious bangle back down to its home. Daya finished fastening her hair, then pinched her cheeks, facilitating a natural blush to match her dark ruby lips. She dipped her right pinky into kohl, then expertly smeared a small thin shadow on her lid. The bangle again slipped, and once more she returned it to her wrist.

"I love you, Daya, and our daughter."

"I love you too, Ram."

"I need to discuss something with you."

Daya looked through the window toward the far clouds, as if steeling herself against what she knew might be coming. "What is it, Ram?"

"I need a son. We need a son."

She spoke deliberately, steadying her voice. "When my body is ready, let us try again."

"There is no easy way to tell you this. The priest read my palm and astrological signs. He informed me another woman will bear me a son."

A lone tear slid down Daya's chiseled face. "Ram, I beg you. Please allow me another chance to give you a son."

"I am sorry, Daya. I must take another wife."

At that moment, an invisible wall rose up to separate me from the woman I loved.

***

The matchmaker found my second bride. In contrast to Daya's petite frame and quiet demeanor, Shanti was a healthy and carefree fifteen year old. During the marriage preparation, Daya dutifully assisted adorning the bride, but made no eye contact with Shanti, nor with me.

On the night before wedding my second wife, I made love to Daya. Afterwards, I held her in my arms. "Daya, I will always honor and love you as my first wife." She remained silent, but her body racked with sobs.

18

A new wing of the house had been built for Shanti, the old and new wings connected by a long corridor. Several months after taking a second wife, Daya confided in me how she occupied herself when I spent time with Shanti. Daya asked the servants to care for our daughter, then took refuge in a small cupola at the top of a narrow staircase ascending from the bedroom we shared. Peering into the sky, she scoured the horizon for pictures made by the clouds. She created stories surrounding the cloud forms, complicated tales designed to relieve her mind of the picture of her husband making love to his new wife.

At times, the clouds themselves represented what she desperately tried to suppress. One early October evening, a grey-blue lightning bolt appeared in the western skies. Daya interpreted the formation as a sign Shanti had conceived. Daya did not know which envy felt greater... her husband inside another woman for a moment of pleasure, or the possibility of Shanti bearing me a son.

The next month, I overheard Daya address the house servant on laundry day. Daya knew that her cycle coincided with Shanti's.

"Do you have enough clean rags this month?"

"Yes," answered the servant.

"But normally there are twice this many, enough for both Shanti and me."

"This is enough. Please...may I go?"

Daya did not need to hear more. She seduced me to her bed often in the next week, utilizing flirtations learned in the Kama Sutra. Following our lovemaking, she reached under the corner of the mattress. In the moonlight or the dark shadows, just before I slept, she rubbed a small phallus symbol made of white marble.

Five weeks after Shanti conceived, Daya became with child. On the surface, the simultaneous pregnancies brought my wives closer to each other. They laid out on a blanket in the sun together, my young daughter between them, while each rubbed her own belly. Yet, I could feel the underlying competitive tension that colored their interactions.

Shanti went into labor three weeks late and Daya two weeks early, on the same day.

***

Life proceeded peacefully with my wives and three children until the Holi Festival of Colors several years later. I watched my two daughters, and one son, Durga Charan, play on the veranda. I found it odd that Daya's son, my only son, gravitated toward Shanti. The young boy touched Shanti's face and stared into her eyes, not fleeting glances, but penetrating gazes reflecting a special bond. Daya shot jealous looks at Shanti, before directing her son, Durga Charan, back to a table laden with fruit.

"What color is this mango, my son?"

"Part of it is yellow."

But try as he might, the child could only distinguish between a red and green mango by feeling their level of firmness, not by identifying their color.

Shanti later told me Durga Charan's difficulty in learning colors was identical to that of her father, afflicted with the rare anomaly of red-green colorblindness. She felt a sickness in the pit of her stomach, and questioned if something deeper hid behind the gazes she and the boy shared.

Reliving the events of the children's shared birthday, she recalled that each wife was attended by a thirteen year old girl. The teenagers sat with the laboring women, but during the actual birthing, stood outside the door and acted as assistants, running for supplies and relaying communications.

That evening, Shanti summoned her birthing attendant to her private wing. In my presence, she asked the girl to relate her memories of the day the two children were born.

***

I left early the next morning for the midwife's home, Daya's mother's home.

We sat down to tea. I skipped the pleasantries.

"Please tell me the story of the birth day of my son and second daughter," I said.

She focused on preparing tea. "Is there something in particular you need to know?"

"The truth."

She set her cup down, then stared out the window.

"I wondered if this day would come," she said. "What has led you to ask me now?"

"The color red," I replied.

She took a deep breath, then began speaking with a quiver in her voice.

***

The midwife arrived late morning and examined both wives. Daya's labor had progressed further than Shanti's. Heavy herbal painkillers were given to Daya, hoping to ease the agony of the strong continuous contractions. Daya fainted after the last push that spewed forth the baby in a gush of blood. She did not hear the baby's first cry, gaze upon the baby's face, nor see its bright red vulva.

Immediately after the delivery of the placenta, the midwife heard her assistant call frantically through the closed door. "Shanti's servant girl ran here from the other wing of the house. She said to tell you to hurry. Shanti is screaming in pain that the baby is coming."

Daya's bleeding had subsided. The midwife prepared to leave her sleeping daughter under the watchful eye of the servant girl, but didn't think it best to leave the newborn. She hurriedly wrapped the unbathed child in a white cotton blanket, and ran down the long hall to Shanti's bedroom, the swaddled baby girl in her arms.

Shanti lay in the center of a large platform bed. The tall removable post that held the mosquito nets remained in place from the previous night, but the netting had been slid open and tied back. The midwife laid Daya's daughter in the corner of the bed where the baby lay nestled out of the way, yet was protected by the post and netting.

The birthing rooms were equipped with pans of clean water and a knife to sever the cord. But the midwife did not like the knife in Shanti's room. She preferred her own sharp knife from her birthing kit, which in a hurry, she'd left in Daya's room. She ordered Shanti's servant girl to fetch the knife, and to make sure it was clean.

The laboring woman cried out. The midwife removed the blanket that hid the vagina. She knelt on the bed, positioned herself between Shanti's legs, and pushed them further apart. The baby's dark wet head, face down, began to protrude. Despite Shanti's exhaustion, at the next contraction she pushed with all of her might, and pee splayed on the midwife. The baby slid out in a gush of milky liquid.

In a voice barely above a whisper, Shanti asked, "Is it over?"

"The hard part is over."

The new mother closed her eyes, laid her head back, and sobbed. The midwife waited for the servant girl to return with her knife. But after a few minutes without the servant's appearance, she used the knife at hand. She did not need to tie the cord in order to cut it, as the elapsed time created a natural clamp which halted the flow of blood. She wrapped the child in a white cotton blanket with only the eyes uncovered.

"Shanti, open your eyes." The midwife held up the baby, who quietly gazed into its Mother's eyes. Shanti then fell into a deep sleep.

The midwife laid Shanti's baby next to Daya's on the corner of the bed near the post. They looked like twins, each born with a dark thick mass of hair on a misshapen head, a scrunched ruddy face, and fetal bent legs. One difference hid under the blanket...instead of a scarlet vulva, Shanti's baby's two swollen red testicles stretched across a scrotum.

My daughter Daya is desperate to have a son. What a cruel twist of fate.

With heart racing, she placed Daya's newborn girl across Shanti's chest. She snatched up the baby boy, and stole away to her daughter Daya's room.

***

The priest's prediction had been accurate. Another woman, not Daya, bore my son. I rose to leave.

The midwife touched my arm. "Ram, what did you mean when you said the color red had raised your suspicions?"

I instinctively pulled away from her. "We discovered Durga Charan is red-green colorblind, like Shanti's father. At Shanti's request, her attending servant girl told us what she remembered about the shared birthday."

"What did she say?" Daya's mother asked.

"Not that you deserve to know, but I will tell you."

***

When directed to retrieve the knife, the girl ran down the hall to Daya's room. She found the bloody knife on the table, but no clean water in the pans with which to wash off the stains. Blood red water filled one pan. The rinse pan's water was stained pink with blood.

The servant girl bounded downstairs with the bloody knife in her hand, and almost tripped on her sari. She ran out the door and across the yard to the separate kitchen structure. After washing and wrapping the knife in a clean cloth, she headed back upstairs.

Shanti and the baby were in the room alone. The baby was lying across Shanti's chest, wrapped in a stained red blanket. No signs of blood were evident anywhere else in the room, not on the sheets or in the pans of water. The lack of blood everywhere but on the blanket puzzled the servant girl, however she never mentioned it, anticipating she would grow to understand such matters.

***

On the walk back home, I reminisced about my family. I loved my son no matter who gave birth to him, and my daughters for the sweetness they brought to my life. I loved my wives, but they had never learned to accept each other. Yet, both needed to be told the midwife's story, the truth.

The three of us gathered in the parlor, sitting on large floor pillows arranged in a triangle. Daya's lovely fair complexion became ashen. Shanti's darker skin turned red. Each pulled up the end of her sari to cover her lowered head. Neither one said a word to each other, but nodded in response to my request. We would delay telling the children until they became older. One day, my son, my golden child, would come to understand why a color he could not recognize revealed the truth about his own beginnings.

Cup

TWO

FRUGAL

Germany 1814
My name is Katharina.
I am the wife of Gerhard Heinrich.

In the predawn light, Father stood by my bedside. "Katharina, it's time to go."

I preferred to savor my lingering dreams.

He burst into spontaneous song at the top of his lungs. *"Market day, market day..."*

"Father, please..." I half-opened my eyes, waking to the comical sight of straw pieces sticking up in his hair. He'd slept in the barn on an old straw mattress to protect the produce we'd loaded on the wagon the previous evening. Despite my attempts to stifle it, a small grin escaped my lips when he continued to sing.

"Time to sell our apples..."

Following breakfast, Father hitched the horses to the loaded wagon and pulled the team up to the house. He wiggled small kegs of apple cider from the root cellar between the homemade baskets filled with apples. My brother, Johann, nestled extra apples wherever he found space in the baskets. I climbed into my seat and wrapped myself in a blanket for the ride. Mother placed a pan of her apple kuchen, cut into squares and covered with a clean kitchen towel, on the floorboard to cradle with my feet.

Father and I waved goodbye to Mother and Johann, then settled in for the familiar ride. We rolled down the rutted road from Merzen to Furstenau, passing through four tiny hill villages on the way. Our songs and ditties were accompanied by the friendly bark of sinewy farm dogs who ran alongside the wagon, lunging at crusts of bread I tossed them.

"Father, how did you meet Mother?"

I knew the story by heart, but hoped he might add a little tidbit he had not yet divulged.

"I happened to stop by the neighbor's on the day your mother came to visit them."

"Was it love at first sight, Papa?"

"Oh Katharina…you are too young to understand," he said.

"I am thirteen years old and understand perfectly fine."

He darted a glance at me, but said no more, instead grinning straight ahead. We arrived in Furstenau shortly after sunrise. Father guided the horses past quiet houses and closed shops to the town square. We parked the wagon in our usual spot, under the protection of the deep shadow of the Furstenau church. Father caught up on the news with fellow farmers while waiting for the townsfolk to trickle into the marketplace.

The morning flew by packing apples for customers, while father counted their coins into the money sock. During the lull brought on by the hot midday sun, Father encouraged me to explore the market and the village. I bought colorful hair ribbons from the smiling chubby mother, who sat in the midst of her happy brood of five, beside their cart of goods.

During a game of hide and seek, I raced through the courtyard by the church and hid behind a rain barrel near the butcher's shop. A boy about my age, wearing a long white apron stained pink and red, peered at me through the open air window. I winked at him, gesturing *sh* in hopes he'd keep my hiding place secret. The boy seemed to understand, carrying on with his work, only glancing surreptitiously at me until I was found.

The boy intrigued me, and I motioned for him to join us. His father, who watched, nodded. Gerhard untied the apron strings behind his back, raised the neck strap over his head, and threw the stained garment on the stool behind the counter.

It didn't bother me that Gerhard smelled of sausages from the shop, and he liked that I didn't mind. Our friendship blossomed during long walks together on market day. Gerhard was practical and straightforward, which I guessed emerged from repeatedly watching cattle and hogs butchered for the shop. We were a good match, a good partnership, and I anticipated his proposal someday.

When Gerhard turned eighteen and I was sixteen, he confided in me he felt no hurry to marry. He told me the story of his grandfather, a quiet man who fell in love with a rich woman. As per the custom of his time, the married couple took the last name of the wealthier partner. Gerhard felt his grandfather lost his individual identity in the process. As a result of his grandfather's experience, whether warranted or not, Gerhard became leery of marriage. Following our conversation, I rarely saw Gerhard and buried my disappointment working in my family's orchards.

***

Ten years passed. I learned of Gerhard's engagement from the ribbon lady. At age twenty-eight, he met Maria, a pretty young Furstenau girl who'd flirted with him in the butcher shop. A short courtship ensued before they married in the fall of 1828 and settled in a small home on a plot of land near Gerhard's parents. Maria gave birth to a daughter, Angela, in 1829.

On a crisp fall Saturday under a bright blue sky, Maria, baby Angela and Gerhard's mother came to market day. Maria carried her beautiful baby and gushed with excitement. "Hello Katharina. Give me your best pie apples. Tomorrow is our first anniversary, and I want to make a special dessert for Gerhard." I managed to hide my feelings of unexpected jealousy behind a smile. Gerhard's mother hung her head avoiding eye contact with me. The trio left my stall and visited a traveler's cart selling homemade grape juice.

As told to me later, Angela felt warm to the touch that same evening. She vomited, followed by a burst of diarrhea. Maria and Gerhard guessed the child caught the flu from exposure to someone at the market. The intensity of the symptoms rapidly increased prompting Maria to recall the traveler's stories of a cholera epidemic in his village in eastern Germany. All three females drank the grape juice the traveler sold, and she remembered thinking the nectar seemed watered down.

The couple stayed up all night with their child, bathed her with cool water, and tried to feed her spoon sips of liquid. By early Sunday morning, the baby burned with fever and went into shock from dehydration. While the church bells rang loud and long, signaling Sunday morning services, the couple begged for their angel's life.

In the middle of the chimes and couple's prayers, Maria's gut wrenched with pain. She ran to the outhouse, and liquid poured out of her. Time and time again, attacks of violent vomiting and diarrhea ravaged her body. Only a few hours elapsed before Maria succumbed to cholera. Helpless and alone, Gerhard extended his arms to the heavens wailing with shock and grief. He dropped his pale and weakened baby on the bed next to her mother.

Down the road, Gerhard's brother woke at dawn to find his father slumped over his mother. No amount of shaking and calling her name brought her back to life. As soon as Gerhard's brother found the strength, he ran to Gerhard's house. He burst into the room and found Gerhard staring at the ghost of his departed wife and the barely breathing baby.

***

News spread as quickly as the cholera epidemic. I felt sorry for Gerhard and once again began to visit the butcher shop on a regular basis. It seemed as if we had never spent years apart. We talked about simple things…work, life in the village, our families. I did not bring up Maria, nor did he, except one time.

While sitting in the front of the shop playing pat-a-cake with Angie, I heard Gerhard behind the counter. He slung the cleaver, hitting the butcher block with a decisive force of anger. I placed the baby in her crib, and walked to him.

"What is it, Gerhard? Tell me what's bothering you."

Without looking up he replied, "Maria and I should be celebrating our two year anniversary tomorrow. Instead I will be grieving the one year anniversary of her death. It's not fair, it's just not fair."

I reached out to squeeze his hand, but he pushed away my arm. Feeling a quandary of emotions, including the hurt and anger of rejection, I walked back to Angie to kiss her goodbye. Managing to put aside my own feelings, I bled for my broken friend. The ooze felt as real as the seeping red blood released with each pound on the beef.

The next market day at noon, as was my habit, I visited the butcher shop. I shouted a subdued greeting to Gerhard, then picked up sweet Angela playing in her crib. Amidst the slaughtered pigs and cows, I had fallen in love with Gerhard's beautiful daughter.

Gerhard walked toward us. He didn't take off his apron. Touching my hand that hugged his baby and looking into my eyes, he spoke. "I need you Katharina. My baby needs you. Will you be my wife?"

I met his gaze, smiled, then turned my eyes to Angela. "Yes."

For the first time in all the years we'd known each other, he leaned down and kissed me. Angela gazed up at our sweet, polite, uncertain touch of lips.

Despite realizing Gerhard would compare me to his first wife, I felt thrilled to marry him. Our parents were delighted, particularly my father when Gerhard formally asked for my hand in marriage. The ceremony took place in the fall of 1831 in my hometown church in Merzen. In our love and partnership born of a solid friendship, Gerhard found strength, I found contentment, and two year old Angela found a mother.

The people of Furstenau considered it a miracle that Angela survived the cholera epidemic. She'd emerged translucent, ethereal, a child of grace. As she knelt with her hands folded for bedtime prayers, a hush fell over the house. She squeezed her eyes closed during our family rosary, and in her innocent childhood voice, told me God was with her in the pretty colors behind her eyes.

I soon conceived and Gerhard beamed with pride at the birth of our son on Christmas Day of 1832. We named him Heinrich Gerhard, the inverse name of his father. Heinrich's temperament surfaced from the moment of his birth. He became raging mad, turning red with anger, as the midwife washed him. Before he could talk, we knew what he wanted through his screams and head butts. He grew into a bold and boisterous child who loved wrestling and roughhousing with his father.

We shared a comfortable love, our children and parents were healthy and business prospered. A new puppy, a Rottweiler mutt, Ralph, made us giggle at his antics. I gave birth to our third child, Anna Maria, in 1834.

***

Our lives began to change the next year. The brutally hot and dry summer withered the rose bushes in my garden and turned the fields brown. We waited and prayed and watched the skies for rain. Late in the fall, we became hopeful seeing the snowflakes fly, but winter snows did not come to renew the parched earth.

Some villagers moved away from Furstenau to find food elsewhere. Those that stayed did not want to leave their roots and parents. Others did not want to give up their land and farm, or business and place of worship. Furstenau's thousand people could not provide for their own needs, and turned to our rulers for support. Help came in spurts, and bits and pieces, in the way of food brought from other districts. But hundreds of mouths still went hungry.

The ruling king, a practical landlord, did not want dissention born of suffering. He wanted to remain rich and powerful. His castle stood not far from the North Sea, and he helped finance and launch the ships being built there. He knew ships traveling to America were half empty and could hold many more passengers.

He announced he would buy the failed farms and businesses of the Furstenau people. Every man, woman and child, rich or poor, who wanted to go to America, would receive thirty-five talers to pay for their passage to America. He demonstrated support of his subjects. Yet, he personally benefited from acquiring much land for little money, in addition to recovering his funds through collection of passage on his own ships.

By late 1836, many families were desperate. The remaining home-canned goods, apples and root vegetables, and smoked meats disappeared from storage. We were surviving the famine primarily because Gerhard brought home scraps from the butcher shop that in previous years were fed to the dogs. I managed to eke out a few vegetables from what was left of the garden by retrieving buckets of water from the natural spring.

The hard work and sacrifice for my family came at my own expense, and gradually I no longer felt like the strong German woman Gerhard married. The three children cried themselves to sleep, or whimpered from hunger in their dreams. I sometimes sobbed along with them from my own weariness and malnutrition.

Looking forward to our Christmas celebration kept me going. My parents traveled from Merzen to celebrate with us, bearing apple cake and cider. I had hidden two jars of canned beef and noodles in a corner of the cellar. We ate one and presented a jar to my parents to take home. My mother gave the girls a doll to share, and my father carved a wooden truck for Henry, who simultaneously celebrated his fourth birthday. I sewed Gerhard a new apron for the shop, and he surprised me with a small pewter wine *cup* he bartered from someone who left for America.

The joyous occasion provided bittersweet memories. For on the way home, the weather turned, with harsh winter winds striking the face and filling the lungs of my parents. Their old and frail bodies held no resistance to fight infection. I could only watch as one, then another, succumbed to pneumonia.

My brother, Johann, had been intrigued with America since his school days. With both of our parents gone, and the apple orchards dried up, I encouraged him to follow his dreams. In the spring of 1837, he sold the farm to the king, and joined twenty-seven other brave souls to become the first group of Furstenau villagers to set sail for America.

Gerhard and I didn't seriously consider the king's offer to go to America. Gerhard's father lived alone, and despite the drought, the butcher shop remained open on market days. We were getting older, both in our late thirties, with three small children. We thought if we prayed hard enough, our prayers would eventually be answered. We endured our third dust laden summer and cold snowless winter scraping by on practically nothing.

A spring shower gave everyone hope, but by the time we ran outside to feel the rain on our faces, it had slowed to a trickle. The moisture stirred up dormant foul smells in the soil, but barely dampened the cracked earth. Gerhard buried his father from a broken will and weakened heart, and watched me and the children grow thinner.

Word reached Furstenau from the first twenty-eight immigrants to America. My brother, Johann, wrote of the wonders of the new land, bounty and beauty, opportunity and freedom. In every corner of the village and the surrounding farms, talk centered on the drought and famine, the king's offer, and who planned to immigrate to America.

In May of 1838, Gerhard and I finally held the conversation both of us anticipated and neither wanted to start. On the way home from church, hot in our Sunday clothes in the late morning sun, Gerhard looked out over the parched countryside.

"Katharina, I think the time has come. The butcher shop and garden can sustain us no longer. I'm losing hope."

I glanced at the children behind me, then stared straight ahead at the bony backsides of the horses pulling the wagon. The wheels of destiny were inching us ever closer to leaving our homeland.

"Are you sure, Gerhard? Our lives are here. Things are bound to improve."

"I have no faith things will get better."

"But this is our homeland, where we were born. I don't want to leave."

"No one is left here. We have a chance to sell our place, to get free passage across to America."

"We may not make it across, Gerhard."

"It's a risk we'll have to take. Katharina, if we don't go, I'm afraid one of the children, or one of us, may die."

I couldn't argue with him. "How will we survive there?"

"We have your brother to help us. Besides, Katharina, we are strong partners. We can make it. We need to seize this opportunity while we are still young enough to go."

I stared at our house up ahead in the distance. Our mutt came running to greet us.

"What about Ralph?"

"I've already talked to my brother. He will take him."

"You've made up your mind then?"

"God helps those who help themselves."

I visited the dried up apple orchards of my beloved childhood home. I walked through the brittle weeds between the rows of dead trees, barely hearing the loud chirping of the day crickets. The smell of ripe apples and bees buzzing around the blossoms filled my imagination. My heart ached realizing I would never again return to my home.

Nostalgia gave way to worry in the darkness of night. I was terrified by the thought of a seventeen day ocean crossing in the dark smelly bowels of a crowded steamship. Those who made the journey wrote of noises and sights unfit for children. They described rats darting about, brazenly stealing food and water. All of us were weak from the famine, and susceptible to illness. We could die on the journey from any number of diseases, or be so seasick we wanted to die. The possibility of drowning in the deep black waters caused me to shake with chills when I allowed myself to dwell on it.

34

In these moments, I did not turn to Gerhard. I felt he would not understand, or did not want to know, my deep paralyzing fear. I was not Gerhard's first choice. He loved me, but expected me to always be strong in this partnership, and he would not know what to do if I were not. Gerhard did not live without fear, but true to his nature, he pushed aside his feelings in favor of moving on. When shaking with terror in the night, I simply tugged on the quilt, hoping Gerhard would stir from his dreams and reach out for me.

Despite acceptance of my fate, I could not help but cry while packing and repacking the one trunk allowed per family. The children too cried at seeing and feeling my anguish, especially Angela. Only nine years old, but perceptive and smart, she understood momentous changes were to come. I saw Gerhard looking at the four of us crying, and tried to shield my eyes from him.

"Katharina, stop crying and pack the trunk," he said, as he turned and walked toward the front door. I winced, but felt compassion for my husband. He hitched the wagon and headed into town to close the butcher shop for the last time.

The children and I spread our most precious belongings on the bed. The trunk stood two feet deep and almost three feet wide, with a rounded top and keyhole lock. I filled the trunk with our essentials, leaving space for Gerhard's things, including the sausage grinder from the butcher shop. Winter woolens and blankets, clothes and shoes, plates and utensils, birth and marriage certificates, pictures and the family bible were packed. I would wear the few pieces of jewelry inherited from my mother.

I weeded out those things that would not fit in our one trunk. It didn't matter what Gerhard said, I was brokenhearted and the tears flowed all over again. Still left on the bed were my children's baby clothes, my wedding gown, and Gerhard's parents' gift of a fragile crystal bowl. My father's hat, and mother's dressing table set would not fit in the trunk. I stuffed the pewter wine cup Gerhard gave me for Christmas into my coat sleeve.

Angela watched me, then ran from the room. She soon returned with her raggedy doll and Henry's carved truck from my parents. Since the little girl rarely asked for anything, I squeezed the toys inside the other sleeve of my winter coat, and slid the coat inside the length of the trunk.

***

I prepared emotionally for the day, crying all the tears inside of me. But in the night, before the morning of our journey, I lay awake listening to the sound of slow steady raindrops on our tin roof. The rain soaked the ground, leaving no puddles behind in the morning. I wondered if we had made the right decision.

Gerhard's brother came early to gather the last of our belongings, including beds and kitchen items we gave him. He and Gerhard drove them to his home, and both returned to pick up the children and me. I looked around the empty little house, and shut the front door for the last time. The worst moment came when we said goodbye to Ralph, no longer a puppy but still my sweet loving friend, who protected me and the children. He would have a decent home on Gerhard's brother's family farm, my only consolation.

Our extended families were gathered near the Furstenau church to see us off. Friends and neighbors sacrificed some of their own food and came with small goodbye gifts of loaves of coarse brown bread, nuts and cheese, and sweet pastries. We drove away from the town square on our brother-in-law's wagon, waving goodbye to the group behind. Our cart held my family and one precious trunk, all that I now possessed in this world. Only my faith and acceptance kept me from breaking down. There was no turning back.

Gerhard and I were numb on our way to meet the canal barge. The range of intense emotions we carried felt overwhelming and rendered us speechless. The younger children, ages five and three, provided some distraction. At once, I felt both acutely aware, and removed from my surroundings. It seemed as if I floated in a dream state, and the farms and fields were being viewed from afar. Under the hot and muggy midday summer sun, the shiny mirror of heat rising above the road ahead reinforced my feeling of being part of a mirage. I shook my head back from illusion into reality when items began shifting and rattling in our trunk.

We traveled northeast for three hours to meet the canal barge destined for the seaport. We boarded with the other Furstenau emigrants, and crowded together on and around our trunks. None of us from landlocked Furstenau had traveled on water, and we sat stiffly, not knowing what to expect. The calm water of the canal gave us the sensation that the barge was standing still and the scenery floated by. I dared to hope the ocean crossing may be less daunting than my fears.

As we became more comfortable on the barge, we began to move about. I opened our parting gifts, and doled out the bread, cheese and a few walnuts to Gerhard and the children. The meticulously planned rations for my family to last the seventeen days on the ship were not touched. Gerhard poured each of us a cup of water from the heavy jugs he'd slung over his shoulder.

The bright orange and red sunset mirrored our feelings of shock and resignation. Darkness fell, the children slept, and the women chatted until nodding off. In the lantern lights, the men talked long into the night, commenting about the villages we passed through. I heard snippets of their conversation in my half-sleep. They shared hopes for life in America. If they felt a knot in their stomach, they did not share their fears.

The night passed slowly, and except for the small children, with more catnaps than deep sleep. In the early morning mist, I continued to feel the surrealism of the journey, and started to relax into the moment. We ate the last of our gifts, the sweet pastries. By mid-morning, the canal merged with the swiftly moving river on the final leg of the journey to the port on the North Sea. Gerhard complained of queasiness, but I attributed his upset stomach to the life changing journey we had set into motion.

One of the children began shouting, "I see it, I see it." We soon disembarked into a bustling world of docks and large ships, beggars and soldiers, people who spoke in foreign languages and were dressed in bright clothes. The fog began to lift while we stood in the midst of chaos, and a clouded sun appeared halfway up the sky. The smell and taste of the salt air, and the sounds of the gull's cries and swoops were new to us. But what struck me most were not the ships or the activity on the dock, but seeing the bay waters and ocean beyond. The sea's white capped waves were both beautiful and frightening. I felt small, but simultaneously the immensity of everything in and around me.

The barge captain pointed to one of several steamships docked in the bay. Before us stood the largest structure Gerhard and I had ever seen. We observed supplies being loaded onto the belly of the ship, and the line of passengers boarding via the long gangway. We looked at each other and took a deep breath. Gerhard patted our papers tucked securely in his pocket, and we each grabbed a handle of the precious trunk. With his free arm, Gerhard carried little Anna, and I held hands with Henry who held hands with Angela. We walked toward the looming, belching, rocking steamship.

We were directed to steerage, the cheapest and lowest of the three passenger levels. We struggled to transport our trunk and the three children down the steep stairs to our assigned deck. The air became increasingly hot and stifling as we descended. In the dim porthole light, we managed to find our adult sleeping bunks stacked one upon the other. High rails surrounded each bunk to prevent falling out when the ship rocked. The children did not have their own bunks, but instead hammocks strung between the rows, in similar fashion to drying laundry. There were no private toilet facilities, only a few filthy overflowing buckets at the end of the row of bunks. The fear and the dread that plagued me in the dark nights resurfaced. But there was nothing I could do to keep my life from unfolding.

Without self-consciousness, Angela dropped to her knees, hands clasped in prayer. "Dear Lord, thank you for all of our blessings. Please keep me and my family safe, and help us find a good life in America. Amen." Her simple words of heartfelt faith gave everyone in her presence strength and courage to begin the journey and face whatever may come.

At that moment, we felt the lurch of the ship as the chains hoisted the anchor and the ropes were released from the dock. We heard the loud shrill whistle of the steamship. We ran up the two flights of stairs with the other passengers to wave to the crowd left behind on the docks below. Gerhard let me squeeze his hand.

Ganesh

THREE

स्पिरितुअल

India 1829

My name is Durga Charan.

I am the only son of Ram Sundar.

In the first few moments following my birth, I've been told, I looked deep into my mother's eyes. I'd emerged from the womb with no need to cry. Knowledge of previous lives and other worlds prepared me for this life as a Kulin Brahmin. After a short time on earth, the rough rub of the rag on my newborn skin should have warned me I would need more than knowledge to thrive as a human being.

I took my place as the only son born into the highest strata of an upper caste Hindu family. The caste system in India consisted of four levels. The highest stood the Brahmins who were the priests and teachers. The lower three castes included warriors, merchants, and laborers. Beneath all castes sat the untouchables, not considered worthy of caste, and fated to perform the menial jobs of society. I came onto this earth not only a Brahmin, but a Kulin Brahmin, believed to have become knowledgeable about spiritual teachings in a previous life.

As a child, people tended to gaze at me, not simply because of my high caste Brahmin status. It was not my appearance that attracted attention, as I looked no different than other young Indian children who lurked in groups staring at interesting scenes. Somehow my very presence caused others to suspend their actions to peer in my direction.

The stories told by my father, uncle and priests about the gods and goddesses of the Hindu faith fascinated me. My elders recited the Bhagavad Gita, specifically the discussion between Lord Krishna and Arjuna on the eve of a great battle. The tale taught that knowledge was supreme and fueled in me a desire to understand the mysteries of the Hindu spiritual stories.

In order to understand the sacred texts, I immersed myself in the study of Sanskrit. At the early age of nine years, the priest pronounced me prepared for Upanyan, the sacred thread ceremony, in which Brahmin responsibilities were assumed. Like most Hindus, I adored the pot-bellied Ganesh, revered as the god who clears the path to success. He was crafted from a child's body and an elephant's head, sitting on a rat. In celebration of Upanyan, my father gave me a miniature ivory *Ganesh* statue carved by a local artisan.

On a simple cloth spread over the grass's early morning dew, the three yogas of the Gita became my practice. Apologizing to the frogs who croaked in protest that I'd disturbed their routine, I began to breathe deeply and slowly. I came to know my essence through these meditations, not fleetingly, but with a sustained attention through which grace flowed. The yellow lotus petals stretched out to the sun while my soul opened to the universe.

***

One morning following yoga, I enjoyed tea and shared bites of biscuits with our dog. My father sat nearby, watching the pup nudge my hand for more.

"Durga Charan, you've turned fifteen. The time has come for you to marry."

"So soon, Father?"

"A suitable girl from Kulpara has been selected. Her name is Padma."

Padma meant lotus, a flower symbolizing the purity of soul. I took the name of my bride-to-be as a sign of good fortune. I later learned her mother named her in honor of the mighty Padma River, a tributary of the holy Ganges. My bride began her entrance onto this earth during her parents' stroll by the wide river to watch the sunset and its reflection on the calm water. In a gush, the amniotic fluid of Padma's birth sack spewed, and she burst forth into this world, while the monkeys watched and chatted in the trees above.

Accepting the decision of my wise father was not difficult, but I felt immediate nostalgia for my carefree life. I feared that my spiritual quest might be usurped by the responsibilities of marriage. I admired the beauty and grace of the Hindu goddesses in the sacred stories, but did not yet feel ready to be a husband.

The two fathers negotiated the details of the marriage. The bride's dowry consisted of exquisite pieces of gold jewelry, silverware, beautiful linens and silk cloths. My father built a new home for Padma and me, on the family compound, near one of the ponds. The astrologer studied our birthdates, along with the days and times of birth. He set the wedding date for December of 1845, when I turned sixteen years old and Padma fourteen years of age. Arrangements were made for the ceremony, two days in length.

Padma and I walked around the fire seven and a half times to the priest's chants, then I looked upon my bride's face for the first time. I didn't quite realize when the actual moment of joining in marriage occurred. We walked to our new home down the path from the main house.

Padma turned fourteen before the marriage, and therefore was not considered a child bride. However, we could not begin our physical relationship because her body had not yet begun a monthly flow. In addition, being intimate with a stranger felt unnatural, and it would happen in due time.

"I want to please you," Padma said.

"Let us sleep," I replied.

We soon became comfortable in our routine. Padma accompanied me to the pond by our home. She positioned herself cross-legged on the bank to watch the fish ripples form rings on the surface of the pond, and the lotus unfold their petals to release their sweet vanilla like fragrance into the dawn air. Focused on my meditations, I did not notice Padma's hormones blossomed into furtive glances at my body holding various yoga poses.

One evening, she flirted with me on our sunset walk back from dinner with my parents. I responded to her lovely eyes and full lips with a gentle kiss and caress of her long silky hair. We finished our walk home hand in hand, in silence, but with the roar of blood in our veins.

We stepped into the dark and cool front room, lit only by rays of moonlight beaming through the cracks of the shutters. Padma shyly removed her sari, unwinding it round and round, finally standing naked in the spotlight of a dust filled ray. We stepped toward each other and embraced. I felt her body tremble when my hardness touched her wet yoni. Her long fingers traced my shoulders and clavicle while I outlined her emerging curves. We lay on the large platform bed, and enclosed the mosquito net around us. Her beauty and the love I experienced for her in that moment astonished me. I felt grateful we did not need to wait for the years to pass and companionship to result in love, as in many arranged marriages.

In July of the next year, similar to the rest of Bengal, we waited for the monsoon clouds to burst free. Under the cool shade of the banyan tree, we told ghost stories and ate ripe mangoes. Padma blushed in embarrassment as sweet mango juice ran down her chin onto her breast. Amused, I began to lick her chin and kiss her juicy lips. With longing and strong arms, I carried her up the entrance steps into the house.

Our beautiful son, Avoya, was born in the spring of 1847.

***

My sister, Tara, and her new husband, Satish, joined our family of three as we gathered at our parents to celebrate Durga puja. The festival honored the goddess Durga, my namesake. Durga Charan literally meant at the feet of Durga, but the figurative interpretation meant at the mercy of Durga. We enjoyed sweets and prepared for the procession to the Padma River the next day with the other villagers.

A village artisan had been commissioned to create a huge straw and clay statue of Durga. She rode a tiger and was adorned with ten octopus like arms. Three brightly painted lotus shaped eyes representing the moon, sun, and fire dominated her face. Traditionally, the villagers in procession carried the statue to the Padma, then transported Durga by boat out to the deepest part of the river. There she glided into the water, while the devotees on the bank chanted and sang. According to the allegory, Durga needed release back to her mother, which symbolized the cycle of eternity. The priest chose me to release the goddess into the river in honor of my name and of my status as a new father.

But the next morning, Avoya became ill, and by the time the procession was ready to leave, the baby felt feverish. Padma and I needed to stay home to care for our son. I asked my brother-in-law, Tara's husband Satish, to take my place in the river ceremony. Satish bowed, indicating acceptance with gratitude and humility.

***

Swollen with rains, the river's water currents ran swift, both on the surface and in the undercurrent below. Satish and several other young men arranged the statue on the decorated fishing boat's place of honor, then climbed onto the vessel with her. Worshippers on the shore navigated the small boat with long attached ropes. The onlookers cheered as the cords slackened, allowing the boat to carry its passengers out into the river.

The mighty river proved too strong and the men on shore not strong enough to control the heavy weight of Durga and her attendants in the small boat. The uneven tension on the ropes caused the boat to rock, and the statue to tip. Top-heavy with ten arms, the goddess slipped over the side of the boat, which caused the men to lose their footholds. They too splashed overboard, and a moment later the boat flipped on top of Satish. His feet became entangled in the ropes. The men on shore still pulled and tugged the lines in an effort to regain control of the boat, further chaining Satish. Rushing water filled the air pocket under the boat and Satish stopped the struggle. I could only imagine how he watched Durga on her tiger, the savior from evil, silently sink into the murky depths of the Padma. Her ten arms waved goodbye to the dying man.

The capsized boat with Satish's lifeless body trapped underneath did not travel far downstream before it came to rest against a tangle of brush near the shore. Tara fainted when she saw her purplish-blue husband pulled from the river that claimed them both. My father and other villagers placed Tara and her dead groom on the bamboo platform that previously carried Durga on her regal procession. A breathless villager ran to our compound and up the path leading to our small home screaming, "Satish is dead".

I helped unload Satish's body. The jute sack covering his body slipped off, revealing the ropes that were still knotted in place from the struggle. While cutting the cords from his body, knowledge and consciousness abandoned me and guilt took their place. I had meditated all of my life, pondered on the soul, death and rebirth, but in this crucial moment, I lost my presence.

Satish's brothers arrived late in the afternoon to take the body to their family home, and prepare for the next day's cremation. In their shock, grief and anger, they cruelly smudged out the vermillion marks of marriage in the center part of Tara's hair. Wracking with sobs, Tara clung to her dead husband, burying her face in his chest.

"I can't live without him. He is my life."

"Tara, they must take him now," I said.

"What terrible Karma has befallen us?"

I tore her away from Satish, but a change came over her. She stared blankly ahead, and repeated in barely a whisper.

I perceived the words, "Satish, Satish, Satish", but quickly realized those were not her words. She had instead murmured, "Sati, sati, sati".

Taking her face into my hands, I turned her head to look at me. "Tara, no." Her glazed faraway eyes showed no signs of comprehension.

***

An image of an old stone marker, worn from the elements, flashed through my mind. One summer when Tara and I were children, we played in a wooded area near our home, not far from the river. We found a marker, into which palm prints had been impressed. Upon our return home, Father explained the stone.

"You probably stumbled across an old sati-stone. The stone venerates a woman who burned herself alive on her husband's funeral pyre," he said.

Tara stared at her father. "Burned herself alive? Why would anyone do that?"

"At one time, Indians considered sati a noble act. In 1829, the year you were born, Durga Charan, the British outlawed the practice as barbaric."

Tara and I recoiled, but remained fascinated by the stone symbol. We learned more about sati, pronounced suttee by the English. Early Brahmin scholars did not think of sati as suicide. Rather they believed true and righteous wives committed sati in order to purge the couple of all accumulated sin. Sati guaranteed salvation and ensured that husband and wife would be reunited in the afterlife. Brahmin women considered sati a religious duty to enhance the status of their family. In addition, many widows preferred sati as they did not want to live on without their husbands. Worse than death would be the ascetic life of a widow or enslavement by the husband's family.

***

Satish's two brothers heard Tara's whispered chant of sati. They glanced at one another with a look that belied their selfish intentions. My gentle soul could not have imagined the depth of their wickedness. The eldest brother immediately considered the family's wealth. Tara's death would result in one less person to drain the value of their estate. The second brother secretly coveted Tara and hoped she remained available for his satisfaction.

By tradition, Tara was required to escort her husband's body home. After observing the brothers' cruelty in rubbing out her marriage marks, I insisted on accompanying her. Disregarding society's rule dictating a man could never touch a woman in public, I hugged Padma an emotion filled goodbye. I kissed my son Avoya, then turned toward the body on the floor. I helped the brothers load Satish onto the oxcart bed, and pulled Tara up next to me. We sat opposite the two brothers, separated by the body. Tara slumped into me, in shock, but once whispered "Sati" when she half opened her eyes and saw the brothers staring at her across the dead body in the faded light of day.

We arrived at the family home in darkness, but managed to carry the stiff and unyielding body to the front room bed. I helped Tara to the upstairs bedroom and I held her before she fell into a fitful half sleep. While the brothers cleansed and anointed the body with oils, snippets of their conversation drifted up the stairwell.

I awoke before dawn and tiptoed past sleeping family members who arrived in the night. Despite the lateness of the season, the pond water had retained its warmth overnight. In my life I had experienced the shock of death, but not this kind of trauma and distress. The soothing water did little to prevent me from hearing the echo of Tara's repeated utterance. Unable to sustain attention to meditation, I quickly finished two prayers, the first to my namesake. "Durga, I am indeed at your mercy." My beloved ivory statue stood on the shelf back home, but I desperately implored, "Ganesh, please help me."

Undetected, I entered the rear door leading into the kitchen, and peeked into the front room where Satish lay cold. Tara had managed to come downstairs. She stood dressed in the white sari of widowhood, but the brothers held Tara's wedding sari in front of her. She sobbed and nodded her head. Fear clutched my chest. Sati committed by women dressed in their marriage finery honored their commitment to their dead husband. I must get Tara away without delay, but feared she or the brothers would resist.

In my panic I glanced around the room. Through the side window, I saw the Hindu priest approach the house. I sneaked out the back door, ran around to the front path that led to the house, and quietly intercepted the priest.

We walked into the house together. Tara's marriage robes covered her white sari, and one of the brothers encouraged her to take another sip of something he'd given her. I slipped my arm around Tara, and in what I planned to look like an accident, knocked the remainder of her drink to the ground. Unfamiliar leaves, not tea leaves, from the bottom of the teacup stuck to the wet floor. Tara's daze resulted from more than shock and a lack of sleep.

The priest chanted, "Hori-bal, in the name of God." The brothers adorned Satish's body with flowers and put him on the coconut fiber stretcher for his final earthly journey to the ghat. They leered at Tara and repeated, "Sati, sati, sati", in the manner she herself previously uttered. The priest nodded at me, and we took our places on both sides of Tara. In a state of intense hatred, I stared at the brothers. No one dared to stop the priest and me as we led Tara out of the door and down the path away from her past life and future death.

***

Father soon passed from this world. I shaved my head, shed my shoes, and carried his body to the ghat for cremation. Within days, Daya, my father's first wife and my second mother, passed away. I inherited my father's property, and the responsibility for my mother, Shanti, and my widowed sister, Tara.

My life studying the Hindu sacred texts did not provide sufficient income to keep the household intact. My maternal grandparents owned a large estate and invited us to live with them. I sold the compound where I'd been born, and Padma, Avoya, my mother, and Tara moved with me to Naria.

Born of my moment of hatred was a moment of clarity...knowledge had not been enough. A tranquil life and quiet mind eluded me for a time. Eventually however, I once again became mesmerized by my newfound depth of meaning in the spiritual teachings. I found where I belonged.

Daguerreotype

FOUR

Tenacious

Indiana 1829

My name is Angie.

I am the eldest daughter of Katharina and Gerhard.

In the village of my birth, I was considered a miracle. No one else who'd contracted the dreaded disease of cholera survived, including the woman who gave birth to me. When Father heard my mother take her last gasp, he raised his arms in grief to wail to the heavens, dropping my tiny body on the bed next to her. Sometimes, even years later, it felt as if I was falling…falling…and landing next to my mother's spirit.

When I was nine years old severe famine gripped Germany, forcing our family to flee to America. The horn's shrill sound followed the lurch of the ship being let loose from its moorings. Grabbing the rail with one hand and covering my ear with the other, I waved to the well-wishers on the dock with my elbow. I glanced at my parents, just as my new mother took Father's hand. The smallest of smiles softened his face.

Germany grew smaller across the ever widening expanse of the glistening sea between ship and shore, while life ahead loomed larger. The boat left the protected water of the harbor, gently rocking the ship. Father's face became ashen. He moaned then vomited over the side of the rail. He climbed below deck to alternately lie on his bunk or crawl to the filthy bucket at the end of the row.

During the dead of night, storm waves crashed relentlessly against the sides of the boat. Mother and my brother Henry were tied down together in a bunk. My three year old sister, Anna, and I were strapped into the hammock. Our thin frail bodies jerked with each crest and fall of the ship. Through the night, my father's dry heaves could be heard above the din of screams, prayers, and thunderclaps. His gagging and gasping scared me. I'd already lost my first mother...the loss of my father would be unbearable. While swinging wildly in the dark, I bargained with God. If He would spare my father, my life belonged to Him.

Calm seas accompanied the morning sun, and remained with us throughout the rest of the journey. We stepped ashore in Baltimore, stayed a few months, then traveled to Cincinnati by flatboat to live with my mother's brother. My uncle helped Father find a job as a butcher, my mother sold baked goods, and we children attended school. One Sunday at church, the priest urged the congregation to buy cheap government wilderness land in Indiana to help form a new parish. We left Cincinnati when I was fourteen.

***

On the farm, my nine year old sister, Anna, became my only friend. I could be grown-up with her one minute and childlike the next. Early on a summer morning, we hacked at the weeds in the space between newly planted rows of corn. During a lull in our chatter, we heard the faint sound of music unlike the fiddle tunes familiar to us. We looked at each other, dropped our tools, and ran to the cabin wondering aloud if a traveling musician had stopped to entertain us. Mother sat in the front room, spinning thread on the wheel. Baby Sam crawled on the dirt floor.

"Where's the music coming from, Mother?" I asked.

"I haven't heard anything. You've been day dreaming."

Anna and I looked at each other, then at Father and Henry who walked in behind us.

Mother told him our story. Father said, "You heard the cowbells in the distance."

Upon waking on Sunday morning, my stomach was queasy. Mother thought it best for me to stay home from church, anticipating the rough road to town might make me feel worse. I sat alone in the remote cabin, reading from my prayer book. I looked up between passages to stare out the window at the rolling hills. Something caught my eye below the cabin window.

A brass cross, a candle, and a prayer book lay spread on a bright cloth, creating a simple altar. A priest clad in white robes rang a bell three times during the celebration of mass. I hurried outside, but saw only the rosebush mother had planted…no altar nor priest. Silence filled the air instead of the sound of bells.

Mother contended I was seeing things. Father told me I had ringing in the ears.

I could not stop thinking about the music of the fields and vision below the window. After finishing chores the next day, I climbed the hill to my favorite spot…a large standing stone that served as a shrine. Kneeling in a bed of leaves before the rock, I recited devotions from my prayer book, then pressed my fingers against my eyes. Kaleidoscope colors flowed one into another. Beautiful voices began to sing the psalms. I opened my eyes, expecting to find a choir. Instead, a white light shone down from above, highlighting two doves hovering above the rock.

I ran to the cabin. Father had come in from the fields early. With joy unlike any I'd ever known, I told my parents of the divine revelation at the rock. "The Almighty called me to live my life in his service. God wants me to join him in marriage."

Father said, "You come home talking foolishness. If people heard you go on about your visions and voices, they would wonder if you were right in the head. Angie, I forbid you to go up to the rock again." He took my prayer book away from me and stuffed it in his pocket. "And thinking that two doves means you've been chosen? That's the craziest notion of all." He turned and walked out the door.

During supper, our family of six sat at the farmhouse kitchen in the two room cabin. We teased and laughed, talked and sang, all the while eating our fill. Following dinner, Father hugged my three younger siblings and asked Mother to tuck them in bed. He requested that I remain downstairs.

"Angie, you are special to me. You survived the cholera epidemic for a reason. You gave me strength to carry on after your mother died. I've always been grateful to you."

My father had never uttered those words to me.

He continued. "This fantasy of yours is a passing whim. At age fourteen, few know what they really want in their life."

"Father, you scared me when you were seasick on the ship coming over. I promised God that if He would spare you, my life would be devoted to Him." I loved and respected my father, but needed to speak my truth. "I have been called to fulfill that promise."

Father's eyes glistened. "You can serve the Lord by being a good wife and mother. I have always imagined you holding my grandchildren. Please don't talk any more about your calling to become a nun."

My dream did not die, yet my father appeared to believe what he wanted to believe. Judging by the way he avoided looking at me, however, it seemed he knew my heart did not waiver. After five years, with the priest's help, my mother finally convinced father my calling could no longer be considered a whim. Despite his reluctance, he gave consent for me to enter the convent.

***

The howling wind rushing through the cracks woke me.

I wonder what time it is. I pulled the covers up over my head, hoping to linger a little longer in my warm cocoon.

The bell already? I peeked through a tiny pinhole between logs, my window to the world.

Pitch black, no hint of dawn yet. I lit the lamp beside my bed, conserving fuel as if it were gold.

Good morning, God.

I took off my nightgown, noticing a red smear on the back. To my relief, no spots had soaked through onto the sheets. Neatly folded rags were stacked in my nightstand drawer. I stuffed them between my legs to catch the flow, then put on my black dress and apron.

Waves of queasiness hit my stomach. *I always get nauseous the first day.*

Negotiating the steep dark stairs while holding both a lantern and my long skirts diverted my attention from my upset stomach. Pre-dawn light had begun to filter through the kitchen window. I blew out the lantern with a quick puff and set it on the bench. My black cloak hung on its assigned peg by the door. In one seamless motion, I held the coat's neck by two hands, outside facing me, then twisted the coat around to wrap my shoulders. I grabbed the large black pot from the fireplace.

Fierce winds of March hit my face like arrows of ice. I put my head down into my chest for the walk across the yard. One of the elderly sisters tapped me on the arm, shuffling past me into the outhouse. While waiting for her to finish, I opened the rain barrel lid, grabbed the ladle and broke through the thin frozen layer to the water below. Water sloshed on my long skirts while filling the pot.

The older nun did not take as long as she often did. She nodded in thanks to me on her return to the convent. Inside the cold wooden shack, a prayer of gratitude was necessary. I thanked the Almighty that I didn't have to sit on my brother's frozen pee like back on my father's farm.

Back in the convent, I built a fire in the kitchen hearth from logs I split the previous summer. I put the water on to boil. Then I took my customary place in the prayer room, kneeling on the floor in the back row behind the other sisters. My calloused hands cradled my black bound book. The pages were barely visible in the dim light, but the prayers had been previously committed to memory.

In leading us, Mother Superior followed a routine order. *ACTS* she called it, an acronym for four purposes of prayer…adoration, contrition, thanksgiving, and supplication. By sheer repetition, her thinking became ingrained in my mind. Throughout the day, an equal amount of prayers in each category became my goal. Kneeling beside my bed each night, the day was reviewed. If I'd asked for too many things, I would berate myself, then adore the infinite, beg for forgiveness, and humbly thank my savior for everything I'd been given.

Sarah, my fellow novice, jabbed me in the ribs with her elbow. She'd poke me when she heard my soft purr instead of prayers. I didn't know it was possible to fall asleep while kneeling on the floor until arriving at the convent four years earlier. Mother Superior stood in the front of the room, signaling the end of daybreak prayers. We followed her toward the door of the room. She allowed the other sisters to go ahead, and waited at the door for me.

"Novice Angie, your wedding day is almost here. Are you ready to commit your life to the service of God?" Mother Superior asked.

"I gladly sacrifice myself."

"You work hard without complaint, and in this you serve."

"Thank you, Mother Superior."

"I will take you and Sarah into town this morning."

Her words astounded me. I had not left the convent grounds since the fall. When we were not working, we prayed. The rules allowed conversation, except after evening prayers, but Mother Superior encouraged us to remain quiet to contemplate the one true word. And suddenly, without any hint beforehand, she planned to take me into town. I tried not to show my excitement.

"Why are we going to town, if I may humbly ask, Mother Superior?"

"Patience, my dear, patience." She walked toward the kitchen, me a step behind.

"Yes, Mother Superior. Please forgive me." I crossed myself. The Lord asked little of me, yet I only demanded more.

While stooping over the fire, frying potatoes, the flickering flames mesmerized me into dreaming about the day ahead. Something was burning... the potatoes had stuck to the bottom of the cast iron pan. I felt ashamed of the lack of attention to my job, which brought more shame for my inadequacies tumbling down upon me. I would try harder to stay awake during prayers. *Oh, no. Is Mother taking us into town to somehow punish me for falling asleep and Sarah for nudging me awake?*

"Breakfast is ready," announced the sister who supervised meals. Soon everyone sat at the table and recited mealtime prayers. Mother Superior began passing the potatoes and boiled eggs. We baked bread the previous day and the smell lingered in the house overnight. My mouth watered thinking about eating a thick piece smeared with butter for breakfast. When the bread plate came to me, only two pieces remained, the middle cut soft thick piece, and the crust. With one person left to receive the plate, I took the crust. Mother Superior nodded "Bless you child. God will provide." I lowered my eyes.

My morning chores were interrupted by Mother Superior. "Novice Angie, get ready to go into town. The other sisters can finish your work. Please take your new habit with you."

I yearned to ask why, but did not. *Don't show impatience or emotion. Stay strong, steady, even tempered. Trust in the Lord's will.*

Mother Superior, Sarah and I hooked the horse to the cart. We sat huddled under the black canopy of the carriage, while Mother Superior guided us toward town. She drove the carriage across the drawbridge spanning the wide river. We hitched our wagon in front of the nicest brick building in the city.

Sarah and I followed Mother up three flights of stairs, my heart pounding. She told me to put on my new habit. A sign above the door read *Daguerreotype: Mirror of Memory.* I did not know what that meant.

I entered the room and saw something I'd only heard about but had never seen, a camera. A man told me to kneel under the skylight and look down slightly. He instructed me to take a deep breath and not move for two minutes. While sucking air into my lungs, the smell of iodine struck me.

It seemed like longer than two minutes before the photographer mumbled that I could breathe. He took the plate out of his box, and told me to send in the other novice. Sarah underwent the same process. After she exited his studio, we waited for over an hour before the photographer came out with four pictures he called daguerreotypes. He handed the silver daguerreotypes, two of each of us, to Mother Superior.

Mother Superior smiled as she studied the photos. "Our founding sisters in France will enjoy these pictures." She did not offer to show us. I wanted to blurt out, *Let me see.* Instead I told myself, *Don't be vain. Sinners are doomed to burn in the fires of hell.*

On the way home to the convent, waves of nausea hit my stomach. Mother Superior guided the horse to pull to the side of the road after we crossed the river. An odd sensation come over my body. I threw up and fell to the ground in my own vomit. Mother Superior and Sarah managed to help me back into the cart, and we continued home to the convent.

The strange sensation returned when entering the kitchen. I slumped to the floor and began to convulse and shake uncontrollably, foaming at the mouth. The other nuns carried me to a bed, and later told me they took turns staying by my side. They reported that while asleep, my closed eyelids twitched, I sporadically mumbled words and my body flailed throughout the night.

The next morning I woke feeling fine. Mother Superior decided we should proceed with the planned ceremony. Sarah and I took our vows before the priest in the prayer room. During the ceremony, my name was changed from Novice Angie to Sister Angie. We prostrated ourselves before the cross, then donned our habits to be worn the rest of our lives. The priest placed a ring on my finger denoting my marriage to the Almighty. The debt for saving my father's life was repaid.

A quiet dinner marked the solemn event. As we prepared to pass the dishes, the now familiar sensation of the previous day returned. A short convulsion, consisting of a few short jerky movements, overtook my body. Sarah glanced my way, and within moments, she too fell to the floor in a fit.

During the next few weeks, five out of the ten of us at the convent including myself, Sarah, and the three youngest nuns experienced vomiting, fainting, and convulsions. One of the nuns gave in to fits of sobbing. Another ran around the convent screaming and yelling. Yet another felt compelled to laugh and cry by turns.

Mother summoned the doctor and the priest to examine us. The doctor found nothing physically wrong, and said the workings of the mind caused our symptoms. The priest whispered Satan was to blame. We needed to pray to rid ourselves of the devil's influence.

Mother Superior left for her scheduled visit to France. No one could understand why the puzzling illnesses in the convent ended as quickly as they began.

***

The summer after I took my vows, priests from Switzerland arrived in Southern Indiana to establish a monastery. They were enchanted by my family's land and home in the rolling hills, and offered to buy it from my father. He'd spent years clearing the trees, developing the farm, and building the homestead, and didn't want to begin again. Mother wrote to me that she convinced Father he could not ignore my apparition of a priest saying mass on an altar under our cabin window. Father sold the property to the priests, and the cabin in which I'd grown up became a chapel. All of my visions had come to life.

Gold Coin

FIVE

INDUSTRIOUS

Indiana 1853

My name is Sophia.

I am the daughter of Katharina and Gerhard.

"...in a few minutes." I heard only the tail end of my father's directive.

"What did you say, Father?"

"The water will be ready for your church-bath in a few minutes," he repeated.

"I don't need to go to church."

His eyes flashed as he yelled, "Yes, you do need to go to church, and you also need to ask The Almighty for forgiveness."

"What have I done wrong?"

"What do you mean? A nine year old should know better. You disobeyed the third and fourth commandments. You must go to Mass on Sunday, and you must honor your parents."

"I feel closer to God in the circle grove of trees near our house than in church."

Father reached out to grab the flour dusted rolling pin Mother was using. Whenever he'd given me a whipping before, he let me choose the weapon: his hand, a wooden spoon, or the hickory switch. I usually chose the wooden spoon before lying face down on the edge of the bed to receive my punishment. The sudden grab for the rolling pin scared me much more than the other choices.

Mother jerked it behind her back. Flour puffed into the air and drifted to the floor. The colander of sliced apples tipped, spewing the fruit across the wooden table. The empty bowl propelled toward the edge of the table, but Father caught it mid-air. He seemed to catch himself in the process, and may not have needed Mother's admonishment, "Gerhard, let the child alone."

She then turned to me. "Best do as your father says, Sophie."

As I ran outside, circling around the cabin to the tub, my father told my mother something about, "past the age of reason, tell her so she'd be thankful." Perhaps he wanted to remind me once again of the hardships they faced back in Germany.

Or maybe he wanted to scare me with the curse. In the year of my birth, 1853, my parents sold their land to Swiss monks to establish a new church. The local priest thought we charged too much for the land, and someone started the notion that a curse would fall on our family…a one-hundred year curse. My parents didn't mention the curse often, but it worried them.

I didn't know what my father meant about being thankful, but I *was* grateful he'd stayed in the house. Taking a deep breath of relief, the scent from late blooming roses calmed me.

Sheets attached to ropes were strung between the house and shed, providing privacy for taking a bath in the wooden barrel tub. I threw my clothes over the linens and wrapped myself in a towel. Mother soon parted the sheets with the top of her head, lugging a heavy pot of steaming water with both hands. Most of the water she hefted to pour into the tub, but some she saved in a small bucket to use for rinsing. She then pushed up one sleeve, reaching far into the barrel to mix the hot water with the tepid my Father put in the tub early in the morning. She helped me climb up a makeshift ladder and into the tub. The warm water sheltered me from the nippy autumn air and soothed me after the jarring exchange with my father.

Dirty soap suds full of sun lit rainbows floated on the surface. Blowing on the suds sent them skimming across the water, magically multiplying into tiny connected round houses. The shimmering rainbows on each little bubble turned the creation into a fairy tale castle. Crouching in a tub of fantasy bubble houses, I prolonged my soak trying to avoid going back in the house.

"Hey, you in there, hurry up. The water will be freezing cold when it's my turn to take a bath." Sam's silhouette visibly lurked on the other side of the sheet. My brother hit a growth spurt in his late teens, making his shadow scary.

"I *am* hurrying, Sam. Besides, mother wants to take her bath before you. You're so filthy, the water turns brown the minute you step in the tub. The only one that can stand to wash after you is Father."

"You just wait, you little stinker. I'll get you for that." I knew what he meant…a torture tickle session. Sam loved to make me squeal until I begged him to quit. His teasing used to be fun, but more and more I dreaded when he caught me in his grasp. The tickles hurt my armpits.

Many times I wished for brothers and sisters closer to my age. I never met my oldest sibling, Angela, who left home before my birth to become a nun. My other sister, Anna, had been married for years. Henry got hitched a few weeks ago. Now only Sam and I lived with my parents.

The sun shone on our hilltop cabin on Sunday morning, but we anticipated cool morning air in the valley near the river. The four of us bundled up and loaded into the wagon to go to church. Not far down the road, we stopped to pick up Henry and his new wife, Philomena.

Mama climbed out of the wagon with the precious apple pie she'd made the day before. We followed her into the kitchen. She placed the dessert in the pie safe for our after church Sunday dinner.

Henry told mother, "You didn't need to bake a pie. You should have let someone younger do the work, like my new wife."

My father teased, "She sure *is* young. You robbed the cradle, Henry." Philomena was ten years younger than Henry, and the same age as Sam.

We took our customary places in the wagon, with me in the front between Father and Mother. On the way into town, the discussion turned to the recent wedding. We chatted about the fiddle music and the guests who came to chivaree the couple with pots and kettles. Glancing behind me to smile at her, I commented that Philomena made a beautiful bride.

She sat squeezed between my brothers, Henry and Sam, hanging her head. Each of my brothers stared at the farms on their side of the wagon. Philomena finally glanced up and saw me, forcing a return smile and saying, "Thank you".

Soon we neared the make-shift church. We celebrated mass in the open air, next to the farmhouse. The chants were nice to hear, but not the long sermon. The priest threatened that if we didn't tithe, the Lord would become angry. We would suffer his wrath upon this earth or worse yet, burn in hell after we died. I didn't need to listen to pleas for money from an angry God, or feel tortured by the flames of my imagination when embraced by my trees.

After church let out, the men talked about President Lincoln. The women gathered in small groups to catch up on gossip. The boys ran to the field to play ball. The girls watched the goldfish circle round and round the edge of the small pond.

The social hour wound down, and we headed towards Henry and Philomena's cabin to eat dinner. While mama cut the pie, I tried not to think about how those apples almost fell to the floor.

We left Henry and Philomena waving goodbye from the doorway of their little cabin. Henry put his arm around Philomena's waist and pulled her close to him. Sam told me to hurry up and climb in the wagon, the sky would soon turn dark.

***

Upon arriving home, Father told Sam and Mother to go on in the house. "I want Sophie to help put up the horses." It struck me as odd, because Sam usually helped him. My brother's old overalls, hanging on a nail in the shed, slipped easily over my Sunday best dress. I rolled up the pants legs four or five times to make them short enough for me. I checked each huge boot for spiders before putting them on.

"Sophie, there's something I want to talk to you about," Father said as he dipped the bucket into the water trough.

Memories of the previous day's comment, "tell her", bubbled up.

"Did you ever think about how your mother and I are older than you might expect, more like a grandparent's age?"

"It doesn't bother me. One of the other girls at church has elderly parents too."

Father dipped the brush into the water, preparing to wash down his horse. "I'd like to explain something to you. Remember the story about my first wife back in Germany...your big sister Angie's real mother? After she died of cholera, I got married again."

"I remember the story, Father."

"Well, you were named in honor of Angie's cousin in Germany."

"Really?"

"But your mother and I didn't name you." He stroked the horse, then looked out at the darkening horizon. Father walked toward the stump next to a woodpile. "Sophie, come here and sit next to me."

I patted my horse, which displayed no inclination to move, and joined Father on the stump.

He continued. "Sophie, Angie's cousin from Germany became a seamstress. She got married to a tailor, and they moved to New York."

"She lives in America too?"

"Yes. Her husband's brother also moved to America. He settled in the Indiana hills north of here. His name was John and he married Christina, and they had two boys and a girl."

"Are we going to go visit them, Father?"

"No, Sophie. We are not going to visit them." He looked up at the horizon, then spit it out. "John and his wife, Christina, were your real parents."

"What do you mean? You and Mama are my parents."

"Sophie, it's time you knew the truth about where you came from. We adopted you when John and Christina died."

He dug into his pocket and placed a *gold coin* in my palm. "This is for you, the only thing we have from your real parents. It is from 1853, the year of your birth."

I stared down at the coin in shock, then looked up at Father. His mouth moved, but I could not hear another thing he said. Before long, I found myself running away from him through the fields, crying aloud, "Stop, stop, you are not making sense."

The phrase real parents rang in my ears, followed by the word adopted, repeating over and over again. My head was spinning, my side hurt, my heart raced. I stumbled in the big old boots until pulling them off one-handed and tossing them aside. I ran barefoot to my safe place in the grove of trees. Barely able to breathe, I sank to my knees in a pile of yellow leaves under a tree. Curling up into fetal position, the circle of trees soothed me in their embrace.

I lost all track of time until Mother's voice interrupted my trance. She gently linked her arm under mine on one side, and father did the same on the other. Too drained to walk on my own, they led me back to the cabin. I couldn't feel anything.

***

Only two good feather beds occupied the farmhouse. Growing up, I'd slept with my parents, while Henry and Sam shared the other bed upstairs in the garret. When Henry got married and moved out, Father told me I'd be more comfortable sleeping with Sam upstairs. I'd already slept there a few weeks, and we each tried to face outward and stick to our half of the bed. That night I lay flat on my back, unable to sleep.

Sam mumbled in his sleep. I didn't understand what he said, except one word, Philomena. He turned and flung his arm across my body. He began to rub my tummy, and repeated her name. Even in my state of shock, the rubbing and talking in his sleep were funny at first. But he kept rubbing harder and harder. I became scared and froze in place pretending to be asleep. Soon he turned back to face his side of the bed.

A few nights later he rubbed my tummy again, but this time it seemed to me that Sam pretended to be asleep. I told him I didn't like when he rubbed my tummy in bed, and added I didn't like the tickling anymore either. He denied the rubbing and said the tickling was just a game. Then he got mad and told me since I wasn't really his sister, whatever he did wouldn't hurt anything.

I believed him. After all, I became part of his family only because no one else wanted me. The rubbing continued to happen every few nights. Sometimes his hand rubbed higher or lower than my belly button.

Philomena got pregnant the next year and the touching changed. Sam said ten year old girls needed to know how babies got out of their mommy's tummies. He put his finger in me. Sometimes far into me, or in and out of me. Sam said if I told anyone what he did, he'd deny my story, and father would believe him and send me away. The civil war raged close to us across the Ohio River in Kentucky, and he said war orphans lived on city streets over there, begging for scraps. Nobody wanted orphans like me.

Henry and Philomena celebrated their baby's baptism in the new church. As the priest poured cold baptismal font water over the tiny girl's head, the baby wailed and her legs straightened in shock. I cried hard too, saying the baby caused me tears of joy.

By my eleventh birthday, Sam said since he touched me in a private place, it was my turn to touch him. He put my little hand around his penis. While he moved my fist up and down, I prayed he'd get drafted and die in the war. But Father and Mother were seventy-two years old, and they didn't want Sam to go off to fight. Father made an agreement with a teenage neighbor boy to substitute for Sam in the war in return for a corner of our farm.

Sam threatened that if I tattled on him, I would be forced to run away with the Negroes we saw sneak through the corn rows on their way north to Chicago. I felt like a slave too and sometimes thought the runaway slaves were better off than me. At least they had somewhere else to go.

The next year Sam told me lots of girls got married not much older than me, so I needed to learn what to do. He made me put my legs apart, and he lay on top of me. My monthly flow had not even begun. Sam told me I'd be shunned if anyone found out what he taught me in the garret. He wasn't doing anything wrong, just his brotherly duty to teach me the ways of life. He rolled off of me, then whispered I'd committed the sin. God loved him, not me, and not even my stupid trees could save me.

In 1866, when I was thirteen, Sam got married to a young girl he met at a dance. Our parents were seventy-four years old and they allowed Sam and his new wife to continue to live with us to help work the farm. The girl took my place in the garret, and I moved back downstairs to sleep on a corner cot my parents set up for me. Still, the fear that Sam would sneak downstairs during the dark of night never left me.

***

A few weeks after Sam's wedding, Father went into town for supplies. He brought back a letter addressed to me, the first one I'd ever received.

Dear Sophia,

My name is John and I am your brother. You probably don't remember me because you were an infant when we parted. But I have never forgotten you and swore to myself one day we would be together again. On my eighteenth birthday, I moved to Cincinnati to work as a tailor. Our other brother, Benjamin, plans to move here too. Please come meet us. I earn enough money for you to stay here for a while. If you like it and want to move to Cincinnati, German girls can always get jobs as household help for the rich people.

I also wanted to tell you about our parents' death. We lived in the bottoms near a stream. Heavy winter snows and spring rains saturated the ground. Late one afternoon, the sky darkened and the clouds let loose an outburst of torrential rain. The lightning flashes illuminated a twelve foot wall of raging waters, full of debris, widening its path and heading in the direction of the cabin. Our father grabbed his two boys, one in each arm. Our mother held you tight, and ran behind father out the cabin and up the hill to safety.

They took shelter in a dug out root cellar in the side of the hill, and waited through the night for the storm to pass. The flash flood waters receded the next day, leaving little trace of the cabin. The horse and wagon stood in a barn out of the path of the flood waters. We drove to the neighbor's house. A few days later, our parents went into town to buy supplies to start rebuilding their lives. On the way back to the neighbors, their wagon slipped off the muddy hilly roads. They died at the bottom of the ravine.

The neighbors kept us three children for a long time until they tracked down our uncle in New York. He and his wife, Sophia, your namesake, took us two boys. But with a struggling tailor shop in their front room, they did not have money or space to raise an infant girl. Our mother had been an orphan, so there was no one from her side to help.

Our aunt and uncle in New York knew Gerhard and Katharina from the old days in Germany, and turned to them for help. I trust you've had a good life with them.

Respond to me at the return address on the envelope. I hope you will come to Cincinnati.

Your brother, John

The day before leaving, I walked into my circle of trees and looked up at the light filtering through the canopy of overhanging branches. The graceful giants embraced me and held me with their love. My cathedral in the woods had been my safe haven my entire life. In the fall, the orange and red leaves made a warm bed for naps. In the winter, the snow outlining each naked limb and twig became my private painting. In the spring, I watched the crocuses push through the wet soil, and collected wild mushrooms for mother. In the summer, the shade provided relief from the hot sun. But in addition to being my church and my refuge, the circle held my most prized possession, my gold coin.

Ever since father told me the truth about myself, and I ran to the woods in despair, the trees hid my treasure. A man's dirty handkerchief had been stuffed in the bottom of a pocket in the overhauls covering my Sunday dress. I placed the gold coin in the middle of the dirty linen square, and tied the opposite corners together. The little package fit precisely, much like a puzzle piece, into a tiny slot formed by two roots jutting out at the bottom of one of my trees. My parents seemed satisfied with the explanation that the coin was in a safe place.

Like so many times before, I knelt down and brushed aside the leaves I'd piled onto the crevice formed by the roots. I peeked inside, preparing to remove the treasure that remained hidden there through the years. Waves of shock hit me. Instead of my gold coin in a white handkerchief, a rock had been wedged into the opening between the tree roots. My only consolation was that the embrace of my trees could never be taken away from me.

I left my parents, Gerhard and Katharina, with many tears, but without a choice. Sam's new wife did not understand why Sam did not return from the fields to say goodbye to me. As Father and I left on the wagon for the journey to the boat, Sam stood across the way, on the rolling hills of my childhood home, waving a white handkerchief at me.

***

John, and my second brother, Benjamin, treated me with kindness. A wealthy family in Cincinnati hired me to cook meals and read to the children. A free world beyond my little Indiana farm opened up to me.

It weighed on me that I never saw my beloved parents or home again. Despite the trauma inflicted on me by Sam, I remained grateful that Father and

Mother had adopted me. Many times I wondered what Sam did with my gold coin, but didn't let his cruelty break or harden me. If the ghosts of childhood spiraled me down into the depths of sadness, I closed my eyes and imagined the embrace of the trees. I found where I belonged.

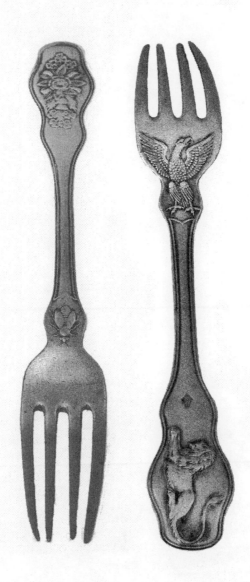

Fork

SIX

stern

India 1858
My name is Avoya.
I am the son of Durga Charan and Padma.
Durga Charan was the son of Ram Sundar, Shanti, and Daya.

In the stillness of morning, skipping stones flew across the calm water like dragonflies. One day after rising, I followed the dirt path to the pond halfway between our small house and the main home of the compound. I reached into the deepest corner of my pocket, feeling for the rounded edges of the flat rock. The day before I'd found the rock jutting out of the ground in the jute field. I'd brushed off the dirt, discovering the perfect stone for repeatedly slicing the water and popping out again.

Mysterious mist rose off the water from the heat of the morning sun. I thought about my one precious natural stone. *Should I skip my treasure now or savor the anticipation a bit longer?* I decided to practice my technique first. I'd collected shards of broken clay pots, then rubbed one against the other until the edges became smooth. I retrieved my fashioned stone, took my stance perpendicular to the pond's edge, and positioned my arm for maximum speed. I side-armed the smooth shard on a flat plane, hoping for a record number of touches.

Each time the clay shard glanced off the water, quick circular ripples fanned out across the pond, setting into motion a sudden eruption of life. The water lilies danced to the rhythm of the waves, while lotus stems undulated in harmonic movement. Frogs jumped from one lily pad to another. The early spring shuly flowers fluttered down from their branches like snow in the mountains, embracing me with their sweet fragrance. The white petals on pumpkin colored stems lay one upon another, thick on the path around the

73

pond, waiting to be collected by the servants to venerate the gods in our family temple.

Father's voice interrupted my world. "Avoya, where are you?"

"On my way to breakfast, Father."

The perfect stone stayed in my pocket, waiting for another day.

Three widows, my great grandmother, my grandmother Shanti, and Auntie Tara, sat on their porch taking tea. Joining them was my grandmother's brother, my great uncle, who lived in separate quarters on the compound with his wife. He carried out the duties of a landlord, a Jamindar, as did his father before him. I lived with my father, Durga Charan, spiritual teacher in the village, and my mother Padma, in a house down the well-worn path.

As required by custom, I paid respects to my elders and in return received their blessings. I bowed with hands folded in prayer, then prostrated before my uncle, kissing each foot. He touched my head, then his own forehead. I prepared to repeat the sequence with each of my elders, anticipating the women would wave off the formal greeting. They shook their heads and simply touched me on the crown of my hair.

My mouth watered from the smell of my favorite breakfast samosa. A light crispy dough, deep fried to a golden brown, encrusted the spiced potato and pea filling. I dipped each bite of samosa in sauce, alternating between tamarind and mint chutney. As grandmother diluted my tea with milk and sugar, I spotted a servant approaching the house. I squinted against the sun to see more clearly. The servant led two horses, my uncle's and mine. The servant's horse, laden with supplies, walked behind without a lead.

"Where are we going, Uncle?"

"A ride in the countryside."

"Why?"

"To visit the tenant farmers. The tax collector reported they complained about the assessment this year."

I pictured the collector riding up to the tenant's small homes. He carried a thick red bound book which contained each name and corresponding amount of taxes owed. For protection, the collector was accompanied by a retired foot soldier, a Sepoy. Despite the rifle slung across the Sepoy's shoulder, I doubted the farmers considered the old man capable of performing his job, especially when he accepted a glass of the best rum offered in every home they visited.

"You are taking me with you to discuss taxes with the tenants?"

"Yes, ten years old is a good age to learn about the ways of the world."

Uncle rode elegantly atop his horse, utilizing minimal hand movements to dodge the sacred cows along the way. I rode next to him when the width of the lane permitted. The rice farmer, his wife and older children in the fields straightened their bent backs as we approached. They collected their young ones playing on the bank, and threaded their way across the land strips to their hut. The peasant's wife spread a cloth under a tree, on which she placed sweet rice cakes and tea. She retreated to the home's doorway to join her stair-stepped children.

The farmer, Uncle, and I sat cross legged in the shade. The adults exchanged small talk. Hearing a commotion near the hut's doorway, I glanced around to see the wife grab something from a boy about my age. It appeared to be two sticks lashed together in an X. Thinking it might be an implement used in a game, I excused myself to the door of the hut to ask the boy if he wanted to play with me. He looked at his mother, who held the sticks in her hand. She retreated with the children into the darkness of the one room house.

I walked back to the shade and sat on the cloth. The farmer's hand shook, causing small splashes of tea to spill on his sleeve. "I am sorry, sir. We do not mean to offend your nephew."

Uncle ignored the spilt tea and the comment. "I am not familiar with the game played with that kind of stick. Please explain it to me."

The farmer excused himself, walking into the house. He emerged a moment later, sticks in hand. "Here, sir."

"This is meant to play a sport?"

"No, sir. It is a cross."

"I didn't know Christians lived in these territories."

The farmer explained that English missionaries, traveling on the Padma River, stopped at the homes of the rice and jute farmers in the district. The men, who called upon both Hindus and Muslims were initially welcomed.

The visitors indicated they held the blessing of the East India Company. The English private enterprise helped colonize India, resulting in the company holding powerful political influence on a broad spectrum of Indian life. The tenant incorrectly surmised my uncle, his landlord Jamindar, bowed to pressure from the East India Company to allow the missionary visits. He also assumed Uncle did not try to prevent the missionaries from converting the farmers to Christianity.

When the Christians called the second time, they told bible stories and preached about one God. They gave the family the crude cross, fashioned from driftwood collected on the Padma River bank. The farmer and his wife found the stories interesting, but they silently held tight to their ingrained belief in the Hindu deities.

During the third visit, the farmer refused the missionaries' request to dismantle the small home altar dedicated to the family's favorite Hindu gods and goddesses. But the farmer felt pressure to comply when the missionaries requested rice and vegetables for the less fortunate. The tenant farmer thought his generosity would be recognized by my uncle, who he still thought acted with complicity in the visitor's activities. The missionary calls occurred several more times, each time resulting in more gifts of rice.

My uncle said, "You shared your rice with the missionaries on three occasions?"

"Yes, sir, as did many of my neighbors." Because of the many bags of rice he'd given to the missionaries, less rice remained to sell than in previous years. As a result, he could not afford to pay the taxes.

Uncle stared at the tea leaves in the bottom of his empty cup. The farmer, seated next to him, and the farmer's wife, watching from the shadow of the doorway, stared at Uncle. He began to speak. "My father made his living as a speculator who gained control of these lands through little more than good fortune. I am now the Jamindar. I accept my fate just as you accept yours."

The farmer rose and bowed to Uncle. "Please, sir, I am sorry for my ignorance."

"Missionaries took your rice. Is this fair? I cannot say. Is there a wrong that needs to be righted? I don't believe so. You are a decent, hardworking man. Please pay whatever you can afford. Let us accept what happened and move on."

Uncle thanked the farmer and his wife for tea, then bowed to them with hands folded in respect. All members of the family returned the bow, then watched us mount the horses and ride away.

***

We traveled in silence, interrupted only by the growl of my stomach. The energy from the breakfast samosas had long since worn off. We reached the river bank, where the servant distributed a substantial lunch of rice, dhal, fried vegetables with greens, and sweets.

"What are we going to do now, Uncle?"

He thought for a minute. "Avoya, there's nothing I can do to remedy the current situation, but in the future will become more aware of what is going on in the district. It saddens me that the poor always pay for the greed of others."

I simply wanted to know if we would be heading home after our meal. Instead my uncle responded to the larger question on his mind.

The dhal and rice left my fingers feeling sticky. I climbed down a small embankment to the shoreline of the mighty river. I rinsed my fingers in the water, and remembered my prized skipping stone still waiting for its moment. I reached into my pocket and rubbed the smooth surface between my thumb and index finger. This would be an exciting place to test my skills.

Far out on the river, dots on the horizon attracted my attention. I slid the rock back into my pocket to concentrate on watching the spots grow larger. Five huge sailboats bearing British military symbols came into focus. I scrambled up the bank to tell my uncle and the servant, waking them from a nap.

The boats changed formation from sailing side by side to a single line in the center part of the Padma River. The lead boat lowered the sails, slowed to a crawl and stopped moving. The other boats followed suit. Soldiers dropped into three small dinghies, and paddled out in front of the large boats. Depending on the monsoons, the Padma alternated between flood stage and drought conditions. The men measured the depth of the water to ensure it was safe to continue.

Uncle and the servant wondered aloud why five boatloads of military personnel traveled the Padma toward Dhaka. We realized one of the dinghies was moving toward where we stood on the bank. Two soldiers hopped out when they reached the shallow water, getting their boots wet. They pulled the dinghy onto the shore, all the while keeping an eye on us.

We bowed Namaste to the men.

One of them spoke. "Have you seen any foot soldiers?"

"No, sir," Uncle said.

"Anything else unusual?"

"No, sir."

"Thank you." They turned and bent to push the boat out into the water.

I could restrain myself no longer. "Why are you traveling on the river?"

The other soldier hesitated, then turned to face us. "There has been a mutiny against the East India Company in Calcutta. The rebellion spread to Lalbugh Fort in Dhaka."

We watched them row back to the lead boat, already in the process of raising the sails. They climbed aboard and gradually disappeared with their convoy downriver toward Dhaka.

The servant packed the remnants of our meal. Uncle told me he planned to stop at a jute farmer's on the way home. He explained that the farmer retired from the service, and had spoken with pride of his youngest son, who joined the British military the prior year.

As we approached the hut, a young man walked into the house. The farmer came out of the doorway, greeted us and asked us to join him for tea. We sat in wicker chairs in the yard. Uncle did not mention the rebellion, but explained he came to discuss the rumors of dissatisfaction with the taxes. The jute farmer corroborated the rice tenant's story of the missionaries, then asked if he could speak freely. Uncle nodded.

The farmer said, "I am sorry you learned of my concerns regarding the taxes. You are a fair administrator of your lands and my dissatisfaction is not directed toward you. Nor is it directed toward the missionaries who seem to believe they are helping their fellow man. My distress stems from a larger force, the East India Company."

The farmer's son came out from the house, bowed to us, and interrupted his father. "Please, Father, say no more."

Uncle spoke to the son. "I am surprised to see you home from the military."

The Father answered for him. "They did not show respect for him."

"My friend, you seem to be upset with both the East India Company and the military. I am interested to hear your views. You can trust me to keep them to myself," Uncle said.

The farmer looked at his son, who sat silently with us.

"My son joined the military last year, excelling in his assignment in Calcutta. Then the army reversed their policy of not placing Hindu soldiers outside of our country. They transferred my son to fight in the Burmese War. I am sure you are aware an assignment elsewhere is considered polluting to our caste because of contact with unsanctified food and people. Of course, my son could not refuse orders. He went to Burma, fought honorably and returned to Calcutta in 1857.

While serving, he discovered he received less regular pay than his comrades from Madras and Bombay. In addition, by the time my son returned to India, the East India Company discontinued bonus pay for Foreign Service. The Company had recently reduced my retirement pension and my son had counted on the bonus pay to help our family. He felt shortchanged on both counts, but continued his service until a disturbing incident occurred on the Calcutta base.

He worked at the arsenal at Dum-Dum, directing civilian laborers in the unloading of a shipment of new rifles, known as the Pattern Enfield rifle. One of his superiors, a high caste Hindu Sepoy foot soldier, checked the ammunition. The Sepoy's job included biting the paper cartridge of the bullet before loading the rifle. One of the men told the Sepoy the rifle cartridges were greased with tallow beef fat, therefore the Sepoy lost his caste status when his lips touched the sacred beef in the lubricant.

From then on, Sepoy Hindus refused to use the rifles containing tallow beef fat in the cartridges. Sepoy Muslims also refused because they discovered another ingredient, unclean lard pork fat. Dissension spread through the base, onto other bases in northern India, and into the streets of Calcutta, in some instances resulting in riots. Soldiers referred to the skirmishes as the Indian Rebellion, or the Sepoy Mutiny. My son decided not to reenlist due to the disrespect demonstrated by the East India Company on four counts…overseas assignment, lack of equal pay, no bonus for Foreign Service, and total disregard of sacred beliefs."

Before my uncle responded, I blurted out, "The Indian rebellion must be the reason why the British Soldiers are headed to Dhaka." Upon my statement, the farmer and his son looked alarmed. They glanced at each other, excused themselves, and retreated into the house.

We later heard the English imprisoned the jute farmer's son in the Mill Barrack at Dhaka for his part in the Sepoy Mutiny. He stood accused of instigating the riots…it was he who first told the Sepoy the contents of the cartridge grease.

Eventually, the East India Company lost their power as a result of the Rebellion, only to be replaced by the British government with their own new rules. Daily life for most people in rural India changed little after the Mutiny, but the complexity of the world had revealed itself to me.

***

Ten years passed.

The cold smooth surface of the white marble bench calmed me as I sat in the anteroom of the maharaja's palace. Light aromas of incense and jasmine scented the clear mountain air. The reflection of the clouds in the man-made lake in the valley below stirred a sense of nostalgia in me. A little more than a year had passed since I accepted a post in Kuchbihar as a tax collector. Now I sat in the palace waiting for an audience with His Highness.

Kuchbihar sat nestled in the foothills of the Himalayas, with roads leading into the city from all directions. For several centuries, the town held the reputation of being a modern trade center. The maharaja lived in a spectacular palace, built into the hillside. Following the Sepoy Mutiny and downfall of the East India Company in 1857, Queen Victoria's crown rule enacted sweeping changes of the country's administration, financial system, and military. The maharaja became a key player in the reorganization, bringing strength to the region. I had never met him, but it was commonly known the British Raj leaders appreciated his progressive attitude. By the same token, they considered his independent character a royal pain in the 'arse'.

Echoed whispers in the nearby rooms stirred me from my thoughts. The maharaja's assistant appeared and led me into the formal audience room. Finely carved mahogany furniture, red beet-root dyed tapestries on the walls, and jeweled ceilings adorned with crystal chandeliers surrounded me. A taxidermied tiger, looming large in both height and breadth, stood guard in the middle of the room. His teeth snarled in a ferocious grin, his nares flared, and his glassy brown eyes stared straight ahead, forever transfixed on an unknown victim.

The assistant announced the maharaja's entrance. The ruler entered the room through a small side archway, and lumbered toward his golden gilded throne. I arose from a deep bow, encountering a double chinned man with a huge belly roll hanging over his waist. He wore informal clothing, a Punjabi shirt and doti, with a silk turban. The attendant poured tea, bowed toward the throne and backed out of the room. Except for the stuffed tiger, I stood alone with the most powerful man in northern India. The maharaja indicated I sit across from him on huge cushions atop a tiger skin rug.

"Avoya, do you know why I called you here today?"

"No, Your Highness."

"You have the reputation of being the most efficient worker in your division. I am promoting you to chief tax collector of Kuchbihar."

I bowed my head. "Thank you, sir. I will prove your confidence in me is well placed."

He nodded and sipped his tea. "The promotion is not the primary reason I summoned you. I hear you are an adventurous fellow."

"Yes, Your Highness."

"I have a proposal for you. The sport of the tiger hunt is like no other. You have proved yourself a clever young fellow through your work. I hope you are also courageous enough to join me on a hunting party."

The maharaja's forays into the foothills to hunt the Royal Bengal tiger were legendary Conflicting emotions surged through me. I grew up listening to my father, Durga Charan, the Khulin Brahmin, the Sanskrit scholar, ingrain in me the ancient Hindu writings. "All life is sacred. Don't kill the fly on the wall, it hasn't hurt you. Your karma will forever follow you."

My ruler could not be refused, even if I had wanted to do so. "Yes, Your Highness."

His Highness continued. "We leave on the trip in a few days. We will hunt a specific tiger, one striking fear in the hearts of people in a village in the foothills. Two children working in the fields disappeared. It seems there is a man-eating tiger on the prowl."

Stunned by the revelation, I not only felt conflict with my moral belief system, but also the profound fear of a man eating tiger. But my ego quickly overrode my trepidation. I would kill a man eating tiger if given a chance. I fancied myself helping the maharaja save the villagers, although at the expense of a tiger's life. For the first time, I convinced myself a life was worth sacrificing to protect others.

***

Traveling through the countryside with the royal hunting party felt luxurious. The servants carried the maharaja on a palanquin when he tired of riding his horse. White tents constructed for the royal hunting parties were set up at dusk. The ruler ordered the traveling chef to prepare rich Indian food and traditional British fare. White linen tablecloths, monogrammed china and full service silverware graced the tables. We slept in comfortable beds, washed ourselves with warm water in the morning, and wore clean traveling clothes each day.

After several days journey, we arrived in the village, a small enclave of dusty huts around a common well. The farmers demonstrated the customary show of respect for the maharaja, but then became agitated while updating us on the situation. A few days previous to our arrival, a wife found her husband's tattered clothes in their backyard garden. His licked-clean skeletal remains lay scattered nearby, and bones trailed toward the woods beyond. Since then, the villagers neglected their crops and stayed in their homes, praying to the gods to save them. They had not tried to hunt the tiger because no one in the village could afford a gun.

A few brave farmers proposed a plan to lure the tiger out into the open, loudly bang drums to disorient the animal, then encircle it with lit torches. The skilled maharaja would shoot the cornered animal.

The ruler felt the farmer's plan would prove too dangerous. Instead, we traveled by elephant to the tiger's presumed favorite watering hole and scouted for a strong tree which provided a vantage point overlooking the pond. The servants built steps to climb the tree and a wooden hunting platform, a machan, on a sturdy limb high up out of the tiger's line of sight. The elephants and workers returned to the village, leaving the maharaja and I perched in the machan, lying in wait for the tiger.

Despite the ruler's girth he climbed the tree, breathing heavily upon reaching the platform. We settled in, our anticipation growing as darkness fell. The full moon rose on the horizon, flooding the clearing in moonlight and creating a shimmering glow on the pond's surface. We sat in silence in the still night air, remaining alert for animals to emerge and quench their thirst at the water's edge. We perceived a few small animals at the pond, but they quickly fled back into the undergrowth.

We waited for what seemed like a long time. Suddenly, we spotted glowing eyes at the thicket's edge on the opposite side of the pond from where we perched. A magnificent tiger crept into the open, the moonlight illuminating his huge frame. He appeared larger than the taxidermied tiger in the palace, probably close to five hundred pounds and twelve feet long. The tiger sniffed the air and stealthily approached the pond, but did not look in our direction. He crouched, drank, and licked his lips. I shuddered when he stretched his neck, cocked his head to the side, and emitted a terrifying roar. We saw into his open mouth and stared at the back of his throat as he let out the blood curdling sound.

The maharaja later explained the tiger revealed himself as the man eater with his mighty roar. Through his monocular lens, the ruler noticed a significant amount of teeth missing in the tiger's mouth. Tigers lived as solitary animals that depended upon themselves for food. The tiger we saw stood in his prime, not old or injured. But because the animal did not have the full set of teeth needed to kill, or shred tough hided prey, circumstances forced him to find another source of food. The farmers in the area did not raise animals, only grew rice and vegetables. In order for the tiger to obtain protein needed for survival, humans became his prey. The tiger developed a taste for human flesh when it killed the children. He became progressively bolder and emerged as a full-fledged man-eater.

Without saying a word, we worked in synchrony. The maharaja gave me the monocular, and I handed him his cocked at the ready rifle. As the man in power, His Highness possessed the honor of the kill. He pointed the gun at the tiger, who sat lounging and licking its fur at the side of the pond. The marksman did not hurry, but methodically shifted his weight into position, brought the gun to his shoulder, looked through the sight and took aim. I held my breath while watching the tiger and waiting for the blast. The maharaja pulled the trigger.

He did not make a clean kill. The tiger wailed and attempted to rise. We saw dark red blood seeping from the side of his belly. The ruler began to reload the rifle to take a second shot. A loud cracking sound, accompanied by the jolt of our bodies and lurch of our stomachs, interrupted him. The tree limbs could no longer support our weight in the machan. Another crack, another body jerk. The maharaja instinctively grabbed the rail to brace himself, letting go of the gun. His rifle slid off the platform and bounced through the limbs to the ground. The tiger heard the commotion and watched the gun fall through the tree.

We needed to get off the platform immediately before it followed the same destiny as the gun. I helped the maharaja climb onto the ladder affixed to the tree trunk. He took a few steps down the rungs, then placed one foot on a lower tree branch to steady himself. I followed behind. He panted, "Shoot him again. We can't let the injured tiger make it back into the wild. It will become even more dangerous."

I scuttled around the maharaja down to the wide fork in the tree, eight feet up from the ground. It was the spot we climbed off the elephant's back onto the start of the built in ladder. I darted glances at the tiger, who had managed to stand. Bracing myself, I slipped my rifle off my shoulder, and loaded it. The tiger's red mirrored eyes bore through the darkness to meet mine. My hands began to shake.

I instinctively reached into my hunting jacket pocket and rubbed the smooth surface of my lucky piece between my thumb and trigger finger. I carried the perfect skipping stone with me since that day with my uncle long ago, the day I left my childhood behind. The treasure reminded me that life's complexities reached far deeper than one could ever comprehend, but life kept moving forward. The skipping stone became a reference point, soothing me into a calm acceptance of my fate.

I took aim. The animal stood still, looking straight at me. It seemed as if he acknowledged *his* fate, and waited for the mercy kill. I pulled the trigger. The animal crumpled to the ground and his body spasmed before he lay still. Blood pools at his side formed red rivulets running toward the water. The pond darkened at the edge where the tiger stood drinking a few moments before.

"Avoya," the maharaja shouted, "you did it, old chap. You saved us from the man-eater."

***

On the way home to Kuchbihar, the maharaja directed his cook to prepare a grand celebration meal of my favorite dishes. I requested traditional Indian food with an appetizer of samosas. The chef surprised me with a desert I'd never tasted, English shortcakes with raisins. While eating my cake, I noticed the engraved lion on the *fork* handle. A bit elated from my conquest, not to mention several shots of scotch, I felt emboldened.

I clinked my glass, stood and made a toast. I thanked His Highness for honoring me. I proclaimed that with the maharaja's help and good graces, one day I would hunt and kill a lion to add to my short list of conquests. He responded he would take me to the dessert in Northwest India to pursue my desire. In the meantime, he presented me with the grand set of silver we used. He said the lion engraving on the utensil handle assured me of having won a lion prize in this life, no matter what the future held.

As time passed, I became more skilled and efficient in my position as chief tax collector. I never forgot my uncle's lament...the poor pay for the greed of others. My understanding of his wise words helped me earn a reputation as a stern but fair administrator. The maharaja appointed me the chief minister of Kuchbihar.

***

Through the years, the luxuries that accompanied my title became familiar. I dreamed of my simple childhood in Naria. I retired early and moved with my wife, Shyamsundari, and our growing family back to my home near the Padma River. I remodeled the old house into a large two story home of brick and teak wood, with marble floors. A central courtyard, roof patios, and a wraparound porch afforded views of the pond.

Several times, when the air was calm and the water surface smooth as glass, I became tempted to walk to the edge and launch the perfect skipping stone. I had dreamed so long and often about how many skips it would take. Instead, I placed my rock in a utensil drawer with the lion engraved silverware the maharaja presented to me. I thought that perhaps someday, someone might find my perfect stone. It rested, waiting for the right person to take their stance, hope for infinite skips, and discover their fate.

Rosary

SEVEN

WHOLESOME

Indiana 1871

My name is Philomena.

I am the wife of Henry, who was the son of Katharina and Gerhard.

In the sun rays piercing the still air of the cold cabin kitchen, errant flour particles danced like miniature windblown snowflakes. My ten year old daughter Katherine stood at the long wood table, kneading endless tears into the white ball of dough. With each push and pull of Katherine's small hands, the drops rolled from the corners of her eyes to the edge of her chin. They plopped onto the mixture, rendering the dough soft and sticky. She reached into the flour bin and sprinkled filtered dustings over the bread dough.

Without speaking, she pushed the dough across the table to her younger sister. Mary kneaded and punched the dough, wiping sniffles on her sleeve, while Katherine began work on another loaf. My baby daughter sat in the high chair, watching her older sisters prepare the bread. My two boys, ages five and six, lay sleeping in their bed.

Henry, my husband, worked outside in the morning sunlight struggling to build a Christmas present for me. I caught glimpses of him selecting the best wood from the pile and splintering the thick pieces into flat slats. He cut and sized the wood, then butted the pieces against each other across the span of two close tree stumps. To complete the box, Henry lay cross beams over the wood at intervals and both ends.

He used wooden pegs and square iron nails to attach the pieces together. The nails had been meant for a house addition planned for the spring. He hit his thumb with the hammer, grabbed his injured hand and cussed under his breath. Neck muscles taut with determination, he continued to work for several more hours constructing the long and short sides of the box. Intermittently shaking his swollen thumb, Henry finished the lid and moved the completed box to the shed.

Henry trudged across the yard and through the farmhouse door. He hung up his coat and hat, then walked to the bed where his boys lay sleeping. Trying to make his children comfortable, he straightened the covers. He returned to the kitchen, poured himself a cup of coffee and sat at the table. The girls served him slices of warm bread spread with butter and molasses, which he devoured in a few bites. Henry wrote a few words on a piece of paper, put his sawdust laden coat back on, and inserted the note into his pocket. He slipped on his hat and as if an afterthought, said, "I'll be back shortly. Keep an eye on the boys."

My husband headed to the stable in the small barn and saddled his horse. Henry rode out through the fields to the edge of the farm, where the fencerow divided his plot from his father's land. The horse stopped in front of a sapling post topped with a rusting tobacco tin. A large flat stone lay on the tin to hold it in place. He took the note from his pocket and folded it to fit inside the tin. Henry briefly glanced across the rolling hills in the direction of his childhood home, where he knew his father and mother waited. He placed the tin back on the post, replaced the rock, and remounted his horse.

That night Henry slept with the boys. Katherine and Mary slept together in the next bed, the baby between them.

At first light, Henry rose from his bed where he'd been lying awake for hours. He looked out over the farm. Glistening frosted snow covered the wintered remains of the crops in the furrowed rows of fields. White powder blanketed the yard. Not even the cat's tracks spoiled the purity of the freshly fallen snow.

Henry shoveled hot embers from the fire into a cast iron pot, grabbed his hat and coat off the peg, and headed outside. He loaded the one horse wagon with dry wood and kindling, an iron tripod, and two cast iron pots, the larger of which held the coals from the fireplace. Cracking the door open, he called for Mary, who sat bundled in her coat waiting by the fire.

Mary climbed into the wagon. Henry guided the horse through the fields to the sapling fencepost. He removed the rock and opened the tin. Nothing lay inside the box, not his note, nor a return note. With deft pulling of the reins, he directed the horse down a gentle slope toward the outer branches of a large tree. The oak stood not far from the creek and served as shade for the animals in the summer. A layer of thin ice protected the shallow still water of the creek. Light powdery snow covered the small rocks jutting above the water's surface, resembling frosting on a myriad of tiny cakes.

My husband helped Mary off the wagon and asked her to fetch water from the creek using the small pot. He surveyed the area, and chose a spot above where the creek flooded last spring. Scraping his boots sideways across the ground, he cleared the light snow from his chosen spot. Henry started a fire on the clearing with wood from the wagon, and the embers. Several yards away, he arranged more wood and kindling for a second fire, and placed the iron tripod over the pile. He poured the water Mary brought him from the creek into the pot hanging above the tripod, and lit the fire underneath.

Both fires roared and sent smoke into the air. Mary watched in silence, but soon pointed to the direction of the sapling post. "Grandpa is watching us." She waved to her grandfather, but made no move to go to him. He waved back at her across the field.

The first fire died down. Henry meticulously pushed the remaining wood and embers a foot away from the original fire, but still within the confines of the cleared area. Mary added a few new logs on top, and stirred the embers to make the flames flare.

Meanwhile Henry dug a small hole in the thawed ground where the first fire burned, carefully placing the thick thawed mud aside in a pile close by. He chipped at the frozen inside walls of the hole with his axe. After pouring the pot of boiling water into the hole, he dug up more thawing mud.

They kept the fires going. Mary fetched and boiled twenty-four pots of water. Henry poured and dug mud and chipped ice. Little by little, the hole in the frozen ground became larger. They worked for three hours in the late morning sun of that day after Christmas.

Henry and Mary rode back to the cabin. They ate apples from the root cellar and leftover bread. They drank reheated two day old coffee to warm themselves. Henry checked on his napping boys, then returned out to the barn with Katherine. They loaded the wagon. Mary bundled the baby, and met her father and sister outside.

Father and three daughters drove to the sapling fencepost. He removed a new folded paper from the tin, and told the girls, "He's too afraid to come." They continued on down the slope to the hole and mud pile under the outer branches of the oak tree near the creek.

Mary looked on while holding her baby sister. Katherine helped her father unload my present that Henry built on Christmas Day. He and Katherine lugged the heavy box made of thick wood to the shallow hole. Thawed mud had slipped back into the hole and started to refreeze on the insides and bottom. Henry used his axe to chip away the frozen mud until the box fit perfectly into the hole.

The three girls huddled by the cart as Henry carried the bundle from the wagon to the box in the frozen earth. He bent down low over the box, struggling with exhaustion and the weight of the load. After positioning the partially frozen wrapped bundle directly above the hole, he let go. The thud of my hard body hitting the bottom of the coffin caused Katherine to scream and Mary to shake uncontrollably. The baby let out a piercing wail.

My husband looked down at me, then up at the heavens. He cried out in despair, "Oh God, not even the priest would come to bless my wife. Why have you forsaken me?" Only the wolves howled in return.

Henry took a last look at my shrouded body in the coffin. Then he picked up the lid, but it slipped out from his muddy hands. He wiped them on his coat and tightly grasped the lid. He tried to lay it over me, but he'd made the lid slightly bigger than the coffin and did not take into account the lid's size when digging my grave. Once again he got out his axe, and the chipped muddy ice flew on my mummy wrapped corpse. After several attempts, he wedged the lid into position. He retrieved four nails out of a coffee sack from his pants pocket. Kneeling at the edge of the hole and leaning over into it, he drove a nail into each corner of my coffin.

Henry dug shovelfuls of the saved thawed mud from the pile. As he slung the heavy wet brown earth on top of the lid, over and over again he repeated, "Oh man, thou art dust, and to dust thou shalt return." He reached into his pocket and retrieved a short piece of jute rope. Henry lashed together two partially burnt large sticks from the fire's remains, then stuck the crude cross into the mud above my head. His filthy hand, fingernails black with dirt, made the sign of the cross into the air. My husband did not weep, nor sing. No flowers grew in the frozen snow to place on my grave. Henry told the girls to get back in the wagon.

***

We had celebrated Thanksgiving at Henry's parents' house. The week after that my two boys came down with bad colds and a sore throat. A red rash covered their gums and tongue. I developed a backache caring for them, made worse by holding my whining baby girl. A few days later I lay in bed with fever and the mouth rash. The skin eruptions on the boys and me spread over our arms and legs, hands and feet. Soon they became raised bumps, and the bumps filled with pus. The house filled with the smell of sickness.

Henry would not give me a mirror. But I stared at the pus filled bumps on my extremities and could feel them on my face. I hoped the disfigured faces of my little boys were not real, rather that they were imagined from my fever induced delirium. Late Christmas Eve morning, after Henry bathed me in cool water, my fever subsided. The girls had prepared soup, and I could not ignore the pleading in their eyes. Despite my pain and pus filled bumps, I got out of bed. Henry helped me to the kitchen table. I sat with him and my three girls on Christmas Eve morning and managed to sip some broth from a spoon. My girls tried to smile at me, not to stare at me. I quickly tired, and peeked at the boys on my way back to bed.

Late in the afternoon, my fever redeveloped and I began to vomit violently. I drew my last breath during fitful sleep on Christmas Eve. When Henry kissed me goodnight, he realized the life had drained from my body.

My husband dressed me in my best dress, my wedding gown. We married ten years before, when I was nineteen. A few moth holes dotted the gown, but he did not notice. Henry folded my arms across my chest, then twined a white *rosary* through my fingers. He tore the two other dresses I owned into long strips. After binding my ankles, he tightly wrapped my body from head to toe with the strips, tying them together at the ends to remain securely in place. The wedding gown and dress strips soaked up the oozing pus and contained the flaking scabs chafing from my rapidly cooling body.

Henry feared that the scabbed over pustules on my dead body would spread the smallpox. He could not transport my body off the farm, nor store me in the chapel repository to wait for the spring thaw and subsequent burial. Nor could he lay me on the ground and cover me with stones for fear animals would carry the scabs to other farms. As a Catholic, he could not cremate my body.

On that dark and cold Christmas Eve, Henry carried me out to the empty barn stall and made sure my body laid straight. He covered me with hay, and left me to stiffen and freeze in the night. He went back in and told the older girls to pray with him, but did not wake the boys.

***

The week following my death, Henry moved in a stupor, taking care of the two sick boys while the girls fended for themselves and tended to the baby. He tried not to think of me lying cold in the grave under the oak tree. At night he felt the burn of several shots of bad whiskey in order to sleep.

He awoke on New Year's Day to half a foot of freshly fallen heavy snow. The neat stack of wood Henry split for the winter's fires lay in disarray since Christmas Day. Henry had chosen the best wood to make my coffin, and in the process scattered the pile of logs. He never restacked the firewood. Except for a small amount of dry wood under the lean-to, the wood hid under the wet snow.

In his grief, Henry had not attended to the wood stack beside the fireplace in the house either. The girls asked for fuel to keep warm and cook breakfast. He brought in the remainder of the dry wood from under the lean-to. With a pitchfork, he probed the snow for the rest of the logs, and brought them into the house to dry. Henry stoked the fire sparingly, and in the snow entombed house, no one stayed warm. The depleted boys' bodies endured no more. Twelve days following my death, my two little boys died in each other's arms. They never realized I lay in my grave.

Henry once again labored in the yard. In the roughhewn casket he made for the boys, gaping holes showed between the uneven slats. The box measured the length of the height of a child, but the width for two children. The lid dimensions matched the size of the coffin.

Henry didn't send a note to his father to fetch the priest. He told his girls the priest didn't need to bless innocent boys who surely went straight to heaven. Henry lamented that I remained unblessed in my grave, but at least my rosary was in my hands. In any case, the priest still feared venturing out of his priory. Nor would he stand at a distance to make the sign of the cross toward the graves.

Our boys' gravesite was next to mine. Henry and Mary again thawed the ground with pots of boiling water, and placed the dug mud into a pile. Katherine helped load the coffin and the wrapped bodies of my two little boys onto the wagon cart. Henry and my three girls drove out to the oak tree across the crusted snow.

My husband guided our oldest son's body gently into the coffin already in the ground. He struggled to fit the second frozen boy into the casket beside his brother. Henry needed to reposition both boys sideways head to toe in order to close the box. Mary, who watched her father from a distance, fainted and slumped to the ground on the snow. Katherine, with the baby in her arms, knelt beside Mary but felt it best to let her remain unconscious until their father finished his grim task. Henry covered the hole with mud and jabbed two stick crosses into the mud at the head of the grave. After one last look at the lashed crosses next to each other, Henry picked up Mary and laid her in the cart. Father and three girls returned to the cabin.

***

The fence posts stood as Henry's only contact with the world that winter. Even then, news of my death, and the death of the boys spread quickly. The neighbors left loaves of bread on the designated saplings dividing their lands. Henry continued to receive bits of folded paper in the tobacco tin from his father.

Henry's mother developed aches and vomiting at the next farm. His sister-in-law acquired an unforgiving headache. Twenty days passed since my death, and eight days since the boys died. Henry checked the sapling on his late afternoon ride. He opened the rusted tin, unfolded the scrap, and read the note, "Sam's wife succumbed a few days ago. Mother died today."

Out on the frozen hills, with no one to see or hear him, all alone in body and mind, he crumpled. His family had been saddled with a one hundred year curse in 1853. Henry felt he had been the prime recipient of the curse. His mind whirled. He lost his senses, lost track of time. For hours he saw fleeting glances of his childhood with his mother, his wife on their wedding day, and his boys playing happily in the summer sun.

The horse wandered off toward the creek, near the graves. Darkness had fallen. Henry walked in the direction of his farmhouse by following the dim kerosene light he saw far off in the distance. His horse soon caught up to him, and they walked together side by side. By the time Henry reached the cabin, he regained his senses.

He found the folded scrap from the tin in his pocket. It smelled of tobacco, not like the apple pies or roses he associated with his mother. Henry downed one nip after another, drinking himself into a fitful sleep. He dreamt of my frozen body in the coffin, unblessed, in limbo, waiting for release to heaven.

Henry requested a proper burial in the spring when the smallpox epidemic passed. He met the gravediggers by the side of the stream where the crooked crosses stood. Thawed mud had seeped into the crudely made coffin and refroze several times. The repeated thawing and freezing caused the wood to expand and contract, thus loosening the nails. The men attempted to raise my body out of the ground. The rotted coffin fell apart. Henry turned away and stared at the creek.

Tattered dress strips gave way and the rosary I grasped slipped from my hands. A gravedigger picked it up and handed it to Henry who put it into his pocket. The horror that took his family resurfaced with a vengeance, rekindling his raw grief to its depths. He could not bear to watch his boys' coffin being dug up.

Henry did not remember to give me back my rosary when the gravediggers reburied me in the church cemetery. It didn't matter. Above my name, Philomena, a cross had been carved into my tombstone. I found where I belonged, blessed in holy ground. Henry hung the prayer beads on the bedpost, drank his bourbon, and prayed to forget all that he had seen.

Frame

EIGHT

PRUDENCE

Switzerland and Indiana 1871

My name is Verena.

I am the second wife of Henry, who was the son of Katharina and Gerhard.

In the dark hall of the old Swiss monastery, I stood alone with a huge basket of dirty linens. I sighed with resignation, hefted the bin and lumbered toward the service stairs. Midway down to the basement, I stopped to rest and gazed through the tiny second-floor window of the stairwell. Only the highest Alpine peaks above the snowline retained their brilliant white caps. During the past few days, arrows of rain shot down from the billowy grey clouds, drenching the rocky terrain and fueling rushing waterfalls of icy cold water.

The sound of laughter redirected my gaze downward. I didn't recognize the man who sat on the creek bank bordering the monastery perimeter walls. He was absorbed in watching a small black dog frolicking in the shallow water. The pair captured my imagination, and I dropped my basket on the floor to observe them.

My entire life had been spent in the same hamlet and I knew all of the townspeople. I'd worked in the monastery six days a week for the past eight years, and the monks and priests who resided there were familiar to me. Everyone knew me as well, and it seems we had become invisible to one another. The steady stream of sick and elderly pilgrims who visited the monastery to pray to Madonna occasionally paid attention to me. But I wished a kind man, perhaps someone like the man by the stream, would notice me.

The chimes finally tolled four o'clock, signaling the end of my ten hour workday. Instead of heading straight home, I meandered along the creek path hoping to encounter the stranger.

The familiar little black dog approached and stopped at my feet. He shook himself dry, the wet spray dotting my skirt with dark spots. A voice from behind startled me.

"Blackie!"

I turned around to face the man I'd seen from the window. He appeared to be about my age, in his early twenties. He smiled when the dog ran to him for a quick pat, before returning to me. I stooped over to pet the dog, whereupon he unexpectedly licked my face.

The stranger spoke. "Sorry about the bath. Blackie likes to chase the guppies in the stream."

"Don't worry about it. He's a sweet dog."

The stranger carried a black leather bound book, larger and thinner than those of the theology students. My unabashed stare at him caused my cheeks to flush when realizing my boldness. "Please excuse me, I need to get home. I'm expected soon to help my parents on the farm."

"So nice to meet you…sorry, I didn't catch your name."

"Verena."

"Verena, my name is John. Maybe we will meet again."

I peered out the tiny window several times the next day, but John was nowhere in sight. My disappointment when fearing he might be forever gone surprised me in its depth. Despite his absence, I took the creek path home, hoping to find him. My heart thumped when Blackie, then John, came toward me. The excited little dog barked, ran up to me, and again shook himself dry at my feet. I laughed in delight, while John again apologized.

Following that day, when the bell chimed four times, I'd hurry to the creek side to meet John. Our friendship blossomed. We walked in the rain to secret corners of the village, and old shelters in the countryside. It poured most of the time we spent together, but I didn't mind. John was a railway worker hired to build bridges over mountainside streams, but thunderstorms in the mountains delayed the start of work on the Alpine railway. The more it rained, the more time I could spend with him.

On our fifth evening together, we discovered a secluded hay barn hideaway. By the light of the filmy spider-webbed window, John showed me his drawings he kept in the black leather bound book. He'd sketched buildings in the city where he grew up, and imagined bridges in the Alps. He then presented to me a small sketch of the shallow stream where we first met.

Overwhelmed with delight, I hugged him. He took my face into his hands, and kissed me. A wave of desire I'd never previously felt stirred in me. I didn't stop him from touching me. We made love in the soft hay, and snuggled together afterwards listening to the rain on the roof of the barn. The next day, the sun appeared and John left to build his railway.

***

One Saturday morning a few weeks after he left, I rushed to work under the reappearance of ominous grey clouds looming over the mountains. I missed my love and hoped that the turn in weather would bring him back to me.

My armful of sheets felt particularly heavy that day. I struggled to carry the load down the hall and pull the door of the laundry chute open. It took all of my strength to heave the sheets high enough to cram into the small opening and release into the bowels of the monastery.

Behind me, an increasingly loud rattle of rosary beads alerted me that a monk walked in my direction. Only new monks acknowledged me, although I wondered if there were others who wanted to look at me, but dared not for fear of the confessional. This man kept his head lowered, and hurried by me, praying his mantra in the hope of salvation.

Relieved at his indifference, I walked down the service stairs to the great white mountains of sheets waiting for me in the basement. Through the years, I'd become oblivious to the lingering odor of sweat and men on the sheets. But that day, while untangling the first few sheets to place them in the large soaking vat, my stomach lurched from the smell. The nausea increased as I scoured the sheets for stains that needed scrubbing on the washboard.

An unscheduled toll of the loudest church bells interrupted my work. An old monk, half deaf from years of aural abuse, tolled the bells. From dawn to dusk, he alone climbed the tower each hour, rang the time of day, and played a simple tune. At noon, and on special feast days, an assistant helped him play complicated hymns. Time dictated his life, and he dictated the lives of the other monks whose schedule of prayer and study revolved around the ringing of the bells. The people of the village lived in harmony with the sounding of his chimes.

Alarmed at the unexpected bells, I abandoned the sheets and ran the length of the long corridor. A flash memory of the hooded monk scurrying down the upstairs hallway came into mind. In retrospect, I recognized that he moved like the bell ringer's assistant, and must have been on his way to the belfry to toll the bells in the seldom used emergency call. I ran up the stairs and into the church.

I hurried through the aisles and out the front doors of the church onto the town square. Steam rose off the creek from the intermittent summer showers that had begun to fall. I spotted my brother, a priest, leaning against the outside church wall. Even though he lived in the monastery, we rarely saw each other. I positioned myself next to him, but before we could talk an official from the railroad shouted orders to those who gathered.

"Hurry, we need men with mules and horses to travel up into the foothills. There's been an accident."

"What happened?" a villager asked.

"Railway laborers were cutting rocks to build a bridge. The boulders were unstable from all the rain and slid down the mountainside. One worker is trapped under the rubble."

I ignored my status as a housekeeper, an invisible person.

"Who is it?" I asked.

"We don't know his name yet, miss. Excuse me, we need to go."

I jumped on the bed of a farmer's wagon, which followed the stream up into the foothills. We approached the bridge building site. Several muddy faced young men stared at a large pile of rocks laying at the bottom of a rocky hillside. John was nowhere to be seen.

"Who's been hurt?" I yelled, while climbing off the wagon.

The men did not look at me, but one rattled off the name, "John".

"Where is he now?"

The same worker pointed toward the rubble. "Under the rocks."

My heart tightened into a solid little ball. I ran toward the heap of rocks, screaming, "Why aren't you working to get him out?"

As I approached the pile, air pockets between the rocks became visible. "Something is moving. He's trying to get out. Come on, help me."

"Ma'am, the pile is shifting. Watch out. Run. Rock-sli-i-i-de."

Instinctively, I turned and ran until the mountain boomed no more. The second avalanche of huge rocks completely covered the original pile of rubble, creating a smoky cloud of debris. I only realized a scream came from my very being when my lungs forced me to take a breath. One of the workers grabbed me round the waist to stop me from going back to the pile.

"Stop flailing, the rocks are unstable. There is nothing anyone can do. He's buried in a grave of boulders."

"No, you are wrong. He can't be gone." In my moment of darkness, the words spilled forth. "My baby and I need him."

Unbeknownst to me, my brother and Father had arrived at the site. They witnessed my despair, my shouting forth of sin. They ran to me. The worker released his hold. I flung myself into my father's arms.

He patted me on the back, saying, "You are not alone. Mother and I will help you, and God will provide for you."

"God? Provide for me? Look at what God did. John is there, under that landslide of rocks." Putting my head down into my hands and sobbing, I proclaimed, "If this is how God provides for me, I don't want anything to do with Him."

Eventually I realized that my hand felt wet and sticky. I slid my palm down the side of my head, and over my ears. My entire hand was covered with bright red blood. The last thing I remembered is my brother lifting the cross of the large rosary hanging from his waist. He turned it toward me and made the sign of the cross.

***

I woke to a gentle wet dog-lick at the corners of my mouth. I giggled and moved my head sideways to escape the tickle. My father came running into the room, immediately followed by my mother. Neither one pushed the little black dog away, although my mother never allowed a dog in the house.

"Verena, how do you feel?" Mother asked.

"I don't know. Alright." I stroked the dog's fur.

"Are you hurting?" said my father.

"I don't think so." My senses were returning. "What happened?"

My parents looked at each other.

"Do you remember going up into the foothills?" said Mother.

The word foothills sparked the scene of the rock pile in my mind. Before I had time to process the memory, she continued. "You were hit by debris from the avalanche and blacked out. Your brother and several monks helped your father bring you home. You've been in bed three days."

"Three days? Wait...I remember, he moved."

"Who moved?" asked Mother.

"John...under the rocks. He was still alive, until more boulders rained down." I began to cry. The dog settled beside me on the bed. He licked my face. "How did Blackie get here?"

"You know this dog?"

The sobs became all encompassing. I nodded, stroking Blackie's soft fur.

"After the accident, he appeared in our yard and stood guard at the front door, day and night. I threw scraps out into the yard for our dogs, and they shared the food with him. He just now jumped into the house through the open window."

I had remembered more. My hands spread across my belly. I looked up into my mother's eyes, and saw neither condemnation nor pity. She put her hand on mine, looked up at my father on the other side of the bed and said, "You did not lose the child."

The days unfolded. Blackie stayed near me. Mother kept an eye on me while working in the house or out in the yard. Father came in from the fields more often than usual. About a week after I woke up, the three of us were sharing breakfast.

"Verena, we are concerned about your future," Mother said.

"I assumed that I...we...would live here with you."

"We love you, and will love your child. We want what is best for you both."

I stared at the dirty dishes on the table and listened to my mother.

"There are tongues wagging. You proclaimed your plight to the world at the rock pile. If you stay in our village, no decent man will want you."

Echoes of her words "no man will want you" bounced around in my mind, drowning out all reason. I wished the rocks buried me along with my love.

"You will be alone and ostracized. The monks won't allow you to work at the monastery unless we give them a fortune in alms. We don't have more money for the church."

My father spoke. "If something happened to us, we don't want you and your child to be destitute." He shocked me into the present with his next words. "I visited the convent in the next village. The nuns will allow you to live there with your child and work as their housekeeper."

"A convent? Me and my baby living with nuns?" Even though my parents thought they were looking out for me, it seemed as if only the little black dog accepted me now.

My parents stared at me. I retreated outside and meandered the hillsides. Despite my fragile state, I did not want to live in a nunnery the rest of my life. I did not want my child confined. I'd heard stories of pregnant women who went to convents being forced to give up their child. Boys were taken from their mother and loaned out to nearby farmers in exchange for providing produce for the nuns. Female children were expected to become nuns.

Why did John die? It's not fair. I don't deserve to be punished.

When I approached the house, my parents stopped hoeing potatoes. The words seemed to rise from somewhere deep within me. "I am sorry if I shamed you. Thank you for trying to help me, but we cannot hide in a convent."

Tears welled in Father's eyes. Mother turned to stare out at the valley.

At three in the morning, a near state of panic enveloped me. *What am I going to do? No one will want me. How are we going to survive?* I lit the kerosene lantern to orient myself, but lay there quietly until early the next morning.

Blackie trotted beside me into town. He ran toward the creek beside the monastery walls and frolicked with the guppies darting about in the shallow water. The first intoxicating moments of love seemed like a dream, but had been only a few weeks ago.

Tears wet my cheeks, but there was my child to think of now. Shaking off the despair, I entered the front door of the church and asked a student to find my brother. I sat in the back pew of the church and listened to monks in the choir loft hypnotize themselves with Gregorian chants. A powerful pipe organ accompanied the voices. Echoes of the familiar music calmed me.

My brother entered the church through the altar vestibule door. His black robes swished as he headed toward the middle aisle. He genuflected in front of the altar then turned and walked toward me, a slight smile crossing his lips. He made the customary silent sign of the cross over me.

"Verena, how nice to see you. I have been praying for you." He reached down to give me a hug. It felt awkward.

"Are you here to be absolved?"

"Yes."

He sat in the pew in front of me, and I knelt behind him.

Over the music of the chants and organ, I whispered my confession into his ear. "I have lusted for a man. I have not honored my father and Mother. I've been angry with the Almighty."

"I absolve you in the name of the Father, the Son, and the Holy Spirit." Another sign of the cross. "Your penance is ten *Our Fathers* and ten *Hail Marys* and daily recitation of the rosary. Each day for a week."

In the deepest part of my soul, I didn't believe any of my actions were wrong. What could be wrong with loving someone, or standing up for myself and my baby? It was normal for people to become angry when an avalanche of rocks steals the one they love. Nevertheless, I would complete my punishment.

"Thank you, Father."

"You are welcome, my child," said my brother.

"There is something else…"

"Yes?"

"I came to you not only for absolution, but as your sister who needs help. Our parents want to send me to the convent." He did not seem surprised. I continued. "I realize they think it would be best for me, but I want more for me and my baby."

***

A week later my brother sent for me. This time no calming music echoed around me in the refuge of the church. I didn't trust that prayers would help. I took deep breaths of the cool humid air in the church. I pressed against my eyes with flattened hands to find peace in the flowing blue colors.

My brother greeted me with a blessing, then sat beside me. He wasted no time.

"Three priests have planned a trip to our sister abbey in America. They are leaving in several weeks, sometime in September. They know you from the many years you've worked in the monastery and are willing to take you along in exchange for your service. You will be expected to cook for them, keep their clothes clean, and tend to them if they became ill."

The unexpected news lifted me above my grief and fear.

"Who is going?" I hoped they were not the lazy or smelly or greedy ones.

My brother told me their names. I felt relieved.

"How long does the trip take?"

"Two months."

For the journey, my mother sewed two new dresses for me, one for weekdays and one for Sunday. The latest fashion, the bustle dress, proved quite practical. The style sported a large bustle in the back, and a pleated gathering in the front. My baby could grow without notice.

Tears flowed as I hugged Blackie for the last time, but felt comforted my parents would care for him. Saying goodbye to my parents and brother, knowing I might never see them again, caused my heart to ache. The only thing keeping me from breaking down was the knowledge that this was the only path that would give me and my baby a chance at happiness.

A combination of morning sickness and seasickness accompanied me during much of the ocean voyage. Yet I managed to assist the priests. In America, we traveled mostly by train, and slept in monasteries and rectories on the way to our destination. We finally arrived in the middle of America in the cold of late November. Figuring conception occurred the last day of June, I was five months pregnant.

The abbey stood nestled in the rolling hills of a beautiful tiny village that reminded me of home. The resident priests greeted my traveling companions with joy, and me with respect. The day following our arrival, we celebrated Thanksgiving... an unfamiliar holiday. During the huge meal, I sat with mothers of students and a few townsfolk. They understood my language. I told them about my life without revealing too much of myself.

Friday morning I managed to wash garments, and presented my Swiss priests with their clean frocks. They asked me to sit and talk, which both surprised and worried me. I hoped they would allow me to stay at the new monastery. Unlike the monastery back home, perhaps the clergy here allowed only male workers in the abbey.

A soft knock at the door signaled the arrival of one of our hosts. He sat in a chair and looked at me. "I've been informed you are looking for a husband."

"Yes, at twenty-two, the time has come for me to marry."

"During the Thanksgiving meal, a local parishioner inquired about you. He lost his wife last December and two boys in January to the smallpox epidemic. His official period of mourning is over soon. He is ready to marry again in order to give his three girls a mother."

"What's his name?"

"Henry."

I had not paid particular attention to the men at the meal. The host priest continued. "Henry visits town for Sunday mass, and wants an answer then."

There was no real choice except to marry him and live my life in this little town. Henry and I were two people who would use each other, but I hoped we would grow to care for each other. I dared not hope for love.

On a cold December night I lay in my honeymoon bed. My thoughts raced.

> *This is the moment of truth.*
> *I hope he won't reject me.*
> *He seems like a good man.*
> *I should have told him.*

> *He's turning toward me.*
> *His whiskey breath is disgusting.*
> *His moustache and beard are prickly.*
> *He's old.*

> *I feel nothing.*
> *This is so different*
> *Take a deep breath.*
> *I hope the girls can't hear.*

Let it be over soon.

Where's the chamber pot?

I hope it's clean.

Relief.

Is he calling me?

Oh no, not again.

Crawl back into bed.

What's that? Did he say he knows?

Henry buried his wife and sons in the frozen ground.

His three little girls need a mother.

He is lonely.

He doesn't care my belly button is protruding.

"Henry, the baby just kicked."

Echoes of my words bounced around in my half-sleeping mind. They bounced over the wedding bed into the corners, through the walls into the girl's room. They bounced outside the door into the hills, up into the sky and across the ocean. They bounced across the Alpine slopes and seeped between the crevices of the rock piles. They filled the silent void.

Henry began to purr. I slung my legs to the side of the bed and crept a few steps to my open trunk. I reached into the bottom, feeling for the heavy scrolled *frame*. In the dark, my finger traced the decorative miniature carved palette and paintbrushes molded into the metal.

I could not see the picture, but felt it with my index finger. Under the photo of my parents flanking my brother on his ordination day, lay another small picture…the sketch John gave me. I imagined Blackie playing in the stream and dreamed of the times John and I sought refuge from the rain. My life became defined as either before or after John on that fateful night when he gave me the sketch. Grateful to my builder of bridges for his gifts and the stars above for providing for me, maybe I could learn to trust life again.

Vermillion Vessel

NINE

respect

India 1888

My name is Kumar.

I was given the title of Rai Saheb.

I am the son of Avoya and Shyamsundari.

Avoya was the son of Durga Charan and Padma.

Durga Charan was the son of Ram Sundar, Shanti, and Daya.

In the corner of the garden shed, a young girl sat lotus style on a thin green cloth. Her head was turned to stare at the sunlit dust rays streaming through the open window. I'd entered the storage building to gather root bulbs needed to make paint, never expecting to encounter anyone inside. She didn't seem to notice my presence, allowing me to study her natural state of being. The free end of the orange sari draping her head slipped partway down, framing her shadowed face in a fiery glow. The effect reminded me of a solar eclipse in which rays of sunlight formed a halo around the dark moon.

She held a clay pot filled with white rice in her left hand. With the fingers of her right, she mashed and rolled a chunk of basmati into a small ball. Our gazes met when she popped the rice into her mouth. The almond shaped eyes dominating her honey toned face startled me in their size and beauty. Hazel centers twinkled in pools of stark white backgrounds. They hid nothing, including her innocence. She put down her bowl and tugged the sari up to cover her head.

"Hello," I said.

"Hello."

I moved closer to her. "Who are you?" I asked, careful to use an inquisitive rather than accusatory tone.

"My father was hired to beautify the grounds for Durga puja. I came along to help, but needed to get out of the sun to rest."

"What's your name?"

"Gulapi."

"A rose."

"My father loves the scent of roses."

"What's your father's name?"

"Abdul."

Gulapi seemed familiar to me. "Have you been here before to help him?"

She nodded. "Several years ago."

"Did you and I play together...near the pond?"

"Yes."

"You've changed. How old are you now?"

"Thirteen. And you must be sixteen, Kumar."

"You remember my name, and age."

Gulapi smiled.

"I am going fishing soon. Would you like to come along?"

"My father needs me. Maybe tomorrow."

***

Several mornings later, noise from downstairs stirred me from dreams of Gulapi staring into my eyes. She wore the Hindu red vermillion mark of marriage in the center part of her rosewater scented hair. I fought waking and pulled the cover over my head in an attempt to return to her eyes.

Within moments, I heard a perfunctory knock on the door followed by footsteps to my bedside. My father's personal assistant shook me fully awake through the mosquito net and summoned me to the study off the entrance hall.

My sandals slapped the hard tiled floor of the foyer leading to the study.

Father said, "Come in, and please close the door behind you."

Father stood in his customary white doti, looking out the window at the mango groves beyond the gate. After I entered, he sat at a small table which held a silver tea service, then motioned me to sit opposite him.

"Tea?" he asked.

114

"No thank you, Father." Only on rare occasion did my father, Avoya, converse with me in his private retreat. I felt too nervous to manage hot tea.

"The servants told me you were with a Muslim girl from the village."

I didn't realize we'd been seen. "Gulapi and I played together as children and met again a few days ago. We're friends."

"They told me you taught her how to fish."

"We have fun together," I said, remembering our excitement when we caught a sunfish.

"You two stood close as you talked."

"I find it easy to talk to her."

"My son, I want you to stop seeing her. She's not one of us. She's a Muslim, and you're a Brahmin Hindu. She's the daughter of a farmer. You've been born into wealth and power. Never forget who you are."

Despite the knot in the pit of my stomach, I protested. "Father, we do nothing wrong."

"Kumar, when you were a child, we allowed you to play with Muslim girls and boys, but now you are a young man. What you call an innocent friendship could evolve into something more. I forbid you to see her again." He signaled the end of the conversation by rising, walking around his desk, and peering into a red bound book laying in the midst of stacks of paper.

Retreating to the shaded veranda, I took a seat at the wicker table where we normally ate breakfast. My progressive father astounded me. He forged social justice and equality in the community by employing all castes and Muslims in his jute rope factories. He built paved roads and canals for the welfare of everyone in the village. I found it inconceivable that he ordered me to stop seeing a Muslim friend. Evidently much more than a silver tea service separated us.

Gulapi and I had prearranged to meet late in the afternoon under the tree by the canal. Echoes of my father's words "evolve into something more" rang in my ears while debating what to do. Perhaps he was right. I'd never felt such an unmistakable pull toward another person. It didn't matter to me that she belonged to the Muslim faith and believed in a prophet, and as a Hindu, I worshipped the gods. We were all human beings, Muslim or Hindu.

I loved and respected my father, but owed it to Gulapi to see her as planned. I resolved to tell her we could no longer meet, despite my mixed feelings. My father would understand that I ignored his words to explain myself to her.

Gulapi waved as I approached, which deepened my trepidation, my guilt and my excitement. She put her nose close to my chest to sniff my shirt, then began to tease me about the faint pepper seed smell. My mother spread the natural bug repellant in each bedroom armoire, resulting in each family member's wardrobe sharing the scent.

As Gulapi smelled my shirt, I looked at the top of her head, recalling vague images of the vermillion mark from my dream. She then looked up at me, hazel eyes suggesting worlds beyond this life. I longed to kiss her, and tilted my head to meet her lips.

"Kumar! What are you doing?"

We both startled. Impervious to our surroundings, we had not seen my father walking toward us. Gulapi dropped her squiggly worm to the ground.

"You cannot be with her." Father grabbed my arm and pulled me away. I looked back to watch Gulapi run away through the field. "You disappoint me Kumar. I forbade you to see her."

"I planned to tell her we could no longer meet."

"It didn't look that way." Father glared at me. "Your mother and I took tea alone today. We discussed this Muslim girl. What is her name? Gulapi?"

"Yes."

"Listen to me. She is a threat to your identity, your future. She will destroy our Brahmin family in this life, and possibly the next. I will not allow it.

"Your mother and I are going to meet with a matchmaker. The time has come to arrange a marriage for you, to a suitable Hindu girl."

***

Despite his disappointment, my father expected me to participate in the festivities of the Durga puja the next day. He'd hired seasonal farmers to construct statues of the sacred deities for the celebration, and artisans to paint and decorate them. I lifted one end of a wooden platform holding a deity onto my shoulders.

My fellow worshippers began to sing the litany of songs for the occasion. Initially I mouthed the words, but eventually I sang aloud with the others, feeling more alive with each note. The long colorful procession snaked toward the river, the trail of flower bedecked people and animals winding through the countryside.

Singing and laughing, we rounded the corner of the dirt road. I spotted Gulapi under a tree, partially hidden behind her father. Her soulful eyes caught mine, causing me to trip on the stray dog following along with the procession. I stared down at the road to regain my footing. When I looked up, my father's eyes met mine. He said nothing, but from the accusatory look on his face, I surmised he had witnessed the exchange between Gulapi and me.

***

The next morning, the entire household slept late. Both adults and children had stayed up to celebrate. I woke to the sounds of a commotion outside, and guessed the noises came from the row of brick outhouses behind the main house. The servants were probably whining about the mess from the festivities, but upon closer listening, I didn't recognize the voices.

My stomach lurched when the pungent smell of the manure cart hit me. The untouchables came once a week and after holidays to empty the outhouse commodes. They managed to eke out a meager living selling the manure to farmers for use in the fields, and the extra work created by puja time helped keep their families fed. I realized I'd probably heard the untouchable's voices, not our own servants.

Slipping out from under the mosquito net, I rose to look out the window. No one labored near the commodes. Rather, the untouchables stood gathered around the side of the road, several hundred yards from the house. They seemed to be staring at something, but their putrid smelling cart blocked my view of the object of their attention. I pulled on my clothes and walked outside to investigate.

From a distance, through the spokes of the wheels, I detected something orange and brown on the ground. Perhaps a manure clay pot fell off the cart, or one of the workers felt the aftereffects of too much rum. The intensity with which they stared, and their halting conversation confused me.

Each of the untouchables, lower than the lowest caste, folded their hands together when I approached. Every man bowed deeply to me while whispering "Namaste", then took a few steps back to let me through. Before rounding the corner of the cart, I respectfully bowed my head to each in return and brought my hands together. "Namaste." *May the peace within me honor the peace within you.*

I took the final steps around the manure cart.

"Gulapi!" I screamed.

She didn't move. I closed my eyes, and reopened them hoping to return to a different reality. Gulapi lay nestled in the grass wearing her orange and brown sari. Her hazel eyes, fixed toward the sky, were exposed to the leer of passerby.

"What happened?" I shouted at the untouchables.

The men nodded toward her lower leg. The hem of her sari had been pushed up, revealing a swollen ankle. First I saw blood, then two telltale holes on her lower leg where fangs pierced her skin…a cobra bite. I knelt and inspected the marks, getting blood on my hands.

"Who has a sharp knife? I'll suck out the venom."

"Sir, it's too late. She's gone."

"No, no," I repeated, cradling her in my arms.

The untouchables began to turn away.

"What was she doing here?" I asked.

One of the men replied. "We don't know, sir. We simply found her lying by the side of the road." The commode cleaners dispersed, leaving me alone with Gulapi and my grief.

I held her, rocking back and forth, my tears dropping on her ashen face. I put my nose to her rosewater imbued hair. The stench from the human waste on the untouchables' cart permeated the air but could not keep me from breathing Gulapi into my very being.

In the days that followed, whether sleeping or awake, the memory of Gulapi preoccupied my thoughts. I remembered when we played as children by the pond. I recalled my discovery of her in the shed and the fun we had fishing at the canal. I recalled her eyes as she stood by the side of the road watching the procession. Those brief moments seemed more important, more real to me than all the rest of my life. No one could understand except Gulapi, and she was gone.

Next to the morning I found my love in the grass, the day I could no longer picture Gulapi's face saddened me the most. Her eyes, nose, and lips were individually clear, but her features melted away before forming her complete face. I asked Durga to bring Gulapi back to me, promising a myriad of devotions, to no avail.

Months passed. Neither my father nor mother mentioned Gulapi. Although my father showed me no sympathy after Gulapi's death, he demonstrated surprising kindness to her family. He gave them a small parcel of farm land on which her father grew and crossbred roses. I had never known my father to give away the soil of his forefathers under any circumstances.

The matchmaker identified several potential brides for me, and astrology readings narrowed the choice to two girls. Dressed in their best, my father and mother visited the girls' parents' homes. With no input from me or the prospective girls, the two sets of parents determined a suitable match. Dowry negotiations followed, until both fathers felt satisfied with the exchange. The astrologer chose an auspicious date for my wedding to Soudamoni.

Days of traditions led up to the actual ceremony. My bride and I walked around the fire seven times. She lifted her veil and I saw her face for the first time. Her beauty took my breath away. I dipped my little finger into the silver *vermillion vessel* and smeared the red powder in the center part of her hair. Even while marking my new wife, the dream in which Gulapi wore the marriage mark flashed before me. I would never forget my first love, but I wanted relief from the pain of her loss and needed room to grow into loving the woman before me.

***

In the year following my marriage, India changed. The British became more accepting of respectable progressive Indians. My father determined that my intelligence and sense of justice would lend themselves to the legal profession. He negotiated my acceptance into law school in England. I would miss my wife and newborn child, but I seized the opportunity given to me.

On the day prior to my departure for England, I decided to visit the tree by the canal to say goodbye to Gulapi one last time. One year had elapsed since her death, and the girl who I once loved seemed like a dream.

I followed a circuitous route to prevent my father from watching me. Now, as a father myself, I better understood that he did what he thought was best when he forbade me from seeing Gulapi. Nevertheless, residual anger and sadness remained in my heart. I did not want to upset my father or reopen my own deep wounds before setting sail for law school in England.

The remote path stood overgrown with tall grasses and brush. I spotted a tattered cloth caught on a prickly plant, and bent down to investigate. A snake slithered by, dangerously close to me. I began to sing loudly to scare away other snakes that might be hidden in the undergrowth or sunbathing on the rocks.

Stepping up onto a tall tree stump gave me a safe vantage point. The snake disappeared into a large man-made hole, partially covered by brush. The five foot square pit went deep into the ground. *If I had fallen in the pit, I could not have climbed out.*

The cobra's bite marks on Gulapi's leg flashed through my mind. My eyes were once again drawn to the tattered cloth stuck to the prickly plant. The pattern of the material seemed familiar. *Probably belonged to a servant, or perhaps I've seen one like it in the bazaars in the village.*

I visually surveyed the area to make sure no other snakes lurked in the grass. Stepping off the stump, a rush of revelation ran through my body. Gulapi sat on a thin green plaid cloth the first time I saw her in the corner of the shed. She put down her bowl of rice on it before pulling her sari back up on her head. I remembered thinking the color of the fabric matched her eyes.

In an attempt to grab the cloth, I pricked myself on a large thorn to which it was attached. Drops of red blood stained the towel. The two ends had been purposefully double-knotted together. As I examined the material, the fleeting scent of rosewater came to me. My imagination ran rampant.

Did this cloth belong to Gulapi? Why were the two ends tied together? Was she gagged and cast into the pit? Stop thinking such crazy thoughts, Kumar. Gulapi died from a snake bite while walking along the road. No one would do such a thing...throw an innocent girl to a painful death, then try to cover up her killing.

I remembered back to the morning of the procession on the day before Gulapi died. My eyes met hers...the shared gaze stunning me in its intensity. I glanced at my father. He knew me in a way only a father could know a son. He must have realized in that moment he might succeed in controlling my actions but he would never be able to control my feelings.

My father's words came flooding back. "She's not one of us. She's a Muslim, and you're a Brahmin Hindu. She's the daughter of a farmer. You've been born into wealth and power. She is a threat to your identity, your future. She will destroy our Brahmin family in this life, and possibly the next. Never forget who you are."

Was my father involved in Gulapi's death? The shocking thought seemed impossible to grasp. *Had I driven him to the unthinkable by ignoring his words? Was Gulapi's blood on my hands?*

Looking toward the sky, the brightness of the setting sun hurt my eyes. I closed them until the warmth of the rays slipped away. When I reopened them, the clouds were under lit with the sun's orange glow, reminding me of Gulapi in the first moment we met. In perfect harmony, her features melded together to create the entirety of her innocent face. My tears flowed for her, for myself, for my father...for the sadness and injustice in this world.

Gradually, the vision of her face melded into the pastels of the muted sky. The colors spread, first horizontally across the thin lines of clouds, then into an upward beam aimed through the higher clouds. Once again, Gulapi left for the other worlds behind her eyes.

The high pitched hiss of the snakes disturbed my transfixed stare at the sky. I let go of the green cloth, and watched as it drifted on the evening breeze toward the cobra pit. I shivered in the cool air, then ran through the fields toward a different world.

Album

TEN

HUMANITY

Indiana 1909

My name is Lizzie.

I am the wife of Paul, who was the son of Verena and Henry.

Henry was the son of Katharina and Gerhard.

In my son's hazel eyes, the reflection of birthday candles glowed as if the light came from within. The beauty inside him was as stunning as freshly fallen snow in a wilderness forest.

"Lizzie, are we ready to cut the cake?" asked my husband, Paul.

"We have to light the candles first."

Ted's lips curved into an embarrassed smile as his three sisters, his father, and I belted out the Happy Birthday tune. Our nine year old sang sweetly, but the only word the four year old produced was the final triumphant, "you". Our baby girl in the high chair babbled along.

Ted spent a few moments pondering his wish, took a deep breath, and leaned in. He blew the air from his puffed-out chipmunk cheeks toward the candles. Our lively middle girl wanted to participate, and in the process her spit flew through the air, landing on the cake. Everyone laughed, Ted most of all.

"Are you going to share your birthday wish with us, Ted?" I asked.

"You know I can't ma, or it won't come true." He added, "But if it does, I'll tell you."

I removed the eleven candles, feeling nostalgia for each year that had passed. Ted's childhood was gone and with it, his attention to me. He'd not chosen the increasing distance, rather duties of life claimed him. I missed Ted in the winter months while he went to school. In the summer months, he worked the farm with his father hours upon end. Perhaps then I missed him the most.

I shook off the melancholy, and busied myself clearing the dishes. On hot July evenings, we retreated to the yard to cool off in the breeze, and let the children burn off energy. Soon the mosquitoes began to bite. I tucked the children in for the night. Paul already lay in bed, and before I could rest my head on the pillow, he pushed up my gown.

***

Anxious nightmares invaded my sleep, waking me in a drenching sweat. I stared at the ceiling in the dim pre-dawn light without waking Paul. He didn't have the patience and understanding needed for heartfelt talks, questioning and self-doubt. His life compass pointed straight ahead, always doing the next thing, with little time or need to reflect.

Paul's demeanor had become increasingly serious after his father's death five years into our marriage. At the funeral he heard unsettling rumors of mysteries surrounding the circumstances of his own birth. He didn't talk much about his parents anymore after that.

I tried to lighten the mood in our home, but Paul told me my fun-loving silliness and antics were stupid. Eventually, he barked orders at me. Instead of being his partner, it felt as if I worked for him. Through the twelve years of our marriage, he became stronger and a stranger, instead of my best friend. I came to feel that if he didn't pay attention to me, it didn't matter. Learning to live without his approval evolved naturally over time. I felt alone within the marriage.

***

The new day dawned. *Today is Friday. I will see Thomas.* My heart lightened.

Thomas was the architect for the house we were building. One day as we studied the architectural drawings at the kitchen table, he noticed my stack of photographs and helped me put together a beautiful picture *album*. We became friends. Paul could not read nor write, but Thomas and I discussed books. Thomas listened to my thoughts, opinions, and dreams, talking with me instead of at me. Rather than focus on farm problems, we discussed art and politics, music and travel.

The baby cried. Time to get up. I shelved my thoughts of Paul and Thomas.

I retrieved the baby and carried her to our bedroom. I sat in the rocker, unbuttoned the top of my gown, and she latched on to my breast. A few of her teeth showed and more hid under the gum line, but four children in eleven years had toughened my nipples. She fed contentedly, cradled in my arms under the quilt. I glanced at Paul, who remained silent as he got dressed.

My eyes focused on a leaf under the bed, which must have been brought in on Paul's shoe. The remnants of autumn leaves congregated in the creek banks, their brilliant color often fading into a dark shade of blood red. The leaf had since dried, but not to the brittle stage in which it began to crackle. I needed to remember to pick it up later.

Before long, the baby sucked harder, turned her head from side to side, and started to fuss. I'd lost track of time and maneuvered her around to my other breast. The baby soon nodded off and her head fell away. I wiped a dribble of spittle from the side of her mouth. I closed my eyes, hoping the older girls would sleep longer before the commotion and nonstop chores started for the day.

Paul headed into the children's room to wake Ted, my cue to start the breakfast biscuits. The girls shuffled into my room, rubbing the corners of their eyes. I put the baby on the bed in-between the two older girls, hoping they'd fall back asleep, while I dragged myself to the kitchen.

Making gravy had become automatic. I melted lard in the cast-iron pan, added a spoon of flour per person plus one for the pot. As I stood stirring the mixture, Ted came in with a fresh pail of milk. He gave me a little kiss on the cheek. "Thanks for baking me the birthday cake, ma."

My smile inside was bigger than the one on my face.

I poured in the milk, working the flour paste and milk together without leaving lumps or letting the bottom scald. The biscuits I'd put in the oven were golden brown by the time the gravy bubbled and thickened. I fixed large plates of biscuits and gravy with fried eggs, and put the butter and molasses on the table in case Paul or Ted wanted an extra biscuit.

I wished for the freedom to eat how they ate. With each new baby came another bit of padding that wouldn't go away.

"Are you going to work on the new house today?" I asked Paul, who had followed Ted inside.

With a mouth full of gravy biscuit, Paul replied, "We will if we get done in the far field."

Ted added, "It might take us a while though. The lower ears on the corn stalks have been eaten away, so Father thinks we have a skunk den out there."

I looked at my husband. "A skunk den?"

Paul finished with his gravy plate, then spread both halves of a dry biscuit with a thick pad of butter. He twirled a spoon full of molasses to put on top of the butter, then put the two halves together. He dipped the masterpiece into his coffee, and took a huge bite. He studied the outline of his bite on the biscuit, then answered "yep" without looking up.

Ted spoke. "Father says since I am quick and strong, he thinks I can catch skunks."

I looked at Paul. "Please don't encourage him. Can you imagine how bad he'll smell?" My husband ignored me.

"Oh come on, Ma. I can learn how to catch skunks without getting sprayed. If they do get me, I'll sleep out in the barn."

Paul addressed his son. "Let's go, Ted. Lots to do today."

***

With Paul and Ted out the door, I sank into the chair and let out a sigh of relief, trying to enjoy a biscuit. But I could smell myself…the sweat from working at the stove in the hot humid weather, and the sex, and my nightmares. The talk about skunks made me feel even dirtier.

I boiled water and carried it to the bedroom, careful not to disturb my sleeping angels on the bed. While occasionally glancing at the children's fuzzy reflection in the silvered vanity mirror, I dipped my rag in the soapy water and rung it out, giving myself a sponge bath. I patted on fancy powder my little sister sent me from Louisville, then put on a clean dress.

When the girls woke up, they got a bath too. By the time I fed and cleaned up after them, it was mid-morning. I wanted to get supper cooked while the stove and oven were still hot. After that, I'd let the fire die out so the house would cool off before evening. Grabbing some potatoes from the cellar, we went outside to the porch.

"Mommy, I see Father Thomas's horse coming up the lane."

My heart skipped. I looked up.

The saddled horse stood rider less. She ambled up to the end of the porch, and started munching at the patch of tall grass that grew where the water ran off the tin roof. I instructed my oldest daughter to keep her little sister and baby away from the stove.

Thomas's horse knew my scent, and she didn't seem to mind my examination of the saddle strappings to make sure they were secure. I grabbed the horn, stepped off the edge of the porch into the stirrups, and swung myself over her. Since my father had no sons, he taught his four girls to ride. The horse readily responded when I directed her out toward the path.

Not far down the lane, Thomas lay on the ground holding his left leg out. I pulled on the reins and swung off the horse in one smooth motion. I squatted down to look at him.

With his face so close to mine, an unfamiliar longing came over me. I yearned to feel his soft lips kiss me. I felt my cheeks blush as I recognized the gravity of what I'd been thinking. *Lizzie, he's a priest. You're married. It can never be.*

Thomas jolted me back to the present. "I think it's broken."

I made him as comfortable as possible. Without an alternative, I headed to the far field to fetch Paul and Ted. They hitched up the wagon, and took Thomas into town. I stayed home to watch the girls.

***

My husband and son returned to the house late in the afternoon. I asked what the doctor said about Father Thomas, but Paul didn't acknowledge my questions. He ate in silence, and told me to get the girls ready for bed. He allowed Ted to go out to the barn. Once the children were settled, Paul motioned me in the direction of our bedroom. He shut the door behind us. His voice trembled from self-restraint.

"Why was Father Thomas coming to see you?"

"To help me make plans for our new house."

"He's the architect for the house."

"I needed to tell him my ideas."

"What a foolish notion. The architect works with the builders, the builders consult me about things, and I tell you...if there is something you need to know." He paused then stared at me. "Has he come to talk to you before?"

"Yes."

"How often?"

"On Fridays when he can get away."

"Does that mean he comes every Friday, Lizzie? How many times has he come?"

"I don't know how many. He's been coming a couple times a month since we started working on the house."

"We began in March when the ground began to thaw. You mean to tell me Father Thomas has been coming here for five months, and you never told me?"

"Why are you so angry, Paul? We're not doing anything wrong. He's helping me with the new house."

"If you aren't doing anything wrong, why did you keep this from me?" Paul looked down and took a deep breath. "I never want you near him again." And he turned to walk out. "One more thing. Clean up the mess from the leaf under the bed. It's cracked into hundreds of tiny little pieces."

Desperate nightmares visited me not only during the night, but during the daylight hours.

***

On a hot evening a few weeks later, Ted ran into the house grinning from ear to ear.

"I can tell you my birthday wish now, Ma."

"It must have come true then." I smiled. "Well, what was it?"

"I wished that I caught a skunk and Father was proud of me and he never whipped me out in the barn again."

Catching my breath, I chose not to respond to the revelation of the whippings. "What, you caught a skunk? Without getting sprayed? How did you do it?"

"Well, ma, skunks spray only what they can see. And they see better in dark than in light. So I snuck up on one at dawn when he first came out of his den."

"Still, skunks are quick. It's a wonder you didn't get sprayed."

"I figured out that if it couldn't lift up his hind end and tail, it couldn't spray me. So I built a short box, just tall enough for a skunk to fit in, but without room to lift its tail."

"But how did you get the skunk in the box?"

"At first light, I snuck up on him, quick put my specially built box over him, and slid the lid shut. It worked ma!"

***

After the accident, I'd only seen Father Thomas saying Mass on Sundays in church. I'd not spoken with him. On the last Sunday in August, Father Thomas announced at the pulpit he'd been transferred to another parish and was leaving that day. The four children sat between Paul and me in the pew. My husband stared at me above the children's heads. I guessed he wanted me to feel shame, but instead I felt overwhelming sadness.

Following mass, the head priest stood by the doors of the church to greet the parishioners as they filed outside. He told us he'd detected a skunk nest in the rectory's basement coal cellar. By this time, Ted's reputation as the skunk catcher had spread. We arranged for Ted to visit the rectory the next day, when we came into town for supplies.

On Monday morning, Paul stayed back at the farm to take advantage of the good weather. He and the builders planned to demolish our current home, which stood about two hundred feet from the massive new structure. Salvaged pieces and fixtures would be reused to finish the upstairs bedrooms. The previous afternoon, I had helped move our possessions into the empty fodder silo, where we would temporarily live. I hoped we wouldn't need to live in the cylindrical echo chamber more than a few weeks. Realistically, the new house probably wouldn't be done before the end of September.

Ted and I got an early start. We dropped the girls off at my sister's before continuing to the village. We finished buying the supplies we needed for living in the silo, then headed to the rectory. No one appeared to be home. We assumed Thomas had departed the previous day as scheduled and that the head priest was called away. We felt comfortable going inside the unlocked door. Ted carried the traps into the house and went downstairs. In case he needed me, I waited for him in the parlor.

The parlor was flanked by two sets of heavy sliding doors. I'd entered through the hall. The other set led into a bedroom. I heard the minutest of whimpers from the opposite side of the bedroom door and became concerned that the head priest was home and needed help. I got up and looked through the crack between the doors.

Thomas faced me with his eyes closed. A man knelt before him. Thomas placed his hands on the kneeling man's head, then whimpered. I realized what they were doing, and put my hand to my mouth to stifle my shock. Thomas must have heard my dress rustle because he opened his eyes. I will never forget his face in that moment.

We moved into our new home in mid-October, a few days before the first frost. A two story round turret framed one corner. Over the long winter, I'd find myself longing for love, or at least freedom from disappointment. At those times, I'd climb the stairs with my children, turn left at the top and take refuge in the tower room.

Our house sat on the highest hill for many miles around. Three windows situated in the turret afforded 270 degree views of the countryside. I craned my neck in every direction to see the fall leaves or the snow diamonds glistening on the rolling hills. Sometimes I'd observe Ted out by the barn splitting wood for the fire.

I sat and rubbed my growing belly while smiling at the girls playing at my feet. Occasionally if the mood struck, I'd turn the pages of my picture album, thinking back to the day Thomas and I had created the treasure. My heavyheartedness subsided. I felt grateful for the gifts of love and joy in my life.

Conch mold

ELEVEN
ᴆᵻꜱᴄᵻᴘᴌᵻᴎᴇ

India 1928
My name is Lily.

In the two years since Father died in the cyclone, my mother never missed a day snuggling his shirt to her face. With eyes closed, she inhaled him, his memory. One evening following her ritual, she thrust the shirt toward me.

"Put it on, Lily," Mother said.

"It's too big for me. And Momi, I don't feel right wearing Father's shirt."

"The plaid material would make a nice dress for you."

"Why do I need a dress?"

"You are almost twelve years old, and time you started to work. They need a sweeper girl down at the Madaripur ferry terminal."

"But Momi, you'll have nothing left of Father."

"I have memories...and his picture. Besides, the shirt doesn't smell like your father anymore."

A few days later, the dress my mother made from Father's shirt replaced my tattered rags. Mother brushed my hair until it shone and secured it with a strip of the leftover shirt material. She cupped my face in her hands and told me I looked pretty. I kissed her on the cheek, then my father's picture hanging over the low door of our shack. Before going to the ferry dock, we said a prayer to Ganesh for protection.

The dress must have impressed the station master because he smiled at me and gave me a chance. Day after day, my dress got filthy squatting down, sweeping the platform side to side with the dried coconut palm broom. I pursued my prey walking like a spider on two legs, holding the swishing broom. During the hot dry weather my target was dust. When boats docked, the water that washed up in waves needed to be chased back to the river. Each evening, I rinsed out my dress and hung it on a jute rope strung above the mat where Mother and I slept.

Between arrivals and departures, the station master checked his pocket watch against the big black clock hanging on the terminal wall. He'd spot a ferry approaching then call out the time. "Prepare for arrival of the 4:10 from Dhaka." Based on his announcements, I taught myself how to read the clock numbers, the ferry schedule, and the discarded ticket stubs. Eventually, I read the signs posted in the station, and the names of enticing foods for sale in the stalls catering to passengers.

One morning, I chased a tiny scrap of paper blowing in circles on the dock. A gust directed it toward the station master. He stomped his foot on it. I looked down at the scrap, then up at his face. He smiled.

"Lily, what are you doing with these little pieces of paper?"

"I take them home to use for cooking fires."

"I've watched you smooth out the papers and study them. Do you know how to read?"

"A little bit sir." I smiled.

The station master began to save his newspapers and helped me decipher unfamiliar words.

During the Puja holidays, a prominent Brahmin family arrived from the countryside. Servants leading a bull cart followed behind. The man at the center of the family often came to the dock. I'd been told he owned a share in the ferry service. During his earlier visits I smiled at him, whereupon he'd touch my head and give me loose coins for sweeping the path before him.

A woman in the midst of the loudly chattering group pointed out toward the wide river. "Here he comes, I see him waving to us." The women and girls trilled their tongues in ululation, the shrill sound drowning out the signal horn and causing babies to cry. The ferry grew larger prompting the children to jostle for position at the end of the gangway. I hated to go near there...I didn't want to get pushed into the water and drown like my father.

Crowds of passengers stood at the railings of the boat, but only a few disembarked at our dock. The eldest son stepped off the boat into the arms of his joyous relatives. I didn't miss the love of a large family until I saw one in front of me. My father perished in the cyclone, my two older sisters left when they became teenagers, and my mother grew older. Perhaps soon I would have no one left.

The young man paid respect to his parents and elders by touching their feet. Then he turned to his wife, smiled and took the crying child from her. The entire family crowded around him while he embraced them with his free arm.

He turned his attention to the cart piled with his luggage.

"Where is my steamer trunk?" he said to the porter.

"It is there, sir. On the cart."

"That is my cabin trunk. I am talking about my large steamer trunk."

"No steamer trunk, sir," the porter replied.

"I watched it being loaded on to the boat before I embarked. It must be here somewhere. My name and address, J. Mukherjee of Madaripur, are written on the trunk in big black letters."

Along with most everyone else, I took a look around. No trunk of any kind sat idly on the dock. I ran toward the back of the boat where a team of workers unloaded heavy bundles of jute into the supply area. A man onboard threw the bundle to his teammate on the dock.

"A passenger's trunk is missing...is it still on the boat?" I called out.

"Don't stand there. You'll get hit by a jute bundle," he said, ignoring my question.

I smiled. "Please search for the trunk, a large steamer marked with the name Mukherjee."

He took a cursory look around. "I don't see it. We're in a hurry. Now go away."

"Listen to me. This is an important passenger. Your jute can wait for a minute."

"If you want to find it so bad, look for it yourself."

The dockworkers probably didn't want to let on they could not read the writing on the trunk. I'd worn pants under my dress that particular day, and asked the worker on the dock to hold me high enough to peek over the side of the boat. He looked at his partner, shrugged, and hoisted me into the air. I felt secure in his grasp. The trunk was on the bottom of a stack of luggage in a far corner of the boat, most likely previously hidden by a jute bundle.

"There it is. See? The one with black markings and the fancy brass bindings?"

The worker lowered me to the ground. I smoothed down my dress, while observing the dockworkers unload the steamer trunk onto the dock.

I turned to call for a porter. The station master and ferry owner stood before me.

The owner said, "It's the child who has a smile for everybody. An unapologetic smile." He addressed me. "Young lady, where did you learn to read?"

"Here…at the dock, from the signs, and ticket stubs…"

"But who taught you?"

The station master replied for me. "She taught herself."

"What is your name?" the ferry owner asked.

"Lily, sir."

"A pretty name. Lily, would you like to go to school?"

"School? Really, sir? I've dreamed of going to school." I felt my hopes deflate. "I have no money, and only this one dress made from my father's shirt."

"Don't worry. The school is free, and we will see to it you have all that you need."

***

Life changed from working on the dock to attending school in the city, and studying in our hut at night. Mother glanced up from her sewing now and then to smile at me, but the hard life took its toll on her. On a rainy morning the day after finishing high school, I allowed myself to sleep late. Upon waking, I discovered my lifeless mother beside me, leaving me completely alone.

***

My teachers helped me get accepted into the army's nursing program. I received my degree a year later and was posted in the military hospital in the Dhaka cantonment. During the English New Year's Eve dance on the base, made even livelier because it was Friday night, I spotted a familiar face.

"Moti? Moti from Madaripur, is that you?" I called out.

He looked my direction, and we danced our way closer to each other in the middle of the crowded floor. He studied my smile for a moment. A spark of recognition seemed to light up his eyes, but it was accompanied by a quizzical look. He said, "I'm sorry, I don't know if it's the scotch, but I can't quite remember…"

"Lily," I said, "…my name is Lily. I went to school with your sisters."

He smiled but before he had a chance to reply, the music stopped. On stage, the base commander began the countdown. "10, 9, 8…" We looked at each other and shouted in unison, "3, 2, 1, Happy New Year!" As Auld Lang Syne crunched over the microphone, I shared a passionate kiss with the handsome captain. Firecrackers ushered us into 1939.

We danced the night away and walked arm in arm to his officer's quarters. He invited me in for a scotch. We sat on the couch close to each other. He took my hand and turned it over, pointing to the crease on my palm.

"I've been studying palm reading. May I?"

"Only if you don't tell me anything bad," I replied.

"Ask me questions you want answered."

"I only want to know one thing…about my career."

"Your Line of Destiny reveals you will be successful."

As he studied my palm further, his brow creased.

A few days later on the first Sunday afternoon of January, we'd cooked his favorite meal of mustard honey sweetened curry in the barracks communal kitchen. For dessert, we made shondesh, sweet treats made with dried milk, in a dented old pot on the small stove. Being careful to avoid scorching the bottom of the pot, we took turns stirring the boiling milk and sugar mixture.

For some reason, I trusted Moti to accept me no matter my roots. Stirring and talking, I shared the story of my childhood as a little sweeper girl.

"Now you know the truth of how I met your sisters, Moti."

"You've come a long way, Lily. You should be proud of yourself."

I didn't really know how to respond to him. Luckily, I didn't need to. He continued.

"I was in that crowd on the dock greeting my older brother, Jitendra."

"Really? We were both there that day? Quite a coincidence."

"I don't know if I believe in coincidences. Things happen for a reason, but we may never know the reason. Anyway, enough philosophy. Is it time to press the shondesh mixture into a design now? I really like the *conch-shell mold.*"

"The mixture is thick enough, but it needs to cool so it's easier to handle." I spread the shondesh on a marble stone. "By the way, how is your older brother?"

"Jitendra? He still resides in our family home in Madaripur. He's over forty years old now, living happily with his wife, Nanibala. He keeps busy at court, and at home with their children and grandchildren."

***

Almost three weeks later, my stomach lurched at the sight of a greasy green chili omelet. I ran out of the mess hall, retched my tea and toast, then dry heaved to the smell of the overcooked eggs wafting out the door. My period had arrived like clockwork for fifteen years, until I missed it the previous week. I'd insisted upon birth control when with Moti, but the dry heaving confirmed our precautions had not worked.

Moti offered to marry me. He was a good man and I felt fond of him, even loved him in a way. But I enjoyed my modern independence and couldn't see myself being married to anyone. I'd worked hard to become a nurse and wanted to help my country doing what I'd been trained to do. I didn't want to be confined to officer's quarters as a housewife raising children. Nor did I want to live in Moti's family home and follow my mother-in-law's rules while the father of my children traveled the world with the military.

I shared my thoughts with Moti and told him I needed time to think about my options. Most things in my life worked out, and this would too. He told me he respected my wishes, and would help me however he could.

Friday evening Moti left to visit his family home in Madaripur. I lounged in my robe all day Saturday and second guessed myself. Although I'd not actually refused his offer of marriage, in effect, I'd dismissed the idea. With no family or other prospects, I struggled to find a way out.

Concentrating on the ritual of high tea helped me think clearly. I boiled the water exactly the right amount of time and rinsed the china pot with hot water. I measured the Darjeeling tea into the sieve, slowly poured water through the leaves, and placed the cozy over the pot. The tea steeped for five minutes, before I filled my china cup with the rich liquid, adding milk and sugar. I sat in my favorite chair, preparing to take my first sip. A knock at the door startled me.

"Telegram and money-wire, ma'am."

Lily. I found a woman who can help you. She wants to meet with you privately. Please come to Madaripur on Sunday afternoon ferry. I will meet you at station. Moti.

Moti could be trusted to act in both mine and the baby's best interests. But the words of the telegram surprised and confused me. What kind of help could this woman provide for me? Someplace to stay while pregnant? Someone who wanted my baby? I decided to find out.

All night long, I tossed and turned dreaming of working at the dock. The next day, the boat from Dhaka arrived at the ferry station on time, 4:10. My days at the dock were far in the past, but nothing much had changed. A little sweeper girl looked at me with big eyes, a strip of unraveling material holding the long hair out of her face. I touched her head and gave her my loose coins.

Moti watched me as I walked in his direction. Our greeting felt awkward, but we both knew eyes were upon us. He carried my bag between us as we walked side by side. In a hushed tone, he related his brother's wife knew a woman, Sachi, who could help me. She'd become a respected herbalist and midwife in Madaripur. Moti would support me financially and emotionally, but any decisions belonged to me.

We arrived at our intended destination, a small market full of aromatics used for cooking and healing. Moti came with me into the shop to make introductions to the owners, Sachi, and her husband. They were seated lotus style on thin cushions on the dirt floor, crowded by burlap bags of fragrant dried spices piled in every nook and cranny. A cat slept on a sundrenched shelf, next to fresh herbs growing in small containers.

Moti introduced us, then explained he needed to return to the Dhaka base the next morning. He gave me money for my return ticket. In the meantime, if I needed him for any reason, send someone. He nodded at me, the shopkeeper and Sachi.

I watched him walk in the direction of the countryside, then turned back to see the couple staring at me.

"Please follow me," Sachi said, exiting through the rear door of the shop. Multiple containers of all types and sizes stood in the hallway and lined the sides of the steps we climbed. She explained they contained special plants used to treat conditions associated with pregnancy.

At the top of the stairs, Sachi opened the single door leading into a small room directly above the spice shop. She slipped off her sandals and sat on one side of the large platform bed. She indicated I sit across from her. I admired the lotus henna tattoo painted on the back of Sachi's hand. She smiled, then looked into my eyes. Her voice sounded kind.

"No need to explain your actions, Lily. However, I do need to know some particulars."

Sachi asked me the normal times of my period, and the exact dates Moti and I slept together. I told her we'd made love for the first time three weeks ago, New Year's Eve. She turned to stare out the wooden latticed window, using her fingers to aid her mental calculations.

"Do you know what you are going to do?" Sachi asked, turning back to face me.

I felt comfortable with her, without the need to hide my feelings. She would not judge me.

"Moti is an honorable man and would support me if I wanted to raise the child by myself. But I want to serve my country and under such circumstances, the military would discharge me from service. I have no one else to help me... no parents, no siblings."

Sachi spoke concisely, with the voice of experience. "You realize you are left with two choices. Give your baby away. Or not have the baby."

I felt shocked that she broached the taboo subject of not having the baby so quickly and matter-of-factly. The thought had crossed my mind a number of times, but I dismissed it as a last resort. The down to earth midwife did not mince words.

"The thought of ending my pregnancy seems drastic," I said.

"I'm not advocating one choice above the other. Only you can decide what is right for you, because you are the person who will live with the consequences. But if you want to end the pregnancy, you need to start taking the herbs within the next few days. You are probably in your fourth week of the pregnancy, the optimal time to begin an herbal abortion. If you wait until the fifth week, inducing a miscarriage using herbs rarely works."

Realizing that I needed to make a rushed decision sent the blood rushing to my brain.

"You should also know, Lily, herbal abortions, even under my guidance during week four, work only half the time. And there are risks, for you…and the baby."

I stared out the window. "What risks?" I asked.

"I will decide if Indian licorice and ginseng, or pennyroyal and blue cohosh will work the best for you. Whatever combination I choose, you could become ill. There exists the remote possibility you could die. And your baby may live, but be deformed."

We both sat quietly for a minute.

She continued. "The alternative is giving up your baby. I know a respected Hindu family who would raise the baby, boy or girl, as their own. Their identity would remain secret to protect Moti's career and your reputation. We also need to safeguard the child from future stigma."

"You'd move here in a few months when your belly starts to grow too big to hide. This room would become your home, and you'd work in the spice shop during the day. Your body would be bombarded with changes, then you'd go through the pain of childbirth."

I looked into Sachi's eyes. She returned my gaze, and continued in a softened voice. "Setting your own life aside for five months would be the easy part. The hard part would be giving up the baby after it becomes a part of you."

She told me I needed to be realistic about the difficulties ahead and confident I'd chosen the right path for me. She'd comforted many girls who once lived in her spare room above the shop. Those who gave up their babies, as well as those who underwent herbal abortions, suffered with torment and guilt.

Following a light meal, I attempted to rest, but tossed all night remembering Sachi's words.

***

Rising to the smells of the mix of spices wafting up to my room, I grabbed a crunchy biscuit I'd brought with me. My stomach could digest only plain crackers or biscuits in the morning. I thought about the day ahead. Moti planned to leave on the morning ferry, but I opted not to seek him out before he left. Speaking with him at this time might only serve to complicate my decision.

I decided to take a stroll in the town of my birth. I wandered until finding the street where my tiny childhood shack should have been. Instead of my home, an empty dirt lot crammed with bicycle rickshaws filled the space. The drivers used it as a gathering place to gossip idle time away. I didn't linger there, but walked toward the park paths fronting the riverbanks.

The Hindu temple stood within the park grounds. I stopped at the door to allow the holy man to smear vermillion on my forehead. I sat on a floor cushion and used the quiet space within the Hindu temple to think beyond this world, closing my eyes to open my mind.

After bidding Namaste to the deities and their worshipers in the temple, I took the path along the riverbank. My beliefs were clear. Souls waiting to reincarnate saw the future and chose their life on earth to work through karma from previous lives. If they chose to manifest for only a short primitive existence, they did so in order to learn a karmic lesson unique to their soul. Spiritually and philosophically, I could live with an herbal abortion.

But I wasn't sure if that's what I wanted. Many people in my life had given me a chance. My mother made a dress for me out of my father's shirt. The station master hired me and helped me read. The ferry owner, Moti's father, invited me to school. Teachers and friends encouraged my nursing career in the military. Moti supported me and Sachi is helping me. Perhaps my baby needed a chance at life too, no matter what the sacrifice.

***

In June, I took a temporary leave of absence to live in Sachi's upstairs room. Earlier that spring, Gandhi had fasted in protest of the British government. And in September, World War II broke out and Britain declared war on Nazi Germany. I wondered if I'd made the right decision to bring a baby into a world of turmoil.

While working in the spice shop one fall morning, my water broke. Sachi guided me through a long labor. She cut my baby boy's cord and tied the stump with a string. She washed the newborn, swathed him in a new yellow blanket and handed the bundle to me. A full head of dark wet matted hair topped a scrunched up red face. I could not take my eyes off of him while he lay cradled in my arms. The few seconds felt like eternity, and simultaneously, a flicker. The midwife touched my arm, breaking the trance.

"It's time," she said.

I wanted to hold onto him and never let him go.

"Lily…"

"I changed my mind. He needs me. I want to keep him."

"Think a little. You know what is best for him, and for you."

"His natural mother is best for him. No one could ever take my place."

"And what is best for you?"

"That's not important."

"Lily, remember when we discussed that this might happen. You asked me, when the time came, to remind you why you are giving him up."

"He won't have me for a mother."

"You've told me that you love your baby enough to let the child go."

"But will he have a better life?"

"Lily, I promise you the child will be loved."

"I don't know. My mind is racing."

"You are giving up your baby because you love him. He is going to a wonderful family. You will be able to work as a nurse to help so many. It is time for him to go."

I trusted Sachi and knew in my heart that she was right.

My son needed something to remind him of me. On the shelf lay the small wooden conch mold that Moti and I used to make shondesh sweets on our first Sunday afternoon together. The conch shell was safe to give my son, and symbolically represented life, the true gift I had given him.

The time came to lay my son in the basket I'd bought in the market. I'd stared at the empty basket on the table many times before this date, each time trying to picture a baby lying there. My imagination could not begin to compare to the unexpected depth of love I actually felt when he I gazed at him sleeping in the basket.

I unfolded the top layer of the blanket which swaddled my child. I placed the conch mold on the first layer of the covering, and rewrapped the top corner of the blanket over both the conch and my baby.

"Here is a conch shell for you my son, a symbol of life," I sobbed. "Perhaps someone you love will make sweets for you. Be happy. I love you more than you will ever know."

My heart broke into pieces when my baby looked at me, knowing that moment would be the last time I would ever see him.

***

I drank the herbal tea Sachi gave me, and fell asleep quickly. In a tortuous nightmare, I wandered through white tiled passageways to large and small rooms trying to find my baby. I heard his repeated cries and desperately searched for him in the huge and confusing maze. I woke with a start and stared at the empty spot on the table where the basket had been. Tears of grief for my son and myself wet my cheeks.

The room had been cleared of any signs of birth, although I smelled lingering traces of blood and urine. Pieces of guava and jackfruit sat on a tin plate on the side table next to my bed. I stared out the latticed window. Through one small section of the scrollwork, a lone star in the early morning sky began to lose its sparkle.

Off in the distance, a sari cloaked huddled figure silently scurried toward the spice shop from the countryside. Soon I discerned footsteps in the room below me and recognized the clop of Sachi's sandals on the stairs. She opened the door to my room, and sat beside me on the bed.

Sachi spoke softly. "Lily, your son found where he belongs."

My grief felt unbearable. "Tell me what happened, Sachi. Help me find peace."

Sachi closed her eyes as if in a trance, and began to speak.

"Under the cover of darkness, your baby journeyed to his new home. He traveled quietly, perhaps soothed by the gentle swing of the basket. Soupy wet fog hung heavy in the air. I had prearranged to leave your baby on the front doorstep of his new home in the night, then intended to sneak away in the darkness before being seen. But the monkeys chattered excitedly in the mango groves, reminding me that lately, bold male monkeys have tried to snatch brightly colored objects. I couldn't risk leaving the baby unattended, an open target for the brazen animals that ruled the predawn world.

I hid behind the family's gate until darkness gave way to breaking dawn. Chirping birds and the call of the rooster signaled the world had begun to rouse. The mango trees rose up like wisps of distant ghosts. Above the tree line the only visible morning star seemed to be a pinpoint of light, a muted diamond misplaced in a white blanket of fog. Mist rose off the side yard pond reflecting a haze of muted colors.

An orange cloaked figure near the banks of the water caught my eye. She moved with the vitality of a teenage girl. I guessed she planned to wash or gather water. But when she stood gazing at the pond, I thought she might be entranced by the frogs playing on the water lily pads.

My chance had arrived. The dim light and spotty fog provided some measure of protection from prying eyes. Avoiding the stone paved path, I snuck around the opposite side of the yard from where the girl stood by the pond. I left the basket holding your son on the doorstep. I bid him peace, then flicked the baby's foot through the blanket. As I'd hoped, he wailed hello to the world through his toothless mouth and trembling lips. The monkeys wouldn't approach the screaming bundle. I ran back and hid behind the gates.

The young girl in the orange shawl looked around. She followed the sound with her eyes, and stared at the veranda. She bolted toward the high pitched cries and ascended the wide stairs onto the porch. She ran up to the jute basket, bent over and lifted the coverlet. I heard her yelling, 'It's a baby, a baby.'

A man, and shortly thereafter, a woman, burst through the front door. They both stood staring down at the basket until the woman reached down. The baby quieted when she picked him up and nestled him in her arms. I saw the girl look at the veranda floor for a second before she bent over to pick up something. I presumed the conch shell mold you gave your son had fallen out of the bundle. The girl showed the man, who peered in my direction. When they took the baby inside, I returned here."

Sachi opened her eyes and touched my arm.

"Lily, you should be proud. You gave life to a human being. You demonstrated the courage to give up your son into the arms of a loving family."

***

Three years later, during the middle of the war, I worked in a military hospital in Dum Dum cantonment. Late in the day, I looked up from rebandaging a soldier's wounds, and there stood Moti, watching me. He looked as surprised as I. His stars and markings told me he'd been promoted.

I saluted. "How nice to see you, sir."

"You are looking well, Lily."

"Thank you, sir."

"I didn't know you were stationed here."

"Yes, sir."

"Would you like to have coffee?"

Neither of us had married, but the war changed both of us. We didn't clamor for one another as we did on New Year's Eve a few years back.

Moti pulled out his wallet. "I have a picture of our son."

I felt shocked. "A picture of our son?"

Moti handed me a small photo with folded edges. A little boy, maybe two years old, dressed as a pirate with a bandana wrapping his head and a patch over his eye, pointed a stick at the camera. He stood on an old trunk, probably his pretend ship. I stared at the little boy's happy face. I studied the rest of the picture, the crop of thick hair, the little white shorts he wore, and his bare feet atop his pirate ship.

Brass fittings and faint black markings decorated the trunk. I held the picture close to my eyes. I could make out an M, a few more letters, then the words J. Mukherjee of Madaripur.

"I know this trunk, it belonged to your brother. This is the steamer trunk I found when I was a little sweeper girl back on the dock."

He took the picture from me. "I never noticed what Ajit stood on."

"Ajit? Is that his name?"

"His parents thought him invincible, therefore named him Ajit."

"Moti, why is our little boy standing on your brother's trunk?"

"I am sorry, Lily. I was told it might be better if you did not know."

I felt as if I had been punched in the stomach. "Tell me now."

"My brother and his wife adopted our baby and raised him as their own. We've kept his parentage secret. To the world, Ajit is my nephew."

Since the birth of my son, I'd thought of him every day. I'd missed him terribly. But I'd made peace with the decision to give him up. Seeing Ajit's picture opened old wounds and I again went through a time of tumultuous emotions. My pain eased when I repeatedly reminded myself that my child had been given a chance at life, and he was safe and happy in the arms of parents who loved him.

Bowl

TWELVE

manliness

India 1924

My name is Motindra.

I am the son of Kumar and Soudamoni, and the younger brother of Jitendra.

Kumar was the son of Avoya and Shyamsundari.

Avoya was the son of Durga Charan and Padma.

Durga Charan was the son of Ram Sundar, Shanti, and Daya.

In what seemed like slow motion, I heard a blast followed by a punch in the gut. My first instinct, to grab at the pain, resulted in sticky crimson blood covering my hand. *What in the hell just happened? This is a mock drill...not a battlefield.* I crumbled to the ground and lay wounded in the fetal position until rushed to triage.

Despite the anesthesia, I did not go completely under and felt the scalpel cut through my skin. The doctor probed deep inside me, the wrenching causing me to moan in my half-conscious state. I would have woken fully had someone not ordered, "Give him some more." Eventually, sleep came until a voice called me to open my eyes.

"Welcome back," she chirped. A nurse's cap held with black bobby pins tilted to one side, obscuring her face. Wisps of brown curls rounded the bottom edge of the cap. She pulled a long strip of bandage from a roll, tore the edge off with her teeth, and studied my stomach.

"What happened?" I asked.

"Seems your training buddy's gun accidentally fired, and you happened to be in the way of a bullet. But you were lucky...you'll live."

She lifted her head to look at my face. She appeared to be about my age, maybe a few years younger...in her early twenties. She didn't shrink from my gaze, rather stared directly at me with lovely hazel eyes. I could not sustain the intensity for long and turned away to look out the window. Once I caught my breath, I made an attempt at conversation in order to cover the awkward moment.

"Sandhurst is lovely in the spring."

Expecting a response, I glanced at her, but she'd regained focus on bandaging my wounds. I studied her name tag...no first name, only her last, Moore.

I'd been with many women, all exotic to me in one way or another. The sensual Indian women back home with long dark hair cascading over the side of the bed became excited at my touch. Light skinned women from many cities in the world were fascinated with my Eastern beliefs in a British influenced society. I didn't consider myself a ladies man, simply a man who appreciated the good things in life. But I'd never been in love. And I'd never locked gazes with another the way I did Nurse Moore's.

Each time she attended to me on daily rounds, I became increasingly comfortable. Common sense told me wounded soldiers often fell for their nurses, especially ones with beautiful eyes and soft curls. I observed Miss Moore perform her duties with other rehabilitation patients in the open ward. She smiled or spoke an encouraging word, and never seemed to run out of energy. The men watched her every move, but from my vantage point, it seemed she didn't gaze into other men's eyes the way she looked into mine.

Part of me wanted to linger in the hospital to continue to see Nurse Moore, but I felt like a released prisoner when discharged. The doctor excused me from regular duty at the Royal Military Academy until I could comfortably tolerate long, fast-paced walks through the neighboring village of College Town.

One afternoon, I returned from my hike later than usual and took the short cut across the parade grounds toward the old college main entrance doors. Six tall pillars gracing the portico led my eyes up to the British flag. The Union Jack flew high above the building, flapping in the spring gusts.

A bicycle's bell commanded my attention. I stopped to let the cyclist cross in front of me. She wore nurse's white shoes, stockings, and dress. A red cape blew behind her.

"Nurse Moore?"

She glided to a stop, put her foot down to stabilize, and turned to look at me.

"Well, if it isn't the lucky Lieutenant! How have you been since we turned you lose a few days ago?"

"Getting stronger every day. And you? Still working hard I see, in your uniform on Easter Sunday."

"I don't really mind. I have off tomorrow instead."

I took a deep breath and a chance. "I hope you don't think me too forward, Miss Moore. Would you like to join me tomorrow on my hike through the village, and perhaps out into the countryside beyond? The doctor recommended the exercise but it gets lonely sometimes."

"A walk through the village sounds lovely. I get rather lonely myself on days off. Let's plan on it, Moti. And by the way, please call me Hazel."

***

We met following breakfast the next day. From our starting point on the edge of the village, a long length of narrow road bordered by yellow daffodils lay ahead. The way initially sloped down toward a cluster of cottages, then began a gradual climb until no more chimneys jutted up from between the trees. From that point on, a silvery lane curved into the countryside.

The pace of our steps synchronized without effort, allowing me to manage glancing at her eyes as we walked side by side. I told her about my life in India, she told me about hers in London. We continued beyond the village where the fortunate lambs not served on Easter dinner tables still grazed in fenced pastures. We followed a small brook, the Wish stream, to a secluded clearing and spread our jackets on the grassy bank to sit and rest.

Hazel lamented she did not have coins to make a wish. I reached into my pocket for a farthing, but found only a halfpenny. She took the coin in her right hand, scooted around until her back was to the stream, closed her eyes and tossed the coin over her left shoulder. She opened her eyes and turned to see where the coin landed in the water. A slight smile crossed her lips.

"Am I allowed to ask what you wished for?" I said.

"Yes, but I'll never tell." She raised her eyebrows, grinned, and looked into my eyes.

"You have beautiful eyes," I said.

"Thank you, Moti." She observed the stream as she spoke. "Most people think I received my name because of my eyes. But my mum named me Hazel at birth, before she really knew what color my eyes would be. Just lucky I guess."

Taking another chance, I caressed her arm. She didn't move away. I tilted my head to kiss her. She leaned into me, returning my kisses with soft lips. We explored each other unhurriedly, leading to gentle lovemaking in the spring grass. Later, when she lay in my arms, she teased me about my Indian accent, and I teased her about her red cape flying in the wind.

I wondered if this was love.

Rain or shine, we stole away to the Wish stream many times that summer. Most often we made love, but sometimes we packed a picnic lunch or simply shared laughs splashing in the brook waters. I harbored no complaints save one. I wished Hazel would stare into my eyes when we made love. She said she could enjoy intimacy more with her eyes closed.

On a hot and muggy morning in late August, I held my lover nestled in the crook of my arm. She lifted her head to stare at my scabbed abdomen. Her tears began to fall on my chest, ran down my midsection and came to rest on my scar. She dipped her pinky in the tiny pool of tears caught by the puckered wound, then sighed as she sucked the salt off her finger.

"You are a good man, smart and kind, and a brilliant lover. I never dreamed we would grow this close."

"I feel the same about you…"

"Moti, I've kept something from you."

Hazel slipped out from my embrace, and lay flat on her back staring at the clouds. "Please know I never meant to hurt you." She took a deep breath. "I am engaged to be married to an army officer. We have known each other for a very long time. He will be returning home soon from his current overseas assignment. We plan to be married in October."

Once again, I felt like I'd been punched in the gut. I had no inkling. *That's why she kept her eyes closed. And what she wished for.*

"Why did you let me fall in love with you, Hazel?"

"I liked you, and trusted you. In my loneliness, I turned to you."

On a crisp October Saturday, from my vantage point across the parade grounds, I watched my lover arrive in front of the Sandhurst chapel. She sat regally beside her father in a black carriage, pulled by two white hoofed dark horses sporting braided manes. The horses wore blinders decorated by Sandhurst's golden insignias glinting in the morning light. The military uniformed driver held a long thin whip upright, but never disciplined the animals.

Hazel's white billowy gown contrasted sharply with the black leather carriage seat and red velvet lined carriage hood folded down behind her. The bride resembled a floating cloud descending from the carriage. She disappeared into the chapel and out of my life. I could not bear to stay and watch the empty carriage patiently waiting for the married couple. My shuffling feet swished through windblown piles of burnished leaves on my way back to the barracks. Never again did I gaze into the eyes of a woman in the same way.

***

I graduated from Sandhurst a few weeks later. The next fifteen years, devoted to my military career, passed quickly. At the beginning of World War II, orders assigned me to Fort William on the eastern banks of Calcutta's Hooghly River. The octagonal fort city was utilized to practice drills. My job consisted of training all military branches in signal communications. I'd studied radiotelephones and telegraphs at Sandhurst, but now taught advanced radar and tactical FM radio technology to those going off to fight. The teaching assignment lasted over three years, but when the war dragged on, I got called up to serve overseas. By then, I'd become a captain in the eighth imperial army.

Much of 1943 I spent in charge of three hundred military in the signal core branch in the Western Desert of the North African Campaign. Following victories in Libya and Tunisia, hundreds of vessels traveled across the neutral Mediterranean Sea bound for Sicily.

The loneliest night of my life was spent hunkered in the belly of a military ship with hundreds of men on New Year's Eve. I watched grown men cry while they reread crumbling letters from their wives and mothers and children, perhaps for the hundredth, or the thousandth time. I thought of all the pretty girls I'd kissed in previous years on the stroke of midnight.

An image of Lily dancing through the revelers to meet me brought tears to my eyes. After Hazel, I had not been serious about any woman until Lily.

Almost unconsciously, I pulled up my right pants leg and reached down into my sock. Safely tucked away was the only memento with me, a small dog-eared photo of a little boy pretending to be a pirate. He looked strong and healthy standing on the trunk, determined to conquer his foes with his pretend sword. I hoped to be as brave as my son.

I arrived on the sun-kissed sands of Italy in early spring of 1944, wondering if it would be the last shore I'd ever climb. Our mission to secure the ancient monastery atop Monte Cassino promised to be dangerous. The allied forces believed the Germans occupied the monastery to protect the main road to Rome, 80 miles to the north. The month before we arrived, the Americans heavily bombed it, killing civilians hiding there. The fortress became a perfect pile of ruins for the German defensive observation post.

Two previous battles failed to reclaim the monastery. A third attempt, which included my division, was underway. We anticipated it would take weeks to reach the inland monastery and hoped by the time we arrived, the front lines of the third offensive would have secured the mountainside. We could then march victoriously through the valley to Rome without resistance.

But as we trudged through the mud on a rainy night, we learned the third allied offensive attempts had already failed. Since my job placed me in the position of being privy to communications, I learned confusion, blunders and accidents contributed to heavy casualties in the battle. Nightmares riddled my sleeping shift with intensified fears the eighth army would also pay a heavy price to regain St Benedict's personal gates of heaven atop Monte Cassino.

We continued our trek inland toward the mountains to become part of the fourth offensive. Patches of snow covered the earth where no sun reached. Large trucks and even tanks could not scale the mountains on roads muddied from melted snow and spring rains. Mule supply lines often did not get through, forcing us to obtain food from peasants. The Italians stared at us suspiciously when given a few foreign coins for their valuable food, and in turn, I did not trust them to keep our position secret.

Our eighth army grew closer to the bombed and deserted little town of Monte Cassino which stood several miles from the actual monastery of the same name. We began to encounter allied troops from all over the world converging to fight the fourth battle. One day our contingent passed a lone American soldier who stood by the side of the road, staring at a sign that said Monte Cassino. From behind, I could see his shoulders racking in sobs. I glanced at his face as we passed, and wondered what demons the small simple road sign brought forth in my comrade.

During the evening, a newly arrived young signal engineer sat down next to me in the dug-out communications trench. He looked me up and down, and extended his hand. "Hello captain. My name is Jimmy and I'm from the good ole USA."

Jimmy fit the stereotype of the handsome friendly Americans in the movie reels. Immediately I recognized his face as the one I'd seen earlier in the day at the roadside sign that delineated the number of miles to the town of Monte Cassino. I decided not to conjure up his demons once again.

"Pleased to meet you, Jimmy. I'm Motindra. My friends call me Moti."

"From India, I presume?"

"Bengal, to be exact."

"Married?"

"No."

"Wow, surprised. At your age." He looked askance at me.

It took me a second to recognize the innuendo. "I've had my share of women, but things just never worked out. Married to the military, you know."

"Your share of women, huh? Why don't you tell me about them? We've got all night to talk...maybe your stories will keep us both awake."

I felt rather shocked by his openness, but comrades in war became instant friends. You didn't have time to involve yourselves in niceties. You could know the deepest thoughts of a man you'd met minutes before. And besides he was right...sometimes it was hard to stay awake just waiting for a voice to come across the radio.

"Bloody hell, why not? Maybe it will take our minds off this lousy war."

"That's the spirit."

"Well, the love of my life was a nurse, back in training at Sandhurst."

"Sandhurst? Shit. Impressive."

Usually I became somewhat closed lipped upon hearing that type of comment. But Jimmy made me laugh, something about the way he said it...so sincere, and crude.

"Hazel didn't work out. I was head over heels in love with her when she told me she was engaged to another man."

"Ooo, hurt. Bet that took a while to get over." He paused to check the equipment. "Anyway, you said wom*en*, plural. How about more recent flings?"

Another chuckle from me. It seemed Jimmy had a way of making the serious less so. I wondered if all Americans were like him. "Well, a few years ago I met another nurse."

"What is it with you and nurses, huh?"

"I've asked myself the same thing. Anyway, I loved Lily too, but in a different kind of way than Hazel. I don't know how to explain it."

"I know what you mean. You can love women in different ways."

"Anyway, I got Lily pregnant, and did the manly thing. I asked her to marry me."

"You old devil you. Got her pregnant? But I thought you said you weren't married."

"She turned me down."

"What? Why?"

"She said she wanted to keep working as a nurse to help in the war effort. I respected her for that. Anyway, much to my relief, my brother and his wife wanted to adopt the baby."

"Your brother adopted your child?"

"You got it. I have my son's picture here, in my sock." I reached down to retrieve it.

Jimmy studied the photo. "Looks like you, except for the pirate patch." He chuckled as he handed me back the picture. "Helluva story. Maybe after we get out of this shit war, you'll find someone who wants to settle down."

"Never know. Anyway, what about your love life?"

"Married my high school sweetheart." Jimmy held up his left hand and pointed to a fat wedding band. "And there's a baby on the way."

"Congratulations, that's wonderful old boy. Won't it be something going home to a new baby?" There were times we soldiers put on our bravado, and tried not to jinx ourselves by thinking of the terrifying possibility we might not go home. "Tell me about your life in America, Jimmy. I only know the movie version."

Jimmy took a deep breath and launched into his story. "Well, I'm from the heart of America. In fact, I saw something today which made me think of home."

I let him continue without revealing I'd seen him earlier.

"While marching on the dirt road through the countryside, I came across a sign that said Monte Cassino. There's a chapel that has the same name near my home in southern Indiana."

The more he talked, the more nostalgic he became. My impression of Jimmy when I first met him was that he made the serious seem less so. Now I realized it might be the opposite.

"It's funny what we think about out here. My grandfather never recovered from shell-shock after World War I," said Jimmy.

"Did he ever talk to you about the war?"

"Not much really, except I do remember he'd make comments about being cold in the winter in the mountains. Come to think of it, this Monte Cassino campaign sounds like the conditions grandfather faced in the First World War. Back then, they engaged in lots of hand to hand combat because they didn't have modern weapons. We are in the same boat on this cold and wet mountain. Instead of our tanks mowing over those damn Germans, we have to use grenades and guns and bayonets to kill them off."

I didn't want either one of us to dwell on what might lie ahead. "Jimmy, what else do you remember about your Grandfather?"

"He experienced bad nightmares, and couldn't tolerate loud noises. I couldn't pretend to shoot my toy guns in his house. I'll never forget the Thanksgiving when I was seven. Grandma started cutting the turkey with a big long knife and Grandpa starting yelling and crying."

Jimmy stopped for a moment and looked at the dirt floor. "Later, my mother told me he hallucinated about not being able to pull his bayonet out of a body of a man he'd killed. I will never forget my Grandfather looking down at that turkey and crying like it was a dead soldier."

The crackle of the radio startled us. We turned the knobs for better reception. The fourth battle would commence the next day.

"I'm scared, Moti. I don't want to end up crazy like my grandfather, or worse."

"Don't worry, Jimmy. We'll be fine."

In the morning fog, Jimmy and I marched with a small troop toward the Rapido River. The river formed a natural moat in front of the abbey in the distance. In the black and white world surrounding me, burnt tree silhouettes of a former olive grove stood out against the morning mist like thin black ghosts. Mutilated bodies of soldiers killed in the previous assault lay on the ground between the trees. Evidently, they'd been missed in the periodic sweep for the dead during the short local truces called for that purpose. Two torsos lay on their stomachs, hiding their last moment of life from my eyes. Another man lay face up with eyes open to the sky. Shredded tendons and a pool of black blood lay where one of his legs should have been. I couldn't look into his eyes, but momentarily slowed at the side of the road to stare at the bloody bare skin seen through the hole in his remaining shoe sole.

A blast startled me from my trance. *Oh no, Jimmy.* He had hurried ahead while I stared at the dead man. I ran up the path. A blown off hand lay in the middle of the road. Despite the blood, I recognized Jimmy's unmistakable fat wedding band glinting in the light. I picked up the hand, and gave it to the medics to place in Jimmy's body bag. No purpose nor consolation for Jimmy's death existed, but I could not allow myself to feel shell-shocked. Not then anyway. I had a job to do.

***

Looming before us was the eighth army's mission to cross the Rapido River and establish bridgeheads on the opposite side. During previous battles, pontoon bridges failed to hold across the steep banks and one hundred foot wide span. My colleagues, Indian divisional engineers, elected to build a truss bridge made of wood and steel. The prefabricated bridge could be constructed without the use of heavy equipment. I helped coordinate the transportation of materials. With equal measure of luck and skill, during the night a sturdy bridge took form across the rapidly flowing water.

The following morning Canadian brigade armor crossed the river into the bridgehead to successfully repel German counterattacks. The Poles followed a few days later, crossing the multilayered defenses of the flatlands. Minefields and barbed wire fences hid in the purposefully flooded quagmire. The Polish military prevailed, although sustaining heavy losses, and eventually climbed the rocky mountain beyond the flatlands, planting their flag atop Monte Cassino in triumph.

In the ruins of the ancient monastery, allied soldiers from across the globe huddled. We leaned our backs on the partially standing limestone walls, sleeping sitting up, guns finally having the chance to rest by our sides. The military had been the only adult life I'd ever known, but I was not prepared for anything like the Monte Cassino battle. I understood how Jimmy's grandfather could have become shell-shocked in the brutality of war.

Jimmy would never get to meet his child. At least I knew my child, and could watch him grow from a distance. Still, I yearned to find something more to fill the emptiness. I stared at a cobweb in the corner of the ruins, and thought of Lily. She'd felt guilty when she swept away the spider's homes at the ferry station. Lily was a good honest person, and even though five years passed since our brief affair, I missed her. I'd last seen her at the base before my overseas deployment. I showed her our little boy's pirate picture. She stared at it long and hard, tears in her eyes. In those ruins, I resolved to find Lily again. Perhaps the war also changed her, and she might feel the need to share the rest of her life with someone who understood.

We marched on to Rome at the end of May, and stayed in Italy a few more months. I sustained minor injuries to my shoulder and leg, but told myself to be grateful. I did not lie dead under the burnt olive trees nor have a severed hand lying in a rut in the road, and a wife and baby crying back in America. I would return home and eventually fulfill my next orders. The Russian backed Afghans had attempted to invade India, and after a short respite, my country required my help to protect its borders with advanced signal techniques.

***

I felt devastated for Lily and for myself when I discovered she had been killed in the war…drowned on a sunken ship, like her father in the cyclone. How could I have had the audacity to hope that something might actually come of my dreams to find a contented love? Hazel, the only woman I'd ever been in love with, devastated me with her rejection. Lily, a woman I cared about deeply and loved as an equal partner, turned down my marriage proposal. And now, she was gone forever.

After discovering Lily's death, I didn't often give in to my loneliness, and never again sought the love of a woman. I contented myself visiting my brother's home and teaching my son, the little pirate boy in the picture, to ride horses and read palms.

In 1947, when India gained independence, I rose in ranks to brigadier general and was assigned to the prime minister detail for a number of years. At the mandatory retirement age of fifty-five, I settled in Simla.

One Monday morning, I strolled through the blooming rhododendrons along the terraced hillsides. Back home in my English style cottage, I sat down to rest in my favorite chair overlooking the red roofs of the village. I enjoyed a pipe of cognac flavored tobacco, turning my head to the side to blow out the smoke. After finishing my pipe, I reached into the *spice bowl* for dried orange rinds to freshen my mouth. My arm suddenly became limp and I slumped in my chair. Closing my eyes for the last time, I knew I'd devoted my life to the greater good.

Rolling Pin

THIRTEEN

HUMOR

Indiana 1900

My name is Clara.

I am the wife of Ted, who was the son of Lizzie and Paul.

Paul was the son of Verena and Henry.

Henry was the son of Katharina and Gerhard.

In a faraway voice, the words, "Clara, wake up," reverberated in my brain. But the warm beckoning glow grew closer and I didn't want to open my eyes. With utter fascination, I was traveling to the white light observing myself star in my own movie. On this stage, the sensations and emotions of each scene accompanied the script. Life changing moments unfolded in sharp detail, beginning with the scene of my birth.

***

My mother grabbed hold of the headboard's white metal rails and pushed hard enough to squirt out two of us. Early in her pregnancy, she'd seen a doe and twin fawns emerge from the woods and stand still in the clearing. For some inexplicable reason, my mother interpreted the sighting as a sign she would give birth to twins. She relished the thought she'd be rocking two little babies at the start of the new century. She'd misinterpreted the fawns standing in the clearing. During the birthing, only one baby emerged...me.

***

"Clara, please wake up." I heard the words, but they evaporated as soon as uttered. The next glimpse of my life took place when I was sixteen years old.

***

The new tooth came in sideways, cutting into my gums and the inside of my cheek. I gargled with salt water, rubbed the tooth with vinegar and doused the area in clove oil. Nothing eased the pain, and before long, feverish chills made me shiver. My gum swelled around the offending tooth, covering the emerging white enamel with angry red tissue. My cheek puffed out like I had the mumps. Mother sent me to town with my older sister, my first visit to a dentist.

Walking into the office in the downstairs parlor of the dentist's home, I could not escape the smell of antiseptics. Waves of nausea hit my stomach, but my sister, in training to be a nurse, didn't seem to be bothered by the odors. I wondered how the dentist's family upstairs tolerated them…probably grew used to them like my sister.

On the shelf, I noticed a medicine bottle adorned by a skull-and-crossbones. Another bottle labeled coca confused me. I didn't understand why the dentist kept chocolate in his office.

I spotted a third bottle. "What's in that container, the one starting with the letter *v?*"

"It's like molding clay," he replied.

"What's it for?"

"Dentures. Now Clara, please sit here."

A red rimmed white enamel bowl sat on a table next to my chair. Rivulets of red ran through the pink water. At the bottom lay a pair of forceps, the source of the blood. Beside the bowl, a cuspidor, the dentist's name for a fancy spittoon, contained pink bubbly liquid. I recoiled at the sight of another item in the receptacle, part of which looked like a tooth.

"How old are you?" the dentist asked.

"Sixteen."

"Open wide." The bright light above blinded me. "Where does it hurt?"

I pointed to the back of my mouth.

He grabbed a probe then stuck his hands into my mouth. "It's not unusual to have dental problems at your age, when the last of the molars come in. We call molars wisdom teeth because you are getting old and wise." He emitted a tired chuckle, giving away the fact he'd probably made that joke more than a few times during his practice.

I couldn't smile back. His fingers filled my mouth, and worse yet, his jabbing caused me to shrink into the chair trying to escape the pain.

He looked at my sister and shook his head. They walked out into the front hall together. I heard her ask, "Are you sure?" He mumbled something about not enough room and best in the long run. My sister looked beyond him through the open door at me. I'd never seen that look on her face and guessed he needed to pull a tooth.

The dentist put a cloth mask over my face. I moaned once or twice, then fell into a deep sleep. It seemed like no time before he allowed me to wake. I couldn't talk. Bloody rags were stuffed in my mouth, and lay strewn about the floor and tables. The enamel bowl and cuspidor were filled with thick red blood. My entire face felt like fire.

My sister bought a bottle of coca and a tin of cocaine toothache drops for me. The doctor helped me climb onto the wagon bed and lay down on patchy hay topped with horsehair blankets. I swooned with each bump in the trail.

We arrived home late in the afternoon, and my mother and sisters helped me to the kitchen table. The smell of baking bread made me gag into the bloody rags still in my mouth. My sister looked at my swollen face, and spoke words I had not yet heard.

"The dentist said it would be best to pull all of her teeth."

My mother bawled like a baby.

***

"Clara, no don't leave us. Come back. It's time for you to wake up. Please."

***

Shortly after turning eighteen, my mild cramps became painful. The next month my flow arrived several weeks late. I looked at the rags in bewilderment. A cluster of little red clumps, like tiny grapes, accompanied the small amount of blood. My mother and sisters insisted I visit the doctor.

"Could you be pregnant?" the doctor asked.

"I've been raised to be a good Catholic girl."

He looked at me in places I didn't know doctors, or anyone else, were allowed to look. While I got dressed behind a screen, he pulled a medical book

169

off his shelf. He studied it for a few minutes, then told me he'd only heard of this condition, never seen it. He gave me a diagnosis of a molar pregnancy. He explained the name had nothing to do with dental molars and nothing to do with a pregnancy. While I grew in my mother's womb, he surmised, I might not have been the only baby. The clots were the remains of my own twin.

The doctor advised an operation to remove my womb. I refused. All of my teeth were pulled two years previously, and I did not want anything else yanked out of me, especially if it left me unable to have children. On the way home, a dead fawn with white spots lay twisted on the side of the dirt road. My twin never caused me further problems.

***

"Clara, are you in pain? Show me where it hurts." I didn't understand why everyone tried to stop me from watching my movie.

***

I'd come home from business college to celebrate my twentieth birthday with my family. We spent the evening on the front porch fanning away the heat. I swatted a mosquito on my knee, and the blood smeared my white petticoat.

The thought of sleeping in the suffocating upstairs bedroom made me cringe, but the nice cool breeze blowing in from the woods and fields usually helped. I plopped down in the feather bed, trying to get comfortable. Just before falling into a deep sleep, my father's shout jarred me awake. "Hurry, Clara, come into the front bedroom." I grabbed my teeth out of the glass of water next to the bed, and slipped them in my mouth.

In the bedroom, Father crouched down under the window framed by white gauze curtains. Only his eyes peeked over the windowsill. I knelt beside him, while my mother and sisters lay in the dark on the floor behind us. The sounds of our heavy breathing were drowned out by the pounding of horses moving closer to the house. I detected movement, perhaps dust in the distance stirred up by the hooves.

Out of nowhere, flickering torches created horizontal white, red and orange line trails in the air. Tiny flecks of fire floated and weaved their way toward the ground until they were wisped off course by the next fast moving blur. A raised torch illuminated the scene. Ghosts were riding horses...not soft and billowy white ghosts, but hard and opaque creatures of the night. They wore pointed hoods on their heads. The frightening shouts of power hungry men barking orders and celebrating their reign of terror filled the air.

The Kluxers...Catholic haters. I felt a gut wrenching fear I'd never known. The Kluxers might lynch me and my family, and the parishioners would study pictures of our bodies swinging from the oak tree in the side yard, with our necks twisted in nooses.

A loud eruption of fire jolted me backwards. But Father still stared out the window, and I forced myself to crouch beside him again. An initial ball of flames subsided and the fire slowly gained definition... a cross burned in our yard. The ghost riders rode around the fire, holding their dying torches high above their heads.

The size of the group was difficult to tell...perhaps four or five, maybe more. I watched them, seemingly in slow motion, circle the fire one last time. And as suddenly as they'd appeared, they began riding in the direction from which they'd come. I followed their movements until the last of them rode off illuminated by the burning cross. They rode past Mama's tobacco patch, her source of spending money, around the barn and out into the fields.

My Father slumped on the windowsill for a few seconds, then put his arm around me. We turned around to see the rest of the family huddled in the corner. The next day I found charred bits of oil-soaked cloth near the ashes where the fiery cross once stood. The smell of the burning torches stayed with me for a long time.

***

"Clara, its Ted, your husband. Come on, wake up."

***

In my twenty-fourth winter, I turned my back against the bone chilling wind howling through the "el" platform. From my seat on the noisy train, the snow covered wooden balconies of three story brick homes were visible. The metal grate steps down to street level had been cleared, but the snow on the sidewalks remained and already looked black from the city dirt.

I entered the revolving door into the lobby of the Harris Bank, almost slipping on the snow melting off everyone's rubber boots onto the white marble floor. Upstairs, I found my desk untouched since the night before. A wire basket on the left hand corner held a stack of papers. My record keeping books lay ready for input. I settled in my chair, and glanced across the heads of coworkers at the light grey Chicago sky holding the promise of more snow.

The boss arrived. He chatted with his secretary, handing her his hat and long black coat. He glanced back across his shoulder and momentarily locked eyes with me, whereupon I quickly put my head down into my books. My older sisters warned me about sophisticated Chicago men like him, but they were old maids, and surely they were wrong about this man.

I passed by his office on my break.

He called to me, "Save me a dance at the company Christmas party this weekend."

"Okay." I smiled.

On Friday morning, I took an extra satchel with me to work in which I'd packed my fancy dress, low heels, white gloves and pearls. Public banking hours were over at five o'clock. The office girls changed into party clothes in the crowded women's restroom. I looked into the mirror and pouted my lips, lining the heart shape with a generous stroke of lipstick, then smeared a touch of rouge on my cheekbones.

I descended the stairs, enjoying the decorations that transformed the lobby into a festive holiday party. The boss gave me a small thrill as he waved to me from the punch bowl table. He brought me a drink, told me I looked lovely, and reminded me to save him a dance.

Near the end of the evening, the boss tapped me on the shoulder. He slipped his arm around my waist and led me to the dance floor. Not surprisingly, he proved to be good at the foxtrot. Following the dance, he said he lived not far from me on the north side. He told me it would be silly for me to take the train home at such a late hour, when he could drop me off. When I hesitated, he informed me he'd offered another couple a ride home too, so we'd have chaperones.

On the way home, he pulled up in front of what appeared to be a funeral parlor. I glanced at it, and then at him.

"This isn't my house," I said.

"I just want to show a small town girl the big city life."

My sisters' warning popped into my head, but I looked at the couple in the back seat, who smiled at me. I didn't want to seem like a prude. Besides, my curiosity gave me courage.

He opened my car door and we piled out. A triple knock let us into a vestibule, attended by an older man dressed in working clothes. As soon as my boss uttered the words, "Joe sent me", the greeter unlocked the inner door. The scene certainly did not look like the inside of a funeral parlor, and I soon realized I'd stepped into a speakeasy. I'd heard about them, but never been in one. A smoky haze hung in the air, and outlawed liquor flowed freely at the long wooden bar. Sexy flappers wearing fringed short dresses demonstrated their best Charleston moves, jockeying for attention from appreciative admirers.

We sat at a round booth, the two men flanking the girls. I'd never developed a taste for moonshine on the farm, and didn't like the speakeasy's liquor any better. Before long, the boss grabbed my knee under the table. My sisters knew what they were talking about, and they were probably wondering why I wasn't back in our Lincoln Park apartment right now. Politely but decisively removing his hand, I commented the time had flown by and suggested he take me home.

While we walked back to the car through the dirty sidewalk snow, he sidled up next to me and patted my behind. He tried to kiss me inside the car, not roughly, almost teasing. His holiday spirit had gone far enough, and I wanted no more excitement with the reputed womanizer. Instead of getting my dander up, which was my inclination when irritated, my sense of humor took over. I pulled away from him, giggled and pronounced, "Home James". My reputation and my job were both too important to risk.

Our car came to a stop in front of my place. My sister, still dressed in her white nurse uniform, flung the front door wide open to glare at us. I thanked my boss for the nice time and the ride home, and let myself out of the car. After whispering in my sister's ear, "Don't worry. I am still a good Catholic girl", a look of relief came over her face.

I felt happy to have experienced the new adventure, and happier still the evening only made me miss Ted back home in southern Indiana. I wished we could snuggle in the car.

***

"Clara, do you hear me? You have so much to live for."

***

Ted took the train to see me during Easter weekend in 1926. We sat on the couch in the living room of my apartment enjoying the spring magnolias blooming on the tree outside our window. My sisters were both gone to work. Ted got down on one knee.

Before he said a word, I summoned my courage. "You need to see me without teeth first." I slipped my dentures out of my mouth.

"Put them in my hand, Clara," Ted said, extending his palm.

"Ted, they're dirty, they were in my mouth."

"Come to the kitchen with me." I followed him to the sink, holding my teeth. He said, "If it makes you feel better, rinse them off." Still unsure, I cocked my head. Ted nodded at the faucet. I ran water over them. "Now, please place your dentures in my hand."

He looked down at my dentures. "These are not who you are." He pointed to my heart. "You are right here." Then he pointed to his heart. "And I love you right here."

I wouldn't kiss him without my teeth in, yet.

I returned to my roots in Southern Indiana after five years in Chicago. I traveled aboard the overnight train, gazing at the haloed moon hanging just above the tree line. My wedding dress lay wrapped in tissue paper in a Marshall Fields' box on the empty seat next to me. The knee length city style matched my short bob haircut. Ted liked the idea of a short dress, but I wondered if Ted's family and the local folks would be shocked. Most brides in small town Indiana wore a long dress and curled tresses pinned on the top of their heads.

Moving back to a tiny place after my exciting big city adventures came with mixed feelings. I gave up living with my sisters in a pretty little rooming house facing Lincoln Park. I would miss having fun with friends and going to movies at the Biograph in our neighborhood.

But I loved Ted with all my heart and soul. He was a well-respected man... intelligent, kind, and hardworking. His favorite prayer *God helps those that help themselves* became mine as well. Ted enjoyed my independence, adventuresome spirit, and touch of rebelliousness. He loved me for myself, teeth or no teeth. I'd have his children, cook, and keep house. I just hoped I wouldn't lose myself.

***

"Clara, why won't you wake up?"

***

My brothers were carpenters. They planned to build my dream home of sandstone with brick accents on the side of the hill near the highway. I'd daydreamed for so long about a big clean kitchen and a real bathroom. I missed the city, and myself in the city. My new house would be the modern part of me I left behind when the train pulled out of the Chicago station.

The great depression had run its course. Ted managed to teach and farm and sell insurance to keep us going. Even after scrimping and saving, I dyed my wedding gown navy blue to have something nice to wear. My dentures were getting old and stained, but new dentures would have to wait. Our family of five shared one small piece of meat cut into six pieces, two for Ted, and one for each of the rest of us. With the depression over, I looked forward to a new house.

Ted came home late one night from teaching all day, followed by work on the farm. I'd not seen him since early morning when he left the house, and knew he'd be hungry and tired. I longed for adult conversation, and especially wanted to share with him details of my daydreams for the new house. Barely looking up, he sat at the kitchen table and ravenously downed the food. He slowed a bit after consuming most of the plate of meat and potatoes.

"How was your day?" I asked.

"I stopped by the home place to see my mother," he said.

"And what's new?"

"She heard the white clapboard foursquare house in the center of town is up for sale."

"Yes, I know."

"She thinks we should buy it, rather than build a house."

My heart sank. I didn't even bother to try to talk Ted out of it. I loved him too much to put him in the middle between his mother and me. No one would win that game.

***

"Clara, Peggy is here. She wants to talk to you."

"Mom, it's me, Peggy. It's time to wake up. Come back, please."

***

Upon first light, I put on my coat over my gown and slipped into my garden shoes. I walked to the backyard coop, hoping the brooding hen that previously laid no eggs had started to produce. Since nothing lay beneath her again, she would be our dinner. Recently, I'd become nauseous at the job of chopping off a chicken's head on the tree stump, then watching the white corpse running around the yard with its head cut off. Concentrating instead on how good the hen would taste after being dipped in milk and flour, and fried to a crispy golden brown, helped me put the bloody image out of my mind. Nevertheless, the nasty job could wait until later.

I took the eggs I had gathered inside and walked to my bedroom. Ted came over and patted my basketball belly while I stood before the mirror. The proud papa informed his brothers about the baby the previous day, Sunday. They'd celebrated with fat cigars and a few shots of whiskey. We hadn't told the children yet. I kept wondering if the two older ones, my fourteen year old boy and twelve year old girl, would notice my growing belly. The ten year old was too young.

"Well, today's a big day. What time are they coming?" Ted said.

"My brand new stove should be here this morning."

"Just in time for you to make your prize winning jam cake."

I couldn't help but tease my husband. "That's not the first thing I'm going to make. If you and your brothers weren't so busy celebrating yesterday after church, you'd have heard the *rolling pin* hitting the table. I rolled out sugar cookie dough to make the first batch of Christmas goodies this season."

Ted smiled a sheepish grin. "They're a lot of work."

"They're your favorite, and mama's too."

Sandies and at least one batch of oatmeal date cookies were also in the works. I knew the ingredients by heart, and made a mental note to buy pecans from the store down the street. I again lamented that my attempt to grow pecan trees failed in the harsh Indiana winters.

Ted kissed me on the cheek and left for school. The children were stirring upstairs. I sat at the kitchen table with my own meal, a glass of milk and a piece of toast, before they came down wanting their breakfast. Through the window I saw the old stove sitting forlornly by the side of the garage. Ted and his brothers struggled to move it there yesterday during their celebration. A moving shadow caught my attention...*Ach Ted*, he must have forgotten something. Or perhaps the hardware store delivery man arrived early.

It was neither.

The back door opened and I recognized the young priest's voice calling out my name. He walked down the short hall directly into the kitchen and looked at me. I didn't have a chance to offer him any refreshments. He blurted out, "Clara, your mother had a stroke. Father Fischer has gone to give her last rites."

Late on Sunday morning, relatives and friends crowded together at the funeral parlor. My mother lay in a black coffin at the front of the main room. The priest led us in praying the rosary. He said the first half of the prayer, and the group answered with the second half. We recited the same prayer fifty times. The automatic responses allowed me to think about my mother, laying there white and cold. She once told me to pluck the black hairs on her chin after she died. She didn't want people to stare at them as she lay in the coffin. I had forgotten.

I need to remember to tell Ted to make sure my dentures are in my mouth when I lie in my coffin.

Following the rosary, most of the crowd dispersed, and others came to console me. Some headed outside to join the funeral caravan to the cemetery. As explained to me later, a passing Western Union man pulled up outside. He talked to a few men in dark hats milling about and smoking cigarettes.

Soon, inside and out, people congregated in small groups, whispering among themselves. I felt a fear in the crowd, not the usual routine of funerals for old persons. Some looked in my direction. My baby kicked hard, and my three children and Ted surrounded me.

"Ted, what's going on?" I asked.

He replied in a hushed voice, as if that might change the content of the words. "Pearl Harbor Base in Hawaii has been attacked by the Japanese. The president has declared war."

***

"Grandma, its Connie. Wake up. You need to answer my question."

***

I remembered when Connie and I stood in the front hallway.

"Grandma, can I ask you a question?"

"Sure."

"What's the secret of being happily married for fifty years?"

Her question took me by surprise. "I need a few days to think about that, Connie."

I hadn't yet found my answer when I checked into the hospital for eye surgery. Before the doctor administered anesthetic, Ted stood by me, teasing me how cute I looked in the blue surgery cap. The answer came to me before slipping into unconsciousness.

Wake up, Clara. Wake up and tell Connie the answer to her question.

***

The movie concluded. I observed myself from above, ashen face and hair, lying on bleached sheets in a sterile hospital room. I felt a whoosh and my eyes popped open.

"Guess it wasn't your time." The voice came from a man in a white coat, my doctor.

"Am I having another baby?" I mumbled.

"No more babies, Clara. You developed complications during your eye surgery. We thought we'd lost you a few times."

Suddenly aware of the pain in my hands, I looked down at my fists. The knobby knuckles protruded at odd angles. Dark spots, wrinkled skin and raised blue veins ran through the translucent thin skin. Stretching out my hands, I rubbed each in turn with the other to relieve the ache. I remembered that I was old.

When I looked up, Ted, Peggy and Connie were standing beside the bed staring at me. I tried to smile at them, but it didn't feel right. "Where's my teeth?" I slurred. "No one ever sees me without my teeth, except Ted." I looked around, nodding at the clear glass of water on my nightstand in which my dentures soaked. Peggy handed me the glass. I grasped the uppers, shook off the water, and slipped them in, repeating the habit with my lowers.

"This is my answer, Connie. To stay happily married for a long time, you need a sense of humor."

***

After the surgery, I never felt quite the same. Someone told me I'd lost oxygen while on the table, but it didn't really matter to me. The details of life became unimportant. Rather, I preferred to study the pictures on the walls of my house, searching for the beautiful warm light.

Years later, in the middle of the night, I again felt a pull to travel toward the unknown. Ted's voice seeped through to me once more. "Clara's gone. Now she will find her light." His soft kiss freed me, and I melded into the warmth.

Buddha

FOURTEEN

Justice

India 1944

My name is Jitendra.

I inherited the title of Rai Saheb from my father, Kumar.

Kumar was the son of Avoya and Shyamsundari.

Avoya was the son of Durga Charan and Padma.

Durga Charan was the son of Ram Sundar, Shanti, and Daya.

In the bright light cast by four petromax kerosene lamps, I faced the children in the last badminton game of the winter season. The servants had spread lime dust in shallow trench lines to form a rectangular court in front of the house. My son, Ajit, and grandson, Haru, both six, stood across the net from me. The children fought hard to win, and in past years, I might have let them. But the time had come for a bit of toughening up. They needed to earn their victory.

After we played three games, all losses for the children, Haru threw down his racket and kicked the shuttlecock across the yard. I ducked under the net and put my arm around him, guiding the small boy to the kitchen. "Perhaps if you ate something, you might feel better."

I fixed a plate and set it in front of Haru. Once again, his frustration boiled over.

"Yesterday we ate fried pumpkin, today smashed pumpkin. Baburchi used to make good things. Now he cooks the same thing every day," he complained.

"Be thankful you have anything to eat." I reached for his untouched plate.

He misunderstood the reason I'd taken his food. "So you will tell our cook to make me something I like?" he said.

"We have nothing else. Perhaps tomorrow we'll have fish to eat with our pumpkin."

The boy's shoulders slumped. He ran out of the kitchen and across the grass toward the main house.

I knew how Haru felt. I too longed for the meals we used to take for granted. Earlier that day, I'd found myself dreaming of saag paneer with freshly made roti.

Our country was in the grip of a famine, brought on by a chain of events. A cyclone spawned a tidal-wave, in turn flooding the fields, which precipitated a fungus that destroyed most of the crops. A long period of drought followed. Priority for available food was given to the military troops, and little remained for anyone else, rich or poor. The situation became more desperate when refugees from Burma fleeing the Japanese poured into our country, increasing the number of mouths to feed.

For a while, we managed to irrigate small plots of rice and lentils from the fresh water of our estate's manmade canal. But as the months dragged on, and still no rain fell, only one crop grew…pumpkins. Their root system reached deep into the ground enabling each plant to draw moisture other crops could not find. The hot dry weather kept away mold and rind rotting disease. I took inspiration from the big orange pumpkins' ability to reach deep to search for what was needed to survive, without giving way to the things that would destroy them.

Haru disappeared into the main house. He would probably tell his mother I confiscated his food. She would question him and guess what really happened before sending him back to me to apologize. Before long, the slap of small sandals on the bare dirt in front of the kitchen door alerted me to his presence.

He bowed his head. "I am sorry, Grandfather." I noticed his eyes glancing sidelong, presumably trying to find his plate.

My voice felt soft and sad. "The servant is giving the beggars your food."

Tears welled up in his eyes. I attempted to share my empathy. "Baburchi ground most of the roasted pumpkin seeds to make flour, but here's a few left in the sack."

My grandson managed to find a handful of seeds. He munched on them as he stared out the window. In the distance just beyond the compound gates, beggars had formed a circle round our trusted servant carrying the plate Haru had rejected. When the starving people noticed him coming out of the side door of our kitchen, plate in hand, they deserted their spot lining the path, thrusting the worst looking of their potbellied children toward him.

Haru turned to look at me. "There are so many of them."

"And more in the village and the cities."

"What if they don't get food?"

"They will starve to death."

"Isn't there anything we can do?"

"Share our coconuts, give them what food we can."

"But we don't have enough to feed everyone."

"It's not fair, but it's their fate."

***

I excused myself to the small family temple across the yard. A bouquet of marigolds perfumed the cool musty room. I waved the air to clear the gnats swarming over the offering of palm dates, which had over ripened. I replaced the fruit with a few fresh pieces.

A statue of the dark deity Kali stood in the center of the altar. The fierce goddess had protected our family for generations, but her grotesque image invoked fear in both children and adults. Two bright red eyes and a third eye in the middle of her forehead bore down on her worshippers. She stuck out her enormous red tongue. She'd grown four arms, one of which held a sword and the other the chopped off bloody head of a demon.

Bowing to Kali, an ancient Sanskrit verse of adoration and thanks rolled off my tongue. I asked for food for my family, and comfort for those starving outside the gates. I begged for understanding of life and acceptance of fate.

Soft moans disturbed my devotions, but finding no source of the sound, I returned to my prayer routine.

The music of the conch shell signaling dusk and the end of the day smoothed my transition from the musty spiritual space to the evening's activities. The women of the house stood at the upstairs window, blowing the shells to ask the gods for protection. During hot and dry weather, the haunting echoes of the spiral instruments carried on the winds for miles, quieting the world with life affirming notes.

I sauntered to the pond at the side of the house. Growing in the murkiness on the opposite side, a tangle of lotus plants supported the pink flowers jutting toward the setting sun. I walked around the edge of the pond watching my reflection in the water. I cradled a lotus leaf, and poured a small amount of water into its center. The leaf repelled the liquid causing it to form into shiny water beads which resembled drops of mercury. I dipped a bucket in the sun-warmed water.

The few prized rose bushes still living in the dust of the once enormous rose garden commanded my attention. I bent down to water each plant, making sure to dispense the precious resource evenly around the base. When the bucket was empty, I lit a cigarette and glanced through the dim light toward the compound gates. The circle of beggars had dispersed, and once again they rested in small groups under trees by the side of the road.

Two boys huddled in the grass caught my eye…Ajit and Haru. I was surprised to see them outside the compound gates at this time of the evening. They usually played marbles in front of the large portico of the main house. I walked toward the boys, following the direction of their gazes down the road.

Volunteers were lifting an uncovered corpse onto a cart. The evening light bathing the skeleton-like body turned the deceased into the most frightening human I'd ever seen. I could not discern if the person was male or female, formerly rich or always poor, Hindu or Muslim. After the ghost had been tossed onto the pile, the men visually surveyed the roadside for additional bodies. Seeing no more, they led the oxen in a half circle to reverse the direction of the cart.

I approached the boys.

Ajit said, "Where are they going?"

"The cremation ghat for the poor."

Ajit had never seen death up close, and began to shake. With Ajit in my arms, and Haru holding tight to my doti, I retraced my steps back through the front gate. I stayed up long into the night at the bedside of the children, patting them if they moaned in their sleep. When they were settled, I snuck out of their room and climbed upstairs to my bedroom.

After I closed the door behind me, my eye was drawn to the brass icon of *Buddha* on my bureau. A shaft of moonlight shining through the crack in the shutters highlighted his hands forever posed in blessing. I took three deep breaths and lifted the edge of the mosquito net to climb into bed with my wife. Nanibala squeezed my hand.

***

Saturday morning, the sound of song and the smell of rising dough in the tandoor woke me. Ajit's voice belted out a lively raga from his perch in the crook of his favorite mango tree. I walked out to greet my son.

"Good morning, Ajit."

"Good morning."

"How are you feeling today?"

"Much better. Do you want to know why?"

Before I had a chance to answer, Ajit continued.

"Jogen Da caught a fish this morning. Baburchi ground the fish bones into a powder, and mixed it with the pumpkin flour to make biscuits. He gave me a warm one."

"So that's what I smelled earlier."

Ajit announced, "He made the biscuits in honor of this special day".

"What is special about today?"

"When Jogen Da went fishing this morning, he spotted a big turtle in the canal. So today he is going on a turtle hunt."

Soon after our head servant, Jogen Da, started working for my grandfather, he became known as the turtle catcher. The tender meat of snapping turtles made tasty curry. He hunted twice a year, once during the early spring egg laying season, and again in late fall during Diwali. Jogen Da shared with me he worried the famine conditions might hurt his chances to catch a turtle this year.

Ajit continued practicing note-runs of the morning raga, and I headed toward the kitchen. Normally, the servants would serve me breakfast on the portico mid-morning. But I couldn't wait until then to taste a freshly made biscuit.

Walking up to the door of the kitchen, I overheard Baburchi speaking to another servant. Evidently he was already working on the noon meal of fish fillets with pumpkin curry. He lamented the scarcity of lemon juice to add to the curry to decrease diarrhea, the effect of pumpkin for every meal. He said he'd sprinkle extra red pepper on the curry instead, hoping the hot spice would work equally as well.

A warm biscuit waited for me in the kitchen. I savored each bite. The sounds of the axe on the grinding stone in the nearby shed let me know that Jogen Da was preparing for the hunt. I asked Baburchi to prepare fish scraps and pumpkin rinds for the most exquisite turtle bait possible. When Jogen Da and I left for the canal a little later, I wanted Baburchi to join us with the enticing lure.

I strode toward the shed. The turtle catcher and I loaded the cart with the sharpened axe, a trap made of bamboo sticks and ropes, and a strong pole with a noose on the end. Jogen Da shared that he was going to allow the two six year old boys to accompany us on the hunt. He had schooled the children in the importance of following instructions and working quietly.

Baburchi joined us as we walked toward the canal, and Ajit and Haru silently caught up to us at water's edge. Using gestures, Jogen Da directed us to tie the chopped vegetables to the inside of the trap. Keeping one side open, we lowered the baited rectangular box into the shallow edge of the canal. Then we waited in the morning sun, each of us intent on being the first to see a turtle swim into the trap.

A short time elapsed before Jogen Da noticed a medium sized turtle taking the bait. We jerked the trap up with the attached ropes, simultaneously rotating the box so the open door was toward the sky. On land, we flipped the cage until the turtle lay on his back, then slid him out onto the ground.

Jogen Da motioned for everyone to move away, and recited a brief prayer for worthiness to take the life of the creature. When the turtle stuck his head out of the shell to right himself, he squarely hit the head with the back of the axe. We laid the unconscious snapper on the tree stump at the side of the canal. Jogen Da chopped off his head with the sharpened axe. He and Baburchi toiled until they broke the shell. They collected the eggs still inside the turtle and placed them into a basket lined with cloth. The two coworkers and friends began to cut the tender meat from the bones.

I heard moans. My first thought was that one of the boys had become ill at the sight of the gruesome turtle kill. But the boys were looking around.

"Did you hear that?" Ajit asked.

"Someone is moaning," Haru answered.

We saw no one, eventually turning our attention back to the turtle. But within seconds, we once again heard the moan.

"I've heard this sound before," I said.

"It sounds like the moans of the beggars," Ajit replied.

I cocked my head. "It's coming from the wrong direction to be the beggars. Follow me."

Jogen Da stopped cutting meat from the turtle bones, swished his bloody hands in the canal and splashed water on his face. He asked Baburchi to stay and get every bit of turtle meat from the carcass. I led the two boys and Jogen Da down the canal path to locate the source of the sound. We were almost ready to give up and turn back when all eyes stared at a shocking sight in the canal. A geyser of water shot from a hole of a dark grey shiny animal.

"What is it?" Ajit asked.

"It looks like a whale," I half-whispered in disbelief.

A small portion of the whale showed above the water. The creature looked long and thin, with three ridges on his head in front of the blowhole. We stood spellbound watching the whale spout twice more, looking at us out of one huge eye. We heard the low repeated moan before the blowhole slid under the water. The animal's curved back, topped with a single fin, soon followed. The dark shadowy form remained visible for only a few seconds.

Ajit said, "Was the whale talking to us?"

"I think he's asking for help," I said.

Haru asked, "Why is it in the canal?"

"It looks like a baby whale. Maybe it got separated from its mother," I replied.

"How could that happen?" Ajit asked.

"The whale may have been hungry and followed a school of herring up the canal."

"Why doesn't it turn around and go back?" Haru asked.

"It seems to have lost its sense of direction," I answered.

We stood staring at the spot where the whale slid under the water. I asked Jogen Da to take the shortcut across the makeshift bridge to the compound to gather help. Ajit soon spotted the blow not much further up the canal. We ran to it, witnessed the same three spouts, the sad eye staring at us, the low moan pleading for help.

Ajit began yelling at the whale. "Go back whale, find your mother."

On my instruction, Ajit and Haru positioned themselves along the canal to track the whale. The thought struck me that perhaps we could use some of the turtle meat to entice the whale to turn around and lure it back toward the river. I hurried back to the place we'd butchered the turtle.

In front of me, the cook squatted low over the turtle mess, pulling meat from the bones and throwing it in the cart. Out of the corner of my eye, I caught movement near the canal edge.

"Run, Baburchi, run!" I shouted at the cook.

He turned his head in time to see a crocodile racing toward him with a huge open jaw full of teeth. The cook screamed and slipped in the blood and intestines of the turtle, so in addition to his bloodied hands, gory turtle remains covered most of his body. He slid backwards on his behind, calling to the heavens for protection.

I charged the spot with arms flailing, hoping to deflect the crocodile from his target. I noticed movement in the canal, then stopped in utter disbelief. The baby whale breached the surface of the water, then flopped down hard on its side. A large splash drenched and distracted the crocodile, allowing the cook enough time to get up and run. The whale repeated his action. The crocodile snatched a piece of turtle intestine lying where the cook had just been, turned back toward the water, and glided off.

I stood at the edge of the canal and bowed in respect to the spot where the whale disappeared under the water. I looked around me. Puddles of water surrounded the turtle mess. The cook kneeled some distance away from the canal, hands in prayer. The two boys ran toward me. From the other direction, Jogen Da led the servants towards us. I felt shaken from the crocodile assault, but knew we could waste no time. I directed the agitated group to place the remaining turtle pieces in the cart and sweep the area to minimize the risk of further crocodile attacks.

When the whale breached, I judged the length to be about twelve feet, with a weight of about 1000 pounds. A plan took shape in my mind. If we could hook its tail with a noosed rope, ten strong men positioned on each side of the canal should be able to pull it backwards.

The rest of that day, and beginning at dawn the next, many men tried to rope the whale. But the whale's tail broke the water too briefly to snare. One servant, a good swimmer, risked getting crushed and joined the whale in the canal, to no avail.

By then, the whale had been traveling the wrong direction in the fresh water canal for at least three days. Its eyes were half-closed, moans barely audible, and blows weak. When I told Ajit the creature may not live much longer, he cried out, "Life is not fair," and ran toward his favorite mango tree. He returned a few minutes before the whale surfaced for the last time.

The entire estate, and other villagers who came to observe the spectacle, stood sobbing on the banks of the canal. Within an hour, the dead whale floated near the top of the water. I knew when the whale's gases dissipated, the animal would sink in the fresh water. We needed to get it out as soon as possible so the rotting body would not ruin the minimal amount of fresh water we had left. We roped the dead whale and many men helped pull it up out of the water.

In the waning light of day, we stood the length of the whale's body shoulder to shoulder to roll it over away from the edge of the canal. When the whale lay fully on its back, the men hushed and backed away. Many touched their foreheads in prayer.

I stared at the belly of the whale. A rudimentary but unmistakable outline of a grotesque face had been formed by shadings of dark grey, purplish-grey and cream. A three eyed female stuck out her long lolling tongue at us. The face of Kali, the face of protection, stared at us. An overwhelming sense of gratitude and humility filled my eyes with tears.

"Sir, may I speak with you?" our cook whispered to me.

"What is it, Baburchi?"

"I am Muslim. Mohammed preaches we may eat whale meat. Sir, so many are starving." He nodded toward the road.

Hundreds stared at me...men standing and staring hollow eyed, women with crying babies at empty breasts, potbellied children.

Hindus did not normally eat mammals, but it was not forbidden. Mohammed spoke to Baburchi, Kali spoke to me.

191

Baburchi, Jogen Da, and I used the sharpened axe to cut the meat from the whale. We handed it out to starving people who lined up for small chunks. That night, long after the song of the spiral shells, small fires lined the path to the compound gate. We heard laughter instead of moans.

***

When I returned home from court the next day, the whale bones had been picked clean by starving wild animals and vultures. The veterinarian was collecting the skeleton to send to the museum.

Jogen Da, Haru, Ajit and I sat together at the long wooden table in the kitchen. Baburchi filled our plates with perfectly spiced turtle curry, then upon my insistence, joined us. The adults and Ajit ate with relish. Haru peered out the window. With food still left on his plate, he asked to be excused from the table.

Through the window lattice, I observed him carrying his leftovers toward the gate. As the mothers with potbellied children surrounded him, the haunting evening melody of the conch began to float on the winds. Kali and the gods had provided protection, yet fate dictated our lives. Perhaps it was not important to understand life, but rather to reach deep and draw upon hidden strength to survive.

Nanibala in Mirror

FIFTEEN

ᴍᴇʀᴄʏ

India 1900

My name is Nanibala.

I am the wife of Jitendra, who was the son of Kumar and Soudamoni.

Kumar was the son of Avoya and Shyamsundari

Avoya was the son of Durga Charan and Padma.

Durga Charan was the son of Ram Sundar, Shanti, and Daya.

In the green and fertile fields of Bengal, well beyond Dhaka's rivers teeming with flimsy boats, my mother felt the pangs of childbirth. The December day fell a month before my expected arrival in January of 1901. Mother previously lamented my due date because she'd wanted a turn-of-the-century baby born in 1900. The labor that gripped her sides before the New Year brought with it physical as well as psychological distress. She didn't know whether to thank the gods for listening to her, or be terrified her wishes jeopardized my life.

Accompanied by her sister, my mother, Shurolata, had traveled to the Bakshi Bazaar in preparation for her baby's welcome feast. They'd spent the morning in the rising heat, admiring six foot lengths of cotton and silk, finally selecting the golden silk sari tinged with red. The traditional color for a mother bearing her first child reminded them of sunset's glow during the hour of mystical light.

On their way home, my mother disregarded the sharp twinges along her hipbones, believing they were a normal part of carrying a child. However she could not ignore her full bladder, made unbearable by the bouncing of the horse drawn cart on the monsoon gouged roads. She directed the male servant to stop between estates on Joogi Nagore Road, an aristocratic neighborhood where large houses stood separated by wide fields.

The driver and Auntie helped my mother down from the cart, and across the narrow drainage ditch bordering the road. Mother hid herself in the cool undergrowth of a stand of bamboo. As she squatted, a slime of mucus slid down her leg, followed by a gush of liquid not as yellow as urine. Only then did she recognize her side pains as those of premature labor. She felt the top of my head bulging between her legs, and cried out for her sister's help.

The laboring woman could not manage to move from the spot, let alone climb back into the cart. The servant flagged down a passerby to find the doctor, and to locate my father, Kamini, a local police lieutenant. Before help arrived, my tiny body slipped out on the soft earth. The sisters found nothing with which to cut the umbilical cord. The afterbirth plopped out shortly after I'd been born. With my belly button still attached to the red and blue lined placenta, Auntie picked me up and wrapped me in her shawl.

Serenaded by the sounds of birds singing in the tangle of bamboo branches, my mother reached out for me. Through her tears, she studied my fair complexion, my strong arms and legs. Realizing that her fears she'd brought me harm by lamenting my due date were unfounded, she thanked the universe.

"This child of lotus birth will bring good fortune," she whispered in awe. "Each pulse of the uncut cord will infuse her with unique nutrients, supplying strength for many in this journey of life."

Eventually I had three sisters and one brother, none petite like me. I never grew to five feet nor weighed a hundred pounds. But as my mother predicted, the lotus birth gave me physical and psychological strength. The priest-astrologer pronounced that despite my small frame, at age eleven, I could withstand the rigors of marriage. My match was the son of a wealthy landowner, a Jamindar, who lived in the countryside a day's journey from my parents' home.

***

Jitendra, my husband, a few years my senior, didn't pursue relations with me until I reached puberty. I quickly grew to love him. At age fourteen, I gave birth to my first child, a little girl. Four more children followed.

One day, as summer break came to a close, I helped my six year old son prepare to start the new term. My fourteen and ten year old daughters sat on the edge of the bed.

"It's not fair he can go to school and I can't. I'm just as smart," said my oldest girl.

"Girls can't go to school," bullied my young son.

"I've taught you how to read and write," I said.

"But I want to learn more," she said.

"Me too," added my younger daughter.

Nehru's leadership toward Indian independence and Gandhi's spiritual advocacy for the downtrodden of our country inspired me. The women's voting rights movement in the western world opened me to possibilities. I recognized the need to stand up for those who couldn't speak for themselves - my own daughters. The servants helped my son finish laying out his clothes and supplies. I walked to my bedroom and addressed myself in the blurry mirror atop the bureau. *My daughters deserve an education, just like my sons.*

I marched downstairs to see if Jitendra had arrived home from court, hoping to speak with him before he left for his bridge game. He sat in the study, reviewing a legal brief.

"I want to start a school," I said to my husband.

"There's already a school," he replied.

"It's for boys. I'm talking about one for girls."

Being open-minded and proud of his daughters, Jitendra didn't need convincing. Over time, with his political pull, my hard work and leadership, and our money, we overcame the many obstacles placed before us. Eventually we rented a space, hired a teacher and adopted the same curriculum the boy's school utilized. We recruited promising girls from the community to join our daughters, allowing all of our children to obtain a good education. Perhaps more importantly, the equality altered the way boys and girls viewed each other, resulting in mutual respect.

***

The years passed quickly. Our two older sons left home to begin their careers. Our three daughters married, and moved into their in-laws' compounds. Following family tradition, our oldest granddaughter, Panna, came to live with Jitendra and me, and we raised her as one of our own. Occasionally I became nostalgic that my children were gone, and our lives were settling into a routine. On New Year's Eve welcoming 1939, a feeling of melancholy struck me.

"Jitendra, I wonder what the future holds for us."

"Why is there sadness in your voice?"

"I am not unhappy, but perhaps I've already lived the most interesting part of my life."

"Only time will tell."

Three weeks into January of 1939, Jitendra's brother, Moti, came to visit from his post in Dhaka. My husband and his brother seemed absorbed in what appeared to be a serious conversation while strolling out in the rose garden. Jitendra later came into the house alone and asked me to join him in the study. He closed the door behind me.

"Moti has gotten a nurse at the base pregnant," Jitendra said. "We know her...Lily, originally from Madaripur."

"Lily...from the girl's school?"

"She recognized Motindra at the New Year's Eve party."

"I remember Lily as a smart girl. I'm happy for both of them."

"She doesn't want to marry."

"Why not?"

"Moti explained she wanted to use her training as a nurse to help in the military efforts to protect our country. She doesn't want simply to be a mother and an officer's wife. Besides helping her financially, Moti doesn't know what else to do. He asked me for both brotherly and legal advice. The problem is... I don't think there is much anyone can do."

During the night, I tossed and turned. I didn't know whether Lily's remaining family, her older sisters, were in contact with their youngest sibling. Lily was smart and educated, but yet I allowed myself to imagine the worst. I worried what would happen to her and the child if she received a dishonorable military discharge. Women who had been tossed aside by society often turned to selling themselves. They and their children were doomed to a life of squalor in the city's ancient brothel slums.

Or perhaps Lily would decide to end her pregnancy.

Jitendra's non-rhythmic breathing patterns revealed he wasn't sleeping soundly. I turned toward him, and waited for my husband to signal he knew of my desire to talk.

"You can't sleep?" Jitendra mumbled.

"Not really. You?" I said.

"Dozed for a bit. I feel so helpless," he said.

"There *is* something we could do, Jitendra."

"What?"

"We could adopt the baby as our own."

He took a deep breath, and reached out to encircle me in his arms. "I love you, Nanibala."

Ajit was born in October of 1939. He became my son the moment I first held him as a newborn. Ajit and our granddaughter, Panna, brought the joy of youth to our home. Our older sons and married daughters, as well as extended relatives and friends, often visited for months at a time. I managed a large household full of life and change, constantly directing the servants to prepare meals for a steady stream of guests. We embarked on a project to construct a six building compound on our estate to accommodate everyone. The remark that the most interesting part of my life might be over was forgotten.

***

One blue-skied morning, I visited the prayer room. A picture of my guru, Sadhu Ramchandra, known to me as the supreme leader Gurudev, adorned the altar. A strange feeling came over me, a sort of premonition. The guru's image rose from his seated lotus position and left the photograph, walking out of the prayer room and beyond the curtain covering the door. The bicycle bell of the Western Union man startled me back to worldly reality. I rushed through devotions and walked to our front veranda to receive the telegram.

The envelope originated from the city of Faridpur, where my second daughter lived with her husband, an attorney. They had three children, a daughter and two young sons. I took the telegram inside the house and hunted for my reading glasses.

I woke up to the sight of our head servant fanning me and encouraging me to take a sip of water. We'd previously known our son-in-law contracted a severe case of the flu, marked by high fever and diarrhea. No one knew the severity of the illness. I must have fainted upon reading the words of the telegram, "Husband expired from typhoid."

Jitendra and I left the next day for Faridpur. We could do nothing for our daughter and grandchildren except share their pain while they wept in our arms. My heart ached for our oldest grandson, age five, when tradition required he helped carry the body of his father on a bier through the town to the ghat. The boy walked around his burning father's pyre seven times. After the cremation, when only ashes could be seen where his father's dead body once laid, a barber shaved my grandson's head.

We brought our daughter and grandchildren back to our home. Friends and acquaintances crying in sympathy met us at our ferry terminal. For many months following our return, wails from the widow and her three children could be heard through our thick walls, and out through the open windows.

As was custom, our son-in-law's parents sent for our daughter and children to move in with them. Out of obligation, she consented. Shortly thereafter, she secretly sent us a message that they were treating her as a slave. Jitendra retrieved his daughter and our grandchildren, silently shaming the in-laws for their inhumane treatment.

***

The next years were difficult. My mother had previously passed away from a sudden stroke, leaving my father alone in his home in Dhaka. Word reached me that he had fallen ill. Jitendra took charge of the household, while seven year old Ajit accompanied me to attend to my father. Scarce and unreliable transportation forced us to walk six miles to find a boat. After a few weeks of nursing, my father regained his strength. It was the last time I visited him in Dhaka before partition in 1947.

Daily struggles with famine and fear occupied us during the pre-partition skirmishes. Our beloved Bengal, a state of India, became East Pakistan in the partition. Instead of Hindus and Muslims coexisting in relative peace, the government decreed our former land a country for Muslims. We wanted to carry out the lives we had built over generations, but in 1949, we were forced to leave our homeland.

We fled across the border, and lived with my husband's sister in Calcutta for a few weeks before renting a flat. Jitendra started a law practice which proved to be unsuccessful. We relocated to an old family property in Barakpur, which required much more income to maintain than what was available to us.

The house was sold, and we moved to the outskirts of Calcutta where many other refugees from Madaripur settled. We'd found a place to live, but I never felt my soul belonged there.

***

Several years following partition, Jitendra worked his way into a judgeship in Calcutta. Through a discreet network, he kept in touch with colleagues in Bengal. My husband received a long letter from one of those friends, detailing the story of a group of young men who had been arrested for a recent rape and murder. Jitendra shared the letter with me.

September 1951
My dearest friend,

My apologies for the horrible story that follows, but I thought you would want to know.

A group of young men were recently arrested for the rape and murder of the daughter of a prominent East Pakistani politician. During pretrial, one of the accused turned against the others. He led the police to a shed where mementos of their conquests were stored, including a box which held a gold earring. The following account, gleaned from a transcript of the interrogation, is part of the information he gave the police regarding the earring.

He and his thugs began their life of violence during the partition uprisings. They participated with other fanatics in one of the horrendous train massacres that occurred while the Hindu-Muslim riots raged. They boarded a train filled with Hindu refugees from the Comilla region in newly formed East Pakistan, raped the women and slaughtered every man, woman, and child on the train. In the middle of an attack on a young woman, he realized he knew her from his home town.

Her name was Bina, and the informant mentioned she might be related to your family, specifically your wife. She traveled with her husband, a physician. Each held a small child in their arms. One of the attackers snatched and stabbed the child in Bina's arms. Another held a machete to the neck of the young doctor, who shielded his child into his chest.

The thugs forced the doctor to watch the clothes being cut off his beautiful wife, piercing her skin with long swipes of the sword. The men threw her down on the bench, held her legs apart, and took turns raping her. The woman turned to look into her husband's eyes during the attack. All of a sudden, the shining blade of the machete struck at her husband's neck. He lay partially decapitated, blood spurting at the wall with each pump of his heart. The child who had been in his arms was stabbed when he fell onto the floor of the train. The woman closed her eyes, pleading for her own death.

One of the attackers laughed as he shoved himself into her mouth. The men finished with her, and one cut off her ear as a trophy. She bled profusely from the side of her head, the cuts on her body, and from between her legs. The men moved on, thinking her dead.

Before sending you this letter, I checked the few records the government kept on file regarding this train slaughter. First class passenger names were on the manifest, and included Bina, her husband and two children.

Also, while doing research, an article in a small newspaper came to light. The paper originated from the nearest town to where the attack occurred. The story stated that one person survived the attack. The train had been parked on a bridge a hundred feet above a river. The morning after the attack, a naked woman washed up on the riverbank near the village. The townspeople assumed she was dead, and grabbed her arms and legs to lift her on top of the pile of dead on the cart. But she moaned.

Horrendous cuts covered her body, but most notably, one ear had been chopped off. A villager took pity on her, and nursed her to physical health. However the victim did not make a mental recovery, and the authorities sent her to a hospital outside of Calcutta. As far as I know, the woman is still there.

My regards to Nanibala.
Sincerely,
Your friend

***

I needed to see for myself if the woman was Bina. A trusted female servant accompanied me to the asylum. The forty-five minute morning train ride to the Alipur station passed quickly. We boarded the bus to the asylum, a foreboding crumbling old building. Upon asking, an attendant informed me a female with one ear cut off did reside there. He seemed surprised by my inquiry, explaining that the patient had received no visitors since being admitted. As prearranged, my servant bid me farewell until early evening when she would meet me at the asylum entrance for the return trip home.

Inside the ward, the attendant cleared a path, motioning me to follow him. He explained the patient's true identity was unknown, so the staff called her Lullaby. I asked why, and he replied the answer would be evident soon enough. While searching for Lullaby, filthy women circled me, touched me, and tried to talk to me. Initially I became fearful, but took my cues from the attendant and shortly grew accustomed to the chaos surrounding me.

He guided me with his left hand toward the far wall, stopped, then with his right he pointed to Lullaby. A thin woman sat naked on the floor in her own waste, staring at the ceiling. Although barely recognizable, I saw remnants of my formerly beautiful cousin.

"Hello Bina. It's me, Nanibala." The attendant stopped me from covering her with my shawl, explaining that she refused to remain clothed, and would destroy my shawl.

Bina gave no sign of recognition, as if I were not present.

The attendant looked at his watch, then warned me it would soon be time for Bina's ritual. As if on cue, my cousin mumbled unintelligibly. She shook her head from side to side, which evolved into jerking her head in every imaginable angle. Next she tore at her matted hair and the scarred skin all over her body. She contorted her mouth in a silent scream. Within seconds, her face relaxed and she began to sing a child's lullaby. She ended the song as abruptly as it had begun, and mutely stared through the ceiling bars and the tree branches to the sky above.

I watched and listened during the first cycle. The attendant swiped the floor with a rag and left me sitting beside Bina. Fourteen motionless minutes elapsed before she worked her way through the sequence again... mumbling, shaking and jerking, hair pulling and silent scream, and the lullaby. I joined Bina in singing the soothing song. She did not look at me, but her eyes seemed to flicker for just a moment before she stared through the ceiling bars once again.

My cousin went through her sequence six more times over the course of the next hour and half. I sang the lullaby along with her each time. She never demonstrated awareness of my presence except for that one brief initial flicker.

Lunchtime ended the morning visiting hours. As the attendant escorted me out, I asked if Bina always did the same thing, day in and day out. He hesitated for a moment, then related the doctors had done all they could. But for the three years she lived in the ward, Bina's behavior never changed. She engaged in the observed sequence during daylight hours. However at night, from the first hint of darkness until the break of dawn, Bina ran through the ward naked, pounding on the door, screaming, "Let me die".

While exiting the insane asylum, the only words Bina ever spoke reverberated in my mind. I fell sobbing to my knees in the dirt outside the main door. Pain and despair I'd known, but never had I seen what a human being became when stripped of all dignity.

During the bus ride from the terminal to the asylum, we'd passed a sweet smelling stall reminding me of a shop back in Madaripur. The fragrance of a blossoming oleander mingled with the aromas of spices in the jute sacks and herbs in small pots. When I left the asylum, I walked to the stall and chatted with the herbalist, who sold me a small sack of oleander seeds. Further along the lane, a kitchen wares dealer sold me a mortar and pestle to grind the seeds. I walked to the park nearby and bought a bowl of rice pudding from a street vendor at the entrance. The shade in the park provided respite before returning to the asylum for the afternoon.

Despite my efforts to reach Bina, her actions never wavered. I wept as I thought of her wretched existence filled with never ending terror. It felt as if a long time passed before the attendant informed me that visiting hours would soon be over. Prior to leaving, I asked to share my extra rice pudding with Bina. He told me to give him a moment to distract the other patients so they would not try to steal it. I placed an oak tree leaf filled with fragrant rice to Bina's mouth. She grabbed it and ate like a wild animal.

My servant waited outside. We made our way back to the bus and the train terminal. The conductor shouted, "All aboard," before the train belched black coal smoke. We settled into our seats under the cool breeze of the ceiling fan. The haunting whistle blew, and as we began to roll along the soothing tracks, tears trickled down my cheeks.

We'd traveled a few miles beyond the last cluster of houses when something moved underneath my seat. I peered into the semi-darkness below me, spotting a calico kitten arching its back. The kitten's ribs were showing through matted hair, while it repeatedly rubbed its fur across the back of my leg. I lifted the kitten into my lap. She purred in my arms, comforting me during the long ride home.

Ajit met us at the station. "Where did you get the kitten?"

"She found me on the train."

The next day we received a telegram stating that shortly after I'd left the asylum, Bina had experienced a massive seizure and died of a heart attack. I cuddled the calico kitten, which I'd christened Lullaby, and stroked her newly groomed fur.

***

Stifling humidity hit me when entering the door of the dimly lit bathroom annex. My hands waved the air in an effort to shoo the pesky insects. I brushed my teeth and freshened up at the wash basin, making sure to dig the sand from the inside corners of my eyes. Looking into the silvered mirror, I combed my hair, briefly lamenting the glistening white strands interspersed in my thinning long dark mane. The damp palms of my hand did little to smooth the unruly wisps at my grey temples.

The nutty smell of cooked basmati rice filled the yard and drifted down the dirt lane that ran beyond the compound walls. Sunny winter mid-afternoons beckoned beggars to our door. Half naked sadhu holy men and widowed women with children in tow carried their plates to our compound in hopes for a scoop of rice. I walked out to a woman standing alone behind the others, her covered head bowed down. She prostrated herself in the patchy grass to kiss my feet.

"Please, that is not necessary," I said.

"You are a Brahmin, I am an Untouchable."

"We are all equal."

I gave the woman rice. She thanked me, then furtively turned her head away from me to eat. I watched her for a moment, but returned to the house to avoid embarrassing her.

In the vegetarian kitchen, I looked over the tray prepared by the servants. My meal consisted of a spoonful of lentil dhal and cooked root vegetables atop a scoop of rice, a fresh poori, a small bowl containing mango chutney, and a cup of milk. I loosely covered the tray with a clean woven cloth. Carrying the tray in one hand and holding up my sari with the other, I ascended the stairs. The dogs, Blackie and Lotu, followed closely behind me onto the protective veranda, wagging their tails.

The front of the balcony remained open to the air except for a low stucco wall, which became a drying rack for my laundered cotton saris. Secured in place with smooth rocks, the garments hung over the wall unfurling six feet down the side of the house to dry. The banners billowed in the breeze, the slow motion ripple of bright colors against neutral walls creating free flowing daydreams.

The servant girl arrived on the veranda with a broom in hand, and a newborn in a shawl tied on her back. She began to sweep the dust and leaves off the floor mat on which I would sit to eat. I found her staring at my tray, focusing on the wet spot where the milk sloshed out.

"Are you hungry?" I asked.

She began to sweep and did not look me in the eye. "No, ma'am."

"Perhaps thirsty?"

"No, ma'am."

"I've never seen you study my tray so intently. Is something wrong?"

"I do not produce enough milk. My baby whimpers from hunger." The servant girl began to cry.

Gently taking the broom from her hands, I gave her the glass of milk and the clean cloth. "Go feed your baby."

"My baby cannot drink from a cup."

"Dip the corner of the cloth in the milk. Your baby will suck it dry."

She bent to kiss my feet.

I touched her head. "Please, no. You don't want to spill the milk."

After I finished sweeping, I positioned myself lotus style on the mat. Lullaby startled me when she landed on the balcony, even though I should have been accustomed to her behavior by now. She nestled in my lap. On cue, three more cats jumped from their rooftop perches to my dining room. One draped across each of my shoulders, and the third perched on my head. They instinctively balanced and kept from scratching me during this ritual. The two dogs, black and white, were seated expectantly in front of me.

I rolled individual balls of rice and dhal, dotted with bits of vegetables, for each one of my six pets. Blackie sniffed the air, but none of the animals tried to snatch the food. I lay the balls in a row in front of me, and only then did they settle in to their customary space to eat.

Each animal ate in a way that reflected its personality. Blackie first separated a small bit of rice from his portion, laid the grains to the side, and inspected the sample before returning to savor his food. Lotu finished her food in three large bites. Lullaby nudged her food apart and picked out vegetable pieces to eat first. One of the cats licked her way from the outside to the inside of the ball. Another ate part of hers and walked away. The small one who perched on my head rolled her ball over to the corner of the balcony and looked warily at the others while she slowly ate her dinner. Observing the animals' habits made me wonder if their personalities mimicked those of their former selves.

***

Years later, Jitendra died from a massive hemorrhage while seated on the judge's seat rendering a sentence. When I became old, cancer invaded my cells. My son, Ajit, came to visit me from America along with his wife, Connie, and their four year old son, Misha. It had been years since I'd seen my son, and the first time I'd met Connie and my grandson.

I lay on a huge Indian platform bed in the corner of a high ceilinged teal room. A second bed and chairs stood in another corner of the room. Pushed against a side wall stood a heavy television that played in the evenings when the moody electricity worked. A translucent white sari swaddled my tiny body, layer upon layer wrapping round me like skins of a pearl onion.

Connie sat beside me in her golden wedding sari, and stroked my forehead, my thin white hair. Nothing else in the room existed but the two of us smiling at each other, connecting on an unspoken level. She understood I loved her.

Two doorways flanked my room. A picture of Jitendra hung above the corner threshold. Connie had been exiting through the doorway below his picture in respect for our custom of obtaining the ancestor's blessing. She kissed me a final goodbye on my forehead, then fled through the wrong door. I observed her hesitate, as if in realization of her error. She continued on, her head lowered as she passed under the arched door frame.

Drawing on the strength from my lotus birth entrance into this world, as I'd done so many times during my life, I'd stayed alive to meet her.

Metronome

SIXTEEN

DUTIFUL

Indiana 1951

My name is Patricia.

I am the daughter of Clara and Ted.

Ted was the son of Lizzie and Paul. Paul was the son of Verena and Henry.

Henry was the son of Katharina and Gerhard.

In the safety of my parents' bedroom, Aunt Betty and my mother sat on the edge of the bed watching me pack. Auntie delivered me twenty-two years ago, on the morning of the big snow that melted before eleven. She nicknamed me Peggy moments after my birth.

"Aunt Betty, am I going to die?"

"You're young and strong, Peggy. You'll have the best care."

"What will they do to me?"

"Give you medicine. Make you sit under heat lamps, or in the sun."

"What about the treatments? Nobody will tell me what happens. Do they cut me?"

She glanced at my mother, then down at her old dirty house slippers.

"They collapse your lungs, one at a time. When there's no oxygen left in your lung, the bacteria will die."

***

Off the beaten track up a gently sloping incline, partially hidden by three tall trees, stood the red brick administration building. On this cool September morning, the sunlight filtering through the dull green leaves of the sycamores provided warmth. As we approached the sanatorium, Dad driving, Mom in the passenger seat, and me in the back, the weight of the moment bore down on me. I had contracted the white plague and been christened with the common nickname, lunger, referring to the diseased state of my lungs. I felt shame where none should have been.

The secretary ushered us into the doctor's office. My mother told him she could take care of me and begged him to let me go back home. My father added that he would drive me to the hospital for treatments. The doctor said I needed to remain in the hospital to get better. Besides, it would be dangerous to live out in society for at least the next six months, maybe even a year. At this last pronouncement, my fragile mental balance teetered, and fear and desperation once again spun out of control. *Why had God punished me?* The doctor's mouth moved, but I couldn't register the meaning of the jumble of words spewing out.

My mother later repeated the remainder of the conversation to me. The doctor told her he used me as an example to the farming communities. If a smart pretty young woman, a college graduate and a teacher, contracted tuberculosis, anyone could be susceptible. He wanted the rural people of southern Indiana to realize that it was not only the WW II veterans who contracted TB. The farmers should take care of their health and get screened for the disease.

***

"Be nice to the nurses and doctor," Mother said, hugging me.

"Don't cry. Get tough. You can beat this," Dad said.

My parents walked away down the long dark hallway. I turned back to my room, spartanly furnished with twin beds and matching nightstands. No dresser, no desks, no chairs. The door of a small closet with shelves and a few hangers stood ajar. My roommate, Mary, looked at my face then quickly away, without uttering a word. Nothing she might have said would have comforted me.

Exhausted from the drive and raw emotions, I stretched out in a lounge chair on the sunny back veranda. A plaid blanket covered my legs and torso up to my neck, but my free hands held *The Diary of Anne Frank*. Seventeen carefully chosen books had been nestled in my suitcase for the stay at the sanatorium. I held the hope that inspirational stories would make me less afraid of my own.

I opened to the first page of text, reading the words repeatedly without comprehension. Normally I did not allow myself to visit far dark corners, but at that point, I possessed no control over anything in life. A frightening thunderstorm from my early youth invaded my thoughts.

***

In the farmhouse kitchen, high up on the hill, I stood in the midst of trembling voices of grown German men praying *The Apostle's Creed*. I felt the baritones resonate deep in my slight eight year old chest, making me aware of the thumps of my heartbeat. Still, human sounds could not drown out the booming thunder that shook the walls nor the deafening cracks of the oaks in the yard when lightning struck. Through the lace kitchen curtains, the electrical show both terrified and fascinated its onlookers. The continuous blinding flashes of lightning, connected across the sky by lines of electricity, seemed to show God's wrath with the world.

My father stood in the midst of his three brothers, all strong hard farmers. The women and children huddled around the periphery. I hid in the folds of my aunt's apron. In German, my Father continued to lead the rosary, reciting the first half of the *Hail Mary*.

Gegrüßet seist du, Maria, voll der Gnade,

der Herr ist mit dir.

Du bist gebenedeit unter den Frauen,

und gebenedeit ist die Frucht deines Leibes, Jesus.

He barely waited for his younger brothers to answer with the second half, before he started the prayer over again.

Every man held a black rosary, counting off the beads as each prayer finished. Their thumb and index finger rubbed one bead at a time, then slid off onto the next. Ten *Hail Marys* were recited in succession, intonation relating pleas for mercy. The men caught their breaths during the refrain prayers, the "Glory Be" and "Our Father". The cycle repeated five times, before my father kissed the cross to end the rosary.

The epic thunderstorm of my childhood eventually quieted, although resulting in a record flood. The effects of wind and water destroyed complete farms, and displaced many rural families. The creeks backed up and the Ohio

River overflowed its banks, fourteen miles north of the river to our little town. We fished in the large backwater ponds caused by the flooding.

***

I closed my book. Perhaps I should pray now, like my father and uncles did then. The storm may not go away, but my fear may subside. I mumbled the ingrained words.

"Hail Mary, full of grace, the Lord is with thee.

Blessed art thou among women, and blessed is the fruit of thy womb, Jesus.

Holy Mary, Mother of God,

Pray for us sinners, now and at the hour of our death. Amen."

Mary's prayer did not quiet my mind. From a grade school nun, I learned a substitute for prayer...the act of making a small cross on the inside of my left wrist with my right thumb. Drawing the cross repeatedly, closing my eyes and taking deep breaths to fortify myself began to calm me.

When a hand touched my arm, I startled and squinted up into the sun at the backlit face of a white capped nurse.

"Peggy, drink this." She handed me a small white medicine cup full of liquid.

"What is it?"

"PAS. Para-amino salicylate sodium. Kills the bacteria."

"Tastes terrible," I said.

She patted me on the arm.

"You'll get used to it. Your first treatment will take place this afternoon."

The cup must have contained several medicines. Before long, I felt the sensation of flying down the hill at the head of the line of children. In the summertime in our little town, children roamed in packs, roller skating up and down and around the hills. We looked like a flock of birds in formation, bunched together then spreading out, and back together again. In the winter, we trudged up and down those same hills with sled in tow, just for a few thrilling seconds of flying back down. Other times too, my body felt light and free...swinging through the air clutching the grapevines in the trees near the little chapel on the hill, or jumping high over the ropes in physical education class.

The doctor's voice came to me from far away. "Peggy, I'm going to give you shots of air into your abdomen." My eyes were blinded by the spotlight on me. I turned my head to the side to look around the white porcelain tiled treatment room. The doctor came into view, filling a large syringe with air. He turned toward me, lifted up my gown, rolled down the elastic on my underwear, and plunged the long thick needle into my belly near my navel. I gritted my teeth to help bear the stinging pain of each shot. He said the air pushed my diaphragm up into the area surrounding the lung to collapse it, thus killing the bacteria from lack of oxygen.

Later that night, my very first night in the sanatorium, my head began to feel as if it were swelling. The pressure produced a headache unlike any other, making me believe my head would explode. Grabbing my head with both hands, I pushed with my palm on one spot, causing the air beneath my scalp to move away from the area undergoing applied pressure. The air bubble reappeared in another spot, as if my head were a partially deflated balloon. The nurse gave me a sedative shot when I became semi-delirious. In the fuzzy state before sleep, the doctor said he probably missed the correct spot. When he shot the air into me, instead of surrounding the space around my lung, the air went up into my brain.

Prior to being admitted to the hospital, I promised myself to survive no matter what happened. Not like the boy across the street. He let me borrow his bicycle while he went to war. He never came back to get it. I would battle this war to come out alive. But in the throes of a debilitating headache, resolve proved hard to muster.

Two days later, the orderly took me to the treatment room again. When I told the doctor the headache pain from the first injections was unbearable, he said it wouldn't happen again. Besides, this was the only treatment available, and if I wanted to live, I had no choice.

The treatment worked, collapsing my lung. It was not easy to breathe with only one lung functioning at a time. Every few days the lung spontaneously refilled with air, necessitating another injection session. Ninety-eight times during my stay, I endured painful injections of air to deprive one lung or the other of oxygen. Each time, I feared that the doctor might miss the right spot and the air would go to my brain.

I gradually began to dread the shots less and the tubes more. The doctor pushed a long tube down the back of my throat and asked me to swallow. My eyes bulged and watered as I repeatedly gagged. The tube was threaded through my vocal cords and into my lungs to obtain a sputum sample.

My throat always felt sore after the tubes. Instead of solid meals, the orderlies served me chamomile tea and soft toast spread with butter and strawberry jam. Each component of breakfast made me homesick. At the house in which I was born, we picked little camilla flowers to make tea. When I ate toast, my mother's words came to me. "Eat the crust, so you are able to whistle." I worked up on the farm milking the cows and churning butter. The jam sparked the memory of picking strawberries by the stem to avoid bruising the fruit.

After a few weeks the routine became familiar, allowing me to be more aware of my surroundings. I made silver Byzantine link necklace chains and volunteered to be the switchboard operator for the hospital. One morning, I peeked through the curtains of my second story dorm window. Some of the multi-colored autumn leaves had fallen off the trees, leaving spaces between the branches. For the first time, a long low red brick structure toward the back of the campus caught my eye. The doctor walked from the direction of his personal residence toward my newly discovered building.

"Where's the doctor going?" I asked the orderly.

"The children's ward, Peggy."

The children's ward? I'd previously been so self-absorbed that the idea of a children's ward had not crossed my mind. Children should be out playing kick the can, or softball, or leaving a rock trail while pretending to be Hansel and Gretel. They should be practicing piano in time with a *metronome* or singing in the choir. I taught children for one year before the patch test left angry red bumps on my arm that changed my life. Imagining children undergoing painful treatments without their parents, I cried for the children, and for myself.

***

On a rare day of rest, no medicine, no injections, no tubes, the doctor summoned me to his office. Perhaps he had good test results for me. After all, I never coughed, let alone produced bloody sputum like the other patients.

Maybe my TB miraculously disappeared and I could go home in time for Thanksgiving.

The doctor sat behind his desk. I had visited his office once before, on my first day at the hospital, but paid little attention to the mess. The walls of his office stood lined with bookshelves, some of which bowed in the middle from heavy medical books piled high one on top of another. Stacks of loose scattered papers littered every surface. He motioned me inside, hustling to clear off a chair for me.

The light shone through the dirty window onto the doctor. I saw him many times, but never studied his face. I guessed he was in his fifties. Lines around his mouth and puffiness under his eyes revealed that he was a tired man.

"Peggy, I have a favor to ask of you."

"Yes?" I choked back tears knowing my hopes of release were dashed.

"Did you know I have been elected president of my medical association?"

I turned to look out the window. "Congratulations," I managed to say.

"I need to give a speech. I've been told you know shorthand. I hope you will help me."

***

Stories regarding the doctor abounded. My aunt told me he'd contracted TB as a child, and his mission in life called to eradicate the disease. But a few disgruntled family members who lost their loved ones said he ran the sanatorium to pad his pockets. I did not know, nor care, but rather focused on recovery. I wanted to go back to the real world, to my life. If the doctor needed me, it was my duty to help him.

I became the doctor's personal assistant. He wrote a controversial speech about the danger of chiropractors. I took dictation from him, and typed his notes. He practiced his speech in front of me. We revised the speech until he felt satisfied. For my efforts, the doctor allowed me to swim in the outdoor pool of his residence on the remaining warm days of Indian summer.

He returned from giving his speech and I assumed my days as his assistant had ended. But he kept finding things for me to do in his office. Clean up his desk. Create a filing system. Organize the bookshelves. His own secretary rarely entered his private office, but kept busy answering calls and making appointments.

One day, the doctor addressed me. "Peggy?"

"Yes, doctor?"

"Does your boyfriend, Mark, I believe is his name, still come to see you?"

"He drives here almost every weekend."

After that brief exchange, there were no more projects to do. I saw the doctor only during my treatments. Late in the spring, I was discharged to finish my recuperation at home.

***

In the summer following my release from the sanatorium, I sat in the upstairs bedroom of my parent's home in our tiny little town. Nat King Cole and Tony Bennett blared from the Shady Inn's jukebox across the empty lot. My diagnosis of tuberculosis left a flood of changes in its wake. My teaching career was interrupted for a year. I became engaged to Mark, the man who stuck by me and who accepted me for myself. I found where I belonged with him.

I realized there were no guarantees in life as destiny often controlled what happened. I felt powerless for a time and lost control of my life. But I got tough and felt since I survived those painful treatments, nothing could hurt me anymore.

Ten years passed and we moved to a large city. In order to continue my teaching career, a yearly TB test was required. My new family physician referred me to a modern lung specialist. I got home from teaching school one day and as always, kicked off my pumps, unpeeled my hose, and threw my dress on the bed. Barefoot in my white slip, I walked to the living room to read the mail before starting supper. The specialist's return address was on the corner of a long white envelope. I tore open the letter, being careful to avoid a finger cut.

> After examining x-rays of the patient's lungs, I have determined they do not have the characteristic appearance of tuberculosis. Rather her lungs suggest a history of histoplasmosis, a fungal infection contracted from soil contaminated by bird or chicken droppings. Histoplasmosis is a common ailment in the Ohio Valley where she grew up.

Shocked, I sank into the chair and reread the report. I looked up, staring into the air beyond my children. The two girls squabbled over a doll and my son tried to dribble a basketball in the middle of the living room. The commotion served as background to my racing mind...and sheer bewilderment.

Over my slip, I instinctively reached down and felt my belly where pinpoint scars dotted my skin. The realization that I was forced to endure the life-changing experience of being diagnosed and treated for a potentially terminal illness that I never had, overwhelmed me.

"Mommy, she won't share."

"Mommy, why do you look that way?"

"Mommy, talk to us."

The three children stood in front of me, staring at my face, the little one tugging on the lace edge of my slip.

"Life isn't fair, children."

My hands came together, wringing in grief for unknown possibilities I'd missed. I closed my eyes and took a deep breath. Unconsciously I began making little crosses on the inside of my wrist. Over and over again.

Doorknobs

SEVENTEEN

DIGNITY

Indiana 2008

My name is Mark.

I am the husband of Pat, who was the daughter of Clara and Ted.

Ted was the son of Lizzie and Paul. Paul was the son of Verena and Henry.

Henry was the son of Katharina and Gerhard.

In a timeless procession of grief, the strong young men carried my coffin up the gently sloping hill. Upturned black collars did not prevent the bitter cold wind from chapping their cheeks, reddening their noses, stinging their eyes. Four of my children sat in the limo, watching the spectacle of darkness, the reverberation of trumpeted Taps in their ears. They did not stay to watch me being lowered into the ground.

Instead, they instructed the driver to go to the hospital. Pat, my wife, and their mother, lay encumbered by a neck brace, leg splints, and wrapped bandages that restricted her every move. Perceiving from beyond, I heard my children comfort my wife. My family discussed my life, the good times and hard times of the last few years. They told her I'd finally found peace.

***

I was born in the back bedroom of a remote southern Indiana farmhouse, the son of Oscar and Bertha, just before the Great Depression. I was the seventh son of a seventh son. My father died when I was two, leaving me to be raised by my dirt poor mother. Mom ruled her brood with love in her heart, and a broom in her hand.

My four oldest brothers were sent off to World War II together, and all came home. I finished high school in three years and joined the army. The military posted me in the Pentagon to set up a record keeping system for veterans.

Upon discharge, the GI bill paid for my education at the State Teachers College. I missed the army life, and considered quitting school to return home to the hills of southern Indiana. Walking across the campus quadrangle one day, I saw ditch diggers far down in a hole, dirty sweat dripping into their eyes. Their hard life spurred me on to finish my degree in teaching math. In addition, I became a high school basketball coach in the heyday of the 1950's Hoosier hysteria.

I married the love of my life, Pat, and had five children, two girls, Connie and Candy, and three boys, Neil, Terry, and Lou. Our family needed extra income to supplement my low teaching salary. A summer business seemed ideal, and the inspiration came to me to build a golf course. At age thirty-three, I found a farm just outside the city limits with a good source of water, and bought it with money borrowed from family and friends. With my knowledge of geometry, I laid out a nine hole golf course and hired high school boys to help me build it. Our family became close working together at the course, and during the winter holiday break we took an annual trip to Florida.

***

Pat and I remained faithful during over fifty years of marriage. But in my seventy-seventh year, hallucinations that she was carrying on an affair haunted me. In my dreams, my wife and her lover were together during broad daylight in a car parked at our business. I insisted my visions were real. The doctor said it may be a form of dementia, Pick's disease, but the dreams disappeared after changing medicines.

In late winter, I developed a sore on the inside of my cheek which eventually was diagnosed as mouth cancer. The doctor recommended immediate surgery with possible post-operative radiation or chemotherapy. Connie, my oldest child, sat with me in the parking lot following my diagnosis, and placed her hand on my knee to comfort me as I wept.

A week later Connie and I drove along the Indianapolis bypass to the hospital for surgery. The safe cocoon of our little world inside the car allowed me the courage to face the possibility of death. I told my daughter what I wanted, and did not want, at the end of my days on earth. If I could not sit and enjoy talking to people at the golf course clubhouse, I did not want to live.

We sat in the pre-op waiting room for what seemed like a long time. I drifted in and out of consciousness in the recovery room, but when Connie was allowed to see me, I managed to mouth, "I am cold." The nurse wrapped me in a silver space-age blanket.

Early the next morning, a rare earthquake on the New Madrid fault shook me awake. I looked in the mirror and was shaken once more. My neck had been cut and stapled from behind my ear, traveling along the jawbone, halfway around my head to my Adam's apple. It appeared as if someone had tried to decapitate me.

Through the summer months, I endured daily radiation sessions. The technician helped me take off my shirt and lay down on the hard cold flat bed of the huge white machine. She inserted a bite guard in my mouth which made me gag. A molded hard fishnet mask over my face and head snapped me into place. Straps were fastened across my torso and legs to hold me still. The radiation bore through my head and neck.

In the fall, the PET scan revealed no more cancer, but the ordeal left me thin and weak. I ate little and slept for long hours in my recliner. My shoulders stooped, and my gait was wobbly. The doctor ordered a CT scan of my brain. Results were negative.

***

We celebrated Thanksgiving with Connie, her husband, Ajit, and dog, Maddie, at their house in Bloomington, about an hour from our home. I ate second helpings of soft foods, dressing, mashed potatoes, and pumpkin pie, bringing a smile to my daughter's face. We settled in front of the TV to watch football games and a special about the White House Christmas decorations.

Connie lay on the couch with Maddie spread out at her feet like a queen. I made the offhand comment that after this life, I would like to come back as a dog, not just any dog, but their dog. I'd received my first dog, Toby, as a young boy in payment for work on a farm four miles away. A few months after I got him, he sat outside and howled all night. I later found out that the dog's original owner, the farmer, had died that evening.

The four of us nodded off from the turkey and feast overload, but forced ourselves awake to play euchre, men versus women. My daughter and I looked at each other during Ajit's crazy card playing antics and laughed hysterically. Despite Connie's declaration that Ajit held the title of the worst card player in the world, the men, Ajit and I, won.

Pat and I headed for home with smiles on our faces.

***

My older brother lived in a nursing home, mind and body feeble with disease. Unbeknownst to me at the time, the Sunday morning following Thanksgiving he was found sobbing inconsolably. "Mark died in a wreck, Mark died in a wreck," he kept repeating. The nurses, believing me to be gone, expressed their condolences to his visiting children walking down the hall to his room.

***

On Monday, Pat and I watched the local six PM news. The weather forecast looked fine for travel to the basketball game that night at the university arena. Candy, our second daughter, drove our big gold Buick we'd purchased for our fiftieth wedding anniversary. I hopped in the passenger seat and Pat climbed into the rear. A few miles down the highway, Candy slowed when she noticed the shiny road, indicating black ice had coated the surface.

BOOM. Disorientation. "Were we in an accident?" I mumbled, holding my head.

"Yes," said Candy, who was pinned behind the air bag and steering wheel. "Mom, are you okay?"

"I think so," said Pat, lying on the floor of the back seat.

I heard Candy talking to Connie on her cell phone. "We've been in an accident on the highway in front of the engineering school. Dad and Mom are both awake and talking, but Mom may have a broken leg."

Pat and I shared an ambulance. We pieced together what happened. An SUV coming from the opposite direction slipped on the black ice and crossed over the center line. Candy T-boned their out-of-control vehicle. The car held three Turkish college exchange students on their way home from Wal-Mart. The impact ejected and killed the male passenger in their car.

My middle son, Terry, arrived at the hospital. We conversed about who was winning the ballgame I was missing. But soon, I developed a pounding headache and sharp stomach pains, which prompted the doctor to order tests. While lying on a stretcher being wheeled down long halls to the MRI machine, I watched the glaring overhead lights roll by one after the other. I traveled through multiple sets of double doors into the mysterious hidden areas of the hospital. The sensation of flying along under the staccato blur of lights through door after door, reminded me of a recurrent dream. I moved from room to room, turning smooth shiny *doorknobs* into bright rooms, looking for answers.

The MRI results indicated internal bleeding. The physicians ordered a transfer to the Indianapolis trauma center seventy miles away. I fell asleep on the gurney waiting for the ambulance.

***

Connie had been spending a quiet evening with Maddie, while Ajit taught class. Following the initial call from Candy in the wrecked car, my older daughter decided to wait until travel conditions improved before attempting to make the trip to my hometown hospital. Driving in the dark on slick, curvy, hilly two-lane roads during a winter ice storm was too dangerous.

However, when I was transferred to the trauma center, Connie determined she needed to make the trip to Indianapolis despite the weather. Terry planned to stay at the hometown hospital with Pat, who was undergoing tests, and Candy, who had suffered pelvic injuries. Connie looked on the computer to find the directions to the Indianapolis trauma center, about two hours up the highway due north from her home in Bloomington.

My youngest son, Lou, on a business trip in Australia, happened to be online and available for instant messaging. He asked Connie to tell me he loved me before I died. That's when it truly hit her that the possibility of my death was real. She found the health care power of attorney document in her file cabinet. She retrieved her luggage from the closet, noticing my college suitcase on the shelf. She put tissues in the car and washed her hair in the sink. Ajit returned home by then, and decided to stay with Maddie. She kissed them goodbye.

Salt treatments had been applied on the highway, but still Connie fought through ice and fear to get to me. Under the cruel glare of the parking lights in the trauma center garage, she prepared herself for whatever may come. She hurried through long corridors to the emergency room desk where the receptionist relayed I had previously arrived by ambulance. Connie walked through the emergency room, seeing accident victims on stretchers in every square inch of available space. Families stood around the stretchers, speaking with the doctors and nurses, staring, crying, and talking on cell phones.

Connie entered the private room where I lay. Two doctors and four nurses turned their eyes from me to her. "Dad, I'm here now."

"He can't hear you," said one of the doctors.

Connie saw the tubes in me. "He knows I'm here," she replied.

"His pupil has blown. You have to make a decision how aggressive you want to be."

Connie was aware of the possibility that I could die, but before that moment, hadn't known that death was probable.

More scans. While I disappeared through the doors into the bowels of the trauma center, Connie got word from Terry that their mother's condition had deteriorated. My wife lay on board a medical helicopter bound for the same trauma center. My daughter stood in the midst of chaos, waiting for me to emerge from my tests, and her mother to arrive on the helipad. She forced herself to make small talk with the minister who barely left her side, feeling as if she needed to entertain him. After the tests, the orderlies wheeled me back to the emergency room into a curtained off examination area rather than returning me to my original private room.

Within minutes, Pat arrived amidst a flurry of activity. The medical team wheeled her into the private room I had previously occupied. She remained conscious, but sustained a broken neck, two broken legs, and deep leg wounds. The doctors determined Pat's broken neck would not paralyze or threaten her life. The wounds would heal with time and treatment if they did not become infected. But she needed surgery to place titanium rods in both of her broken legs. It would be a miracle if she ever walked again. Connie was allowed only a brief conversation with her mother. Pat asked, "Where's Mark?" My daughter said that they were running tests on me.

Connie walked to my bedside. The doctor slid the curtain aside and asked her to step out with him. They found a space near a pillar which offered a small measure of privacy. The brain scans showed surprising results, the doctor explained. They found old blood, indicating my brain had been in the process of a slow hemorrhage *prior* to the accident. When my head hit the window during the wreck, the radiation weakened blood vessels could not hold back what the slow hemorrhage began. During the trip from my local hospital to the trauma center, while I slept peacefully, half my brain exploded. The doctor would be willing to attempt surgery but with the understanding the prognosis was extremely poor. If I survived the operation, I would almost certainly be a vegetable in a nursing home the rest of my life.

Connie remembered our long conversations in the car on the way to cancer appointments.

"No. Dad would not want to live like that. Let him go," she said.

In the past several years, my mind tried to leave reality through hallucinatory dreams. My body tried to leave this earth from mouth cancer, and a hidden slow brain hemorrhage. The car accident came out of nowhere to relieve me of pain.

***

The physician assistant led Connie to a computer cubicle near the nurse's station and showed her my brain images. "Twenty-two cuts," the assistant said. "The MRI revealed hemorrhaging on twenty-two slices of the scan. The more MRI slices showing the bleed, the worse the prognosis. Your father sustained one of the most severe bleeds we have ever seen."

Both Connie and I had been born on the twenty-second day of the month. She often said twenty-two was her lucky number. My daughter would never wish me dead. But because of the previously undetected slow hemorrhage which probably would have led to lingering suffering, and because I was in a weakened state and tired of all the pain I'd endured, she realized the extended bleed evident on twenty-two cuts may have been a blessing in disguise.

Connie held my head while the nurses turned me to change my gown and sheets. She felt something wet on her hand and looked down. Blood from the wound where I hit my head in the car covered her hand.

She watched the doctor unplug the machine, unhook tubes and remove medical drains. On the monitor, the life lines began to flatten. The diminished peaks signaled I would leave this earth shortly. In a resigned voice, she asked the nurse, "He doesn't have long, does he?" The nurse shook her head.

Medical staff walked in and out of the area, but did not stay with us. Connie remained with me, tried to stay present for me. I gave her life, she helped me leave mine. She whispered to me not to be afraid, to find where I belonged. She stroked my arms, stood at the head of my bed and kissed my forehead. She told me she loved me, my family loved me.

She did not recoil when I began to gag, and green fluid gushed out of my nose. She asked the doctor to give me morphine to quiet my racking chest. She did not want me to feel the panic of suffocation, though she realized by then I felt no pain or suffering. Giving me the medicine made her feel better.

The nurses could not find a Catholic priest to give me last rites and my daughter refused a Protestant minister. She no longer practiced Catholicism, but she blessed me in a way she thought that I might want. She told the nurses it didn't really matter; we were all going to the same place anyway.

I flat lined in less than an hour. A priest arrived after I passed, but administered last rites before the doctors actually pronounced me gone. Connie told the reverend that her mother lay in the other room. He seemed to be shocked by her revelation.

Connie called her siblings and husband. Ajit told her that Maddie was sitting out on the deck, her sorrowful soulful howling echoing through the woods.

***

Connie felt conflicted whether Pat should be told of my death prior to her surgery. My daughter asked the universe for grace to guide her. Among the many staff rotating in and out, a new nurse came in and stood beside the bed. The lovely innocent girl with reddish hair introduced herself as Grace. She counseled if Pat did not make it through the surgery, my daughter may be sorry her mother didn't know of my passing. Until then, Connie had not fully realized she could lose her mother too.

My oldest son, Neil, arrived at the trauma center. My daughter steeled herself before the two walked into Pat's room. Several doctors and nurses joined them.

Connie held her mother's hand. "Mom, please look at me. I need to tell you something."

"Yes?"

Connie took a breath. "Dad died. He hit his head in the accident...and he died."

"No, Connie. That can't be."

"Yes, Mom, he is gone."

Pat stared at the ceiling.

"Would you like to say goodbye to him?" said my daughter.

"I don't know. I don't know."

The staff wheeled me into the room with Pat. I lay on the gurney, white as a ghost, a raw picture of death. A bandage covered the small cut on my forehead where I bumped the car window. Pat also looked ghostlike from her blood loss and trauma. She could not turn her head to see me due to the medical collar restricting the movement of her broken neck. The nurses wheeled me close enough for Pat to touch me. My body had not yet turned cold. Connie snapped a picture of us in order to confirm the reality of the surreal moment.

"It feels like a dream," Pat said. She began to shake uncontrollably.

Connie spoke to the nurse. "Please give her something. She is going into shock."

"I don't want anything for sleep. I want to be awake," Pat said.

"Just a little something, Mom. Just a little something."

Connie and Neil whispered their last goodbyes to me. An orderly wheeled my body to a back hallway to await the coroner. I was finally at peace.

233

Horse

EIGHTEEN

ग्रविटय

India 1947
My name is Ajit. I am the last Rai Sahib of my family.
I am the adopted son of Jitendra and Nanibala,
and the natural son of Motindra and Lily.
Jitendra and Motindra were brothers, the sons of Kumar and Soudamoni.
Kumar was the son of Avoya and Shyamsundari.
Avoya was the son of Durga Charan and Padma.
Durga Charan was the son of Ram Sundar, Shanti, and Daya.

In the summer of my twenty-seventh year, I climbed aboard an early train bound for the Red Sea. My six week summer vacation had been spent exploring Ethiopia in rickety old buses or perched on the backs of farmers' trucks. Where available, I rode the Italian built rail line, basking in luxury and protection from the hot sun. A fellow Indian teacher of mathematics at Haile Selassie University in Addis Ababa was my summer traveling companion. He offered me the window seat on the train to enjoy the views, explaining he'd probably fall asleep.

We boarded before first light, when the windows appeared to be framed black views of nothingness. I settled into my space under the dim glare of the flickering overhead lamps. The tea vendor took my breakfast order. "Yes, Mr. Mukherjee, I will bring you a hot cheese puff, with strong tea and milk. Very soon sir." I'd learned to enjoy more than triangle-cut toast in the morning while attending college in London.

The train began its slow three hour descent from Asmera at 7600 feet above sea level, creaking and squeaking its way around curves down through the mountains to the Red Sea city of Massawa. I wet my index finger to gather the pastry flakes left on the plate, then lifted my hand to lick off the crumbs. The windows were black no more.

Entranced by the light of the morning sunrise in the mountains, I sat back in my seat to enjoy the view. Conical mountain shapes stood outlined by the breaking dawn light behind them, their shadows shifting with each minute the sun rose higher in the sky. Low lying clouds nestled in the valleys subtly changed colors as the day became brighter. The feeling reminded me of a childhood train ride that changed my life. Time slipped away.

***

"I bet you can't get it this time, Ajit. The coin hit the middle, in the deepest part," Haru taunted.

My cousin's words resonated in my ears as I dove off the bank into the pond. Haru was eight, the same age as me, but one month older. He had not won the diving-for-the-coin competition the entire summer. The final afternoon of vacation we held one last diving contest, his final opportunity to defeat me and crown himself king of the swimmers. During his turn to throw the coin and my turn to retrieve it, he took no chances. He circled the large pond for the best vantage point, then aimed at his chosen target spot. The coin plopped into the water, then Haru pointed at the water ripples issuing his dare.

With each powerful downward stroke of my arms and cupped hands, the water darkened as less light filtered from above. I angled down fifteen feet then extended my arm to feel for the bottom. My hand patted the floor of the pond to detect the coin. The wet soil felt soft and silky, a blend of solid and liquid so enticing I ran my hands along the bottom longer than necessary. The murkiness stirred up from the dirty muddy water caused my eyes to burn.

A rare bright shaft of light penetrated the darkness up ahead. The sun's rays refracted through the water to shine upon a concentrated small circle of light. Kicking my legs hard behind me, I reached to grab the coin. Beating my cousin and remaining the champion was within my grasp. I pushed off from the bottom of the pond, anxious to emerge from the surface of the water with my arm raised in triumph, displaying the coin for all to see.

Picturing the disappointment on Haru's face, I assuaged my guilt with the justification that he'd been mean-spirited when he threw the coin into the deepest water. My female cousin and her neighborhood girlfriends lining the shore of the pond would cheer in admiration. Servant girls who stood on the steps leading into the water would clap. Filled with anticipation, I decided to make my breakthrough more exciting and impressive by unexpectedly emerging opposite my entrance spot.

I propelled toward the surface near the edge of the pond. In the process of jabbing my foot at a fish that nipped my toes, my leg became entangled on a water lily root. Kicking back and forth only made the situation worse. Looking up through the water, I saw the blurry brown bodies of Haru and his little brother standing on the banks in their swim trunks. The glittery embroidered edges of the girl's pink and yellow saris formed a golden rainbow shimmering through the water. The long wavy silhouettes of the standing servant girls stared at me so intently that even through the water, I could see the white corners of their wide open eyes.

Holding my breath became increasingly difficult and the burning pain in my eyes worse. I turned to face the long dark roots wrapped between my toes and around my foot. In my struggle to unwrap the tentacles, the coin dropped from my hand. An inward calm came over me. With a bit of untying of knots, plus a hard yank, I slipped the bonds that held me. One strong instinctive stroke launched me upward to erupt through the surface, gasping for air.

Everyone but Haru cheered and applauded. The roar of fear in my ears subsided, and the exhilaration of breaking free took its place. Haru yelled above the din of the celebration.

"Where's the coin? You didn't get it, did you? I won, I won!"

The coin no longer was important to me. I simply felt relief. Besides, Haru and I both knew that despite coming up empty handed on the final dive, I was the better swimmer. No need for me to protest or explain, even when Haru started his victory dance around the edge of the pond repeating the words, "I won, I won," in a familiar children's tune.

I dog paddled toward the pond steps. Open petaled water lilies at eye level on the water's surface caught my attention. I'd become accustomed to flowers in our ponds, but never studied them from this vantage point. The full blooming soft white lilies released a sweet fragrance. Their green pad bases glistened with water drops splayed during my emergence. A few moments before, the lily roots held me captive in their grasp, but staring at the beauty of the flowers made me feel the magic of being alive.

Early the next day, the muted sweet song of a raga woke me. The seasonal traveling musician sat in the alcove of our large brick entrance gate during summer dawns. I climbed out from under the mosquito net and opened the window to let the voice float into my room. The haunting melody of the music enchanted me until Mother knocked on my door. I became caught in the whirlwind of dressing, last minute gathering of belongings, saying tearful goodbyes.

Returning to boarding school in the Himalayan foothills took two travel days, or more with delays. Our house assistant, along with a luggage toting servant, accompanied me on several connecting boat rides to Faridpur. There I joined my friends and fellow students traveling by train back to school. On the train, I sat mesmerized by the terraced rows of plantings on the hillside farms and mighty rivers roaring through quiet canyons. We slept in the first class bunk at night, and woke early to a morning breakfast of tea and toast slathered with butter. In Siliguri, the school bus picked us up for the six hour trip to Kalingpong.

The unchanging structure at the Jesuit boy's boarding school suited me well. We wore uniforms consisting of a white shirt, red and blue striped tie, and a navy blue lion-emblemed blazer, with khaki pants and black shoes. We rose at seven and attended classes until four. After school, we ate a light snack packed in a portable three tiered tin tiffin. We played soccer until seven in the evening, showered, ate dinner and studied.

Saturday we attended half a day of class, with sports in the afternoon. Sunday, the Catholics attended mass, and non-Catholics slept and read the paper. One of our classmates charged each boy a rupee to peek at bra ads from his confiscated Calcutta Statesman. In the afternoon we studied, played cricket or took day trips.

About a month into the school year, Brother Thomas called me aside during math class. He told me the principal rector wanted to see me. Walking down the dim hall, I wondered why. Heavy brown wood comprised the bottom of the door. Wavy opaque glass adorned with shiny gold stenciled letters spelling Rector formed the top half.

After I knocked three times, the Rector responded, "Come in." He motioned me to sit in front of his desk. Reaching into his drawer, he pulled out a folded piece of paper, then walked toward me. The starched material of his white cassock jangled the large rosary beads tied around his waist, which in turn rattled my nerves.

What did the principal hold? Was I in trouble? Was it a math award? Maybe a special note from home? Letters were usually frequent when I began the new term, but this year I'd received only one since the beginning of the school year.

The Rector must have noticed that I'd started to fidget, and he put his hand on my shoulder. He'd done this once before as he comforted me during a soccer game mishap. "I received a telegram from your father. Let me read it to you."

> *Ajit, My assistant will be in Kalingpong Saturday 28/8/48 to bring*
> *you home. Father.*

"Why do I need to go home? I love it here, please don't make me leave."

"You haven't done anything wrong. You're a wonderful student."

"Then what is going on? I don't understand."

"Have you noticed some of your classmates left school the last few days?"

"Yes, Rector."

"My son, last year when the Partition divided our country into India and Pakistan, we all hoped and prayed people would learn to accept each other and live in peace. That has not happened. Neighbors are fighting each other and everyone is scared. Muslims are moving out of Hindu controlled land. Hindus are moving out of Muslim controlled land. Your parents want you to come home because they feel you will be safer with them."

"But I don't want to get behind in my studies."

"You can take your books home with you, Ajit. You are smart enough to work on your own and if you need help, your family will guide you. Once the situation calms, you will be able to come back to school."

"I will miss my teachers and friends."

"Don't worry, Ajit. Things will work out. Now then, you can skip soccer training and go to the dorm to pack."

"Sir, I'd rather go to practice. I don't have much to get ready."

***

I arrived home to a feeling of uncertainty. Father's colleagues, our family friends, and many relatives were coming and going. The adults closed the doors when speaking to each other in the house. Out on the veranda they stopped their conversation if I approached. The servants finished their work without lingering to talk or tease. The Partition changed the boundaries of people as well as countries.

Although we lived in our same house on the outskirts of Madaripur, we found ourselves no longer living in India, but residents of East Pakistan. We were Hindu, but our home and our land, the area where we lived for generations had been decreed Muslim. Riots between Hindus and Muslims broke out in Madaripur, and it became unsafe for us to go into town to shop at the markets. Many of our Muslim servants remained loyal to our family. At risk to their own safety, they surreptitiously bought food for us and relayed rumors they heard in the city.

On a clear fall day in 1948, after having been home a few weeks, I sat on the veranda pondering a math problem Brother Thomas had given me before leaving school. We'd finished tea time and the house was quiet while people rested. My eye caught sight of our most respected servant running toward our compound through the gate, gasping for breath and holding his side. He hurried toward Father, who stood smoking a cigarette surveying his large rose garden. I jumped off the veranda and ran toward the edge of the garden to hear their exchange.

Father addressed the servant. "Why are you in such a hurry?"

"Babu Sir, there is a rumor the young Muslim students in Madaripur are going to attack this Hindu neighborhood. They are fanatics and everyone is afraid of them. Please take precautions, Babu. I believe the situation is serious."

"Where did you hear this?"

"One of my cousins is a servant to a wealthy Muslim family in the city. On the way home from the market, I passed by his house and my cousin came out in the yard under the pretext of tending to flowers. He told me that he overheard the son of his employer speaking with friends last night. The son is known to be a ringleader in college militant groups."

All eyes turned toward the gate when we heard a car approaching the house. The servant backed away and retreated into the side yard. Few in town owned private cars, but as a judge and landowner, Father maintained friendships with important people. The manager of the newspaper stepped out into the yard. He and my father walked side by side deep into the rose garden, beyond the reach of my hearing.

He stayed a few minutes. The smell of the dust kicked up by his car speeding away stung my nostrils and made me sneeze. Father glanced in my direction, then he called for Mother as he hurried toward the rear of the house. I entered the front door in time to see my parents walk through the foyer and retreat into his private study. A few minutes later, the door creaked open, and Mother emerged from the room ashen faced. She saw me standing in the front doorway watching her. She motioned to me and told me to gather the family in the study.

I ran to get my three cousins, actually my nephews and my niece, the children of my much older widowed sister. I'd seen them earlier in the vegetable garden with their mother and my father's cousin, Pishi. She had become a destitute childless widow at age nineteen, and Father took her in. She became part of the background fabric of our lives, carving out a simple existence for herself by supporting us in ours. Within minutes, everyone gathered in the study and Father closed the door.

Tears were streaming down Mother's face. Father looked at her and addressed his family in a sad soft voice. "We must leave. The fanatic Muslim students from the university are full of hatred for the Hindu people. They are planning to rid Madaripur of wealthy Hindu families."

I spoke first. "When are we leaving?"

Father replied, "Tonight. In a few hours."

"When are we coming back?"

"We are not," Father said.

My sister cried out, "What about our home? Our things? Our life here?"

Father said, "We have no choice. If we stay, we could be killed. Or worse." He glanced at my niece, a beautiful thirteen year old girl.

After that statement, his voice became stronger, filled with resolve. He directed us how to proceed. We were to take only what we could carry. Wear our sturdiest shoes. Put on layers of traveling clothes, and take another set in a small satchel. Grab a few tiny sentimental or valuable things. He told my sister to go to the kitchen and direct the servants to prepare a quick hot meal, and to pack a snack to take with us. He told me to stay behind with him and Mother for a moment. He closed the door once again.

"Ajit," he said, "you must be brave. We need money for our journey. If I carry it, someone will confiscate the money. Your mother and I think you can help us."

I looked at Mother's tear stained face. "I will do whatever you want me to do."

We heard running through the house, then pounding on the door. The rumors of the attack and our impending departure spread in a flash.

"Babu, Babu Sir, please talk to us. What is happening?"

Father got up and opened the door. Two families of Hindu servants lived in our compound: two husbands, two wives, and children of varying ages. Most of them poured into the room, wailing wives shuffling behind their husbands with children in tow.

"Please, Babu Sir, what should we do? Please tell us. What to do, Babu?"

"You may come with us," my father said to them. He glanced at my mother, who nodded as she surveyed the mob in the room. She looked from one to another of the servant children as if she were counting the danger. I could understand the source of fear in her eyes. Escaping with our family of eight, plus an additional nine more people would not be easy.

"Thank you, sir, thank you, sir," they recited repeatedly en masse as they lay on the floor to kiss my father's feet. He instructed them to pack in the same manner he'd told us.

In the commotion another car pulled up to the house. Father's lifelong Hindu friend, Shibnarand, walked into the house and through the study door. He saw the commotion, heard the crying, and looked at my father with knowing eyes.

"My friend, you are going?" Shibnarand asked.

"I must. The situation is too dangerous for us. And you?"

"I cannot go. I will stay here to protect our store."

Father sank into the chair, tears in his eyes. He heaved a sigh. "This is goodbye then?"

Shibnarand seemed unable to speak. He kissed my father's forehead, touched his feet, and left the room wiping his tear stained face.

I'd been standing back toward the corner of the room with Mother, witnessing the end of life as we knew it. After Shibnarand left, Mother guided me toward the door, patting my father's arm as she passed by him in the chair. At her touch Father seemed to regain focus. "Ajit, go to your room and start packing. Your mother will be there soon."

The clock read a little before six in the evening. Less than an hour had passed since our servant ran through the gate. It seemed so long ago when I sat on the veranda with pencil in hand, working a math problem. Now I began to change into my most comfortable traveling clothes and pack a few trinkets in preparation to leave my home. Mother walked into the room and straight to the wardrobe.

"Here, son, put these on instead. You need to wear pants with two deep pockets. Hurry, and don't forget a jacket. Your father is waiting for you in the study."

I slid a small math book in my satchel and headed downstairs in time to see Father open the safe. He took out papers, stuffed them in an envelope, and put them on the desk. He glimpsed at me standing in the doorway, waved me inside, then peered back inside the safe.

"Ajit, here are our gold coins. We have no time to sew them into your pants."

I put them in my pocket. "You can trust me, Father."

We looked up to see another of my father's Muslim friends in the doorway.

"I heard you are leaving tonight."

Father replied, "Yes, dear friend. It is true."

"Is there anything I can do to help you?"

Father stared at his trusted friend. "There is something."

"Anything, name it."

"When you return to town, go to the river services office. Purchase passage on tonight's steamboat for the eight in our family, and nine in our servant families."

Father loosely counted out the last of the money from the safe. "This should cover the cost. Be sure to tell them the tickets are for me. Please wait for us at the dock with the tickets."

We left our lives at nine o'clock that evening. In pitch dark, seventeen travelers including eight adults and nine children walked four miles to the ferry dock. We snuck along a circuitous route hugging the tree line, avoiding the main road. Besides quiet splashes as we crossed the streams, the lone sound was an occasional sniffle from Mother. When we neared the river, we began to hear the rumble of shouts and cries from the crowd at the boat launch. We were shocked to see people shoving and fighting under the dim lanterns of the platform.

My father told us to stay together and follow him when we entered the sea of swarming men, women, and children. I put my hands in my pockets to secure the gold coins. Pandemonium ensued as word spread through the crowd that Father had picked up tickets from his assistant. If our prominent family was being forced to leave their birth land, then others realized the gravity of the situation. My small frame was pushed along with the wave of the mob trying to get on the boat. All I saw were the legs of those in front of me, and got separated from my family.

The loud speaker announced the boat could take no more passengers and would soon depart. I tried to find my way to the gangway plank, but there were too many bodies in the way. The horn sounded, signifying the imminent departure of the boat. I called out desperately to my parents, "Wait, I am coming."

Someone's arms abruptly picked me up and hoisted me high into the air at the edge of the dock. I didn't know who held me, or what they were going to do with me. My eyes caught a glimpse of the wooden plank being retracted and the boat beginning to pull away. A voice said, "You are in the hands of God." Without warning, I was flying across the water between the edge of the dock and the departing riverboat. White foamy peaks slapped against the side of the boat. The black water churned, dark and deep, far below me.

"Gio, gio…long live, long live," came from the crowd. I feared drowning in the foamy black waters. Instead I landed in the arms of my father, who hugged me and would not let go. Father nodded at a tall fair skinned man who stood in the dim light on the dock, hands folded in prayer. It was his friend, Shibnarand, who nodded in return, then closed his eyes and lowered his head. I buried my face in my father's chest, encircled by his embrace.

"Why did you let go of my hand?" I said to Father. "I screamed for you but could hear only the sound of the horn." The words spilled out of me, leaving me breathless.

Tears streamed down my father's face. "Please forgive me, Son. I tried to make a path for us through the crowd, and thought you were holding on to your mother's hand. People were pushing, and shoving, and please, please thank God you are safe. I love you." Father hugged me and we were alone in the middle of the masses.

***

With at least a thousand refugees crowded onboard, twice the five hundred person capacity, the dark ship was bedlam. Normally the first deck held second class, the second deck first class, but in this disordered world cooperation triumphed over rules. Regardless of social status, people settled where they could find room. My father's legal assistant and his family squeezed into small open deck spaces to sleep, as did many others we knew. Our servants entrenched themselves in the second class cabin Father purchased for them.

Our family was still considered members of the privileged class, one of the wealthy landowner Brahmin families of Madaripur. Since Father owned a small share of the river services company, we occupied a private first class cabin. Once everyone settled in our cabin, Father and I returned to the deck, where he smoked cigarettes with the other men. Father stood tall, even when we rocked from the wake of boats traveling the opposite direction. A smell of diesel hung in the air, but little smoke accompanied the odor. We watched as the lights of the Madaripur faded into the distance. Father and I sat in the cool evening air, on the deck of the steamship, along with other shocked refugees on their way to the unknown. The boat rounded the bend, and we could no longer detect signs of civilization. Shadowy shorelines and filtered moonlight on the water guided us on our way.

I looked up toward the heavens. Clouds were heavy in the night sky, dark grey with white marbleized veins running throughout. Not a star could be seen, but the full moon shone brightly. The clouds moved across the moon, from right to left as if reading ancient Hindu script, creating a halo. Mother said God's hand saved me when Shibnarand threw me across the water. Now it seemed as if God's eye shone through the clouds of life, a life that kept moving.

Father and I returned to the cabin. Mother sat on the cot, her slight body racking with sobs. My sister tried to comfort her. Although rare for my father to show affection to Mother in front of us, he put his arms around her. His embrace was both strong and tender. Her cries were not loud, but every so often we heard her lung's staccato attempts to catch her breath.

Until then, I'd been preoccupied with my terrifying flight over the water and fascinated with observing life on board the overcrowded boat. Mother's sadness disturbed and confused me. I couldn't understand why we were forced to leave. We were all people, Hindus and Muslims. We played and studied together and lived in peace before the Partition. The same sun warmed us, and the same stars and moon graced our night sky.

We tried to make ourselves comfortable in the small room. We didn't mind being crowded, as we needed each other's closeness to alleviate the fear. Our family had traveled on this same journey many times for pleasure, or trips to school. We knew we should arrive at the train station in Khulna the next evening, barring delays. Father tried to reassure and comfort us.

"I know this journey is hard for all of us. But we must be strong. The situation at home was deteriorating. We had no choice but to leave."

As if making a confession, he began the story of our exodus. "Yesterday I heard a rumor a radical student at the college in Madaripur stirred up trouble. He became a ringleader of a posse formed to hunt down Hindus. I didn't want to believe it, but in the middle of the night, last night..." here he took a deep breath "...as all of you slept, an unfamiliar low rumbling sound came from out beyond the canal bordering our lands, near the outbuildings. I went outside to my rose garden, lit by the almost full moon. One of our Muslim servants had also come outside to investigate the sound, which had evolved into a kind of chanting. The servant advised me to take refuge in the house. He knew the posse already burned some buildings in town, and might try to set fire to our compound."

"I no longer felt like I could protect us." He looked directly at my teenage niece. "A few days ago, rumors had surfaced that religious radicals were trying to kidnap Hindu girls to become slave brides to the Muslims. I am friends with many Muslim families with sons, and did not want to believe this. But the rumor proved true. A Hindu teenage girl was raped last night, and the ringleader announced it would happen to other Hindus if they did not leave."

When my father said the words, "a Hindu teenage girl was raped", the color from my niece's high cheekbones drained. To me, she seemed years older in an instant.

Rest did not come easy that night, but exhaustion took over. All night long, dreams of my beloved brave black horse, Bahadur, invaded my sleep. In the sunset hour before we fled, I stood at the edge of a field and watched a servant lead him away. I would never see him again, let him eat from my hand, feel him nuzzle me. My early morning rides in late fall or winter along the sandy shore of the river were no more. I woke and reached up to dig the sleep out of the corner of my eye. Instead my finger felt wet from the tears shed during my nightmare. I retrieved my *statue of Bahadur* from my satchel and held it tight. I must also be brave.

In the morning, the commodes were filthy and overflowing. We saw men and women using the river as their toilet. Except for dreaded bathroom trips, the women and my youngest nephew stayed in the cabin the rest of the boat journey. Father ventured out to talk to others, but did not stay away from the frightened women for any length of time.

My nephew, Haru, and I walked around the boat, entertaining ourselves by watching people on the decks, and trying to engage the armed police in conversation. On previous journeys, I'd never seen guards on the boat. This ship contained only Hindus fleeing Muslim controlled land. I did not understand why the police were on board. One of the guards explained. About a week before, on another boat full of Hindus leaving East Pakistan, militants on the shoreline wrapped the tips of arrows in cloth, doused them with gasoline, lit them, and shot the burning arrows toward the boat.

Upon hearing the guard's story, Mother would not allow me to leave the cabin to visit the small food counter. It didn't matter, my father told me, because the counter closed when they ran out of food. He asked my sister to unwrap the flat bread chapattis and halua cereal she brought from home.

In the past, when we had stopped at the next shallow water port, the fresh fruit vendors on their dinghies would row out to greet our boat. That didn't happen. We glided by the port without stopping. In any case, there were no dinghies to be seen, no vendors, and no fruit. I lay on the cot in our cabin, pressing against my stomach to make it stop growling. All I could think of was food: fish and cauliflower from the farmer's fresh stalls, pooris and naan, kulfi and molasses coconut dates our servants prepared. I consoled myself by picturing the food at the upcoming Khulna train station, samosas made by the old man with a curvy handlebar moustache.

The port adjacent to the train station neared. We gathered ourselves and stood by the gangplank opening. Pushing and shoving began, but we held tight to each other as we disembarked. Chaos reigned. Hundreds, maybe thousands, of Westbound Hindus, and eastbound Muslims spilled off the platform. In each case, people had left homes behind that would soon be occupied by strangers coming in to the country. The old man with the amazing moustache who sold samosas on the platform was nowhere to be seen.

In addition to the many armed railway police, northwestern Punjabi soldiers guarded the station. Father explained that ever since the Sepoy Mutiny almost one hundred years before the Partition, the Britishers did not trust the Bengalis. The Bengali regiment of soldiers had been disbanded and the local police kept order. Riots erupted in Khulna the day previous to our arrival. The neutral well trained Punjabi military were brought in to East Pakistan to help the local railway police restore order. I wondered if they helped or hurt. From a short distance away, we saw Father's legal assistant get butted in the head for trying to push through the crowd to get water. Blood ran through his hair, onto his face.

The soldiers guided the Hindus leaving the country into the station house to be searched. My sister dressed my niece like a young boy, and covered her face and head with a wrapped shawl. But the soldiers spotted the glint of her gold chain. One reached up to rip the necklace off my niece's neck, but my father acted faster to prevent him from touching her. With one swift continuous movement, Father tugged hard at the chain, then handed it to the soldier. In the process, the guard spotted and confiscated Father's opal ring. They searched our satchels for hidden silverware, but found none. They did not search the children.

We were allowed to go back out on the platform. I watched my father's eyes as he surreptitiously scanned the crowd. Before we'd gone inside the station house, we caught a brief glimpse of our servants and their children across the platform. Following the search, we looked again in the direction we'd last seen the servants, but they were nowhere in sight.

Father averted scrutiny by glancing down at his family when the soldiers looked his way. Soon he took my niece's hand and the rest of us followed them, snaking our way through the crowd. I saw flashbacks of black churning water, and held tight to Mother's hand.

I assumed we were looking for the servants, or my father's legal assistant who'd been struck with the gun, but instead Father stopped to talk with a distinguished rotund gentleman. The stranger wore a lunghi, a checkered sarong-like cloth around his waist, typical of a Bengali Muslim. From snippets of the conversation, I gathered he and Father were both judges. I heard no more of their brief exchange but Father looked shaken after the man walked away. Father told us to sit down on the floor of the platform to wait for the train.

My father still held tight to my niece's hand. He motioned her to sit directly in front of him. He instructed us three boys to flank my niece, and asked the three women to surround the four children. We were not to get up for any reason until the train arrived and he told us what car to board.

The train did not arrive on time, and it didn't arrive in the next hour, or the next hour either. My stomach hurt from hunger. The lights of the station were murky, the noise constant, and the stench disgusting. But more than what we could hear and see and smell, the din of fear seemed to grip everyone on the platform. Like electricity, it built to a crescendo, ready to jolt the massive amounts of exiles waiting for the train.

I wanted to stretch my legs. Father told me not to get up. He looked at me, and all around us, and leaned into our circle. He whispered, "I must tell you to muster your courage." Mother breathed, "Don't." When he lifted his eyes to her, she shook her head. He said, "They are old enough to understand."

Just then, we felt the low rattle of the rails, and the rush of the crowd rising to their feet. People were pushing once again, this time toward the tracks. The warning whistle of the train approaching the station did nothing to thwart the oncoming panic. Father told my niece to hold hands with her mother. He told all of us to stand, secure our few belongings, and stay together while we followed him.

He scanned the crowd once again, and lifted me up onto his shoulders. I made sure the contents of my deep pockets were secure. Father told me to search for his friend, the fat man he spoke with earlier, without calling attention to him or to us. Father grabbed my niece's free hand, and began walking toward a center car of the train.

From my high vantage point, I spotted the Muslim judge and directed Father to go straight ahead. I looked back and everyone followed close behind. We forged through the crazed crowd, and made our way to Father's friend at the entrance to our car. The judge pushed the crowd away to let us through, and nodded at the guard while slyly slipping him more than the customary note. We climbed aboard the dimly lit train.

Previously, I'd only traveled by train in a first class car or cabin. During the exodus, class distinctions on the trains did not exist. We made our way on and crowded onto two rows of narrow benches closely facing each other. Father directed us precisely where to sit. The four adults occupied the four corners, knees touching, with two children between each two adults. The trunk and our small satchels were on the floor between the children in the middle.

When I sat down, the seat of my pants felt wet. I stood, rubbing my bottom. My niece turned my back to the light from the station shining through the open window. She let out a stifled scream. "It's red," she whispered. "Red...blood." She then stood and felt her own seat. Someone nearby shouted, "There's blood on our seats. What happened?"

Father tried to calm us in the midst of the storm. "Sit. Don't call attention to yourself. It doesn't matter if your pants are wet. We are alive and together and we made it onto the train. Look at all those still left on the platform with their arms outstretched. Let the train pull out of the station. When we are on our way, I'll tell you what I know." We sat in stunned silence.

Passengers filled the aisles, stood between the cars, sat on top of the train. The train blew its whistle and left the station immediately after the doors closed. People on the platform screamed that someone had been pushed onto the tracks. But we did not stop.

The refugees sat and stood rigidly at first, then jostled to get comfortable for the ten hour trip. Babies cried. An old man with tear stained cheeks sat impassively, rocking and mumbling to himself while hugging a framed picture. My nephews fell asleep despite the commotion.

Father leaned in toward all of us. "I will tell you about the blood."

I felt afraid.

"Remember the man who helped us get on this train, the Muslim judge? He has been my friend for many years. When we spoke at the station, he told me the train would be late. He said there had been a problem at one of the previous stops along route, in Jessore."

Mother once again tried to dissuade him from telling us, but he said, "They need to know what is happening in their own lives." He took a deep breath.

"Jessore district was split down the middle in the Partition. Both sides were angry about the division of the area, and the situation became increasingly tense. Just like in Madaripur, militants incited fanatics to protest. Many trains came through the central station carrying refugees. The protest built to a frenzy and the crowd marched to the station. The militants overpowered the poor security at the station. When the last train stopped, the protesters boarded the train and slaughtered anyone in their path. Innocent men, women, children. The unarmed passengers were powerless to stop the pillage.

"When the murderers finished, they celebrated on the platform. The dead hung out of the windows, bloodied arms or legs dangling down the sides of the cars in futile efforts to escape. The protesters did not kill the conductor, who pulled out of the station.

"The engineer stopped the train at the next small rural station, the one before Khulna. The locals tended to the injured and buried the dead in a mass grave, then sloshed the train with buckets of water."

He paused. "Ajit, now you know why your pants are wet and stained with blood."

He then looked at my mother. "One more thing you must know. The people slaughtered were ... Muslims."

***

Black soot layered my face, my clothes, my soul.

I'd switched places with Mother in order to put my face by the open air window. The coal fired steam engine chugged away. In the waning moonlight, the flat rice paddies and farmlands became a backdrop for my shock and overload. Clickety-clack. Clickety-clack. I slumped against Mother's shoulder, lulled to sleep by the sounds and steady movement of the train. I dreamed of swimming in the pond, and flying kites, but woke with a start, seeing the black churning water below me.

The cool heavy air of dawn shivered me fully awake. Morning mist settled on the farmer's fields reminded me the world remained the same. But yet everything had changed. The glimpses of standing water between the rows precipitated my urge to use the bathroom. Except for a few chapattis and water from home we'd consumed for breakfast on the boat, I hadn't drunk or eaten during the previous day. Still the body's rhythms were at work.

While picking my way through the crowded aisles, I observed the passengers on the train. Many were dozing, a few snorting and snoring, gnats gathering on their drool. Others were awake, staring out the window, or digging in their belongings.

Mosquitos swarmed the filthy bathrooms. I peed into the hole that opened onto the tracks, hoping the train did not jerk. I didn't want to have to touch anything to steady myself, especially since there was no water with which to wash.

I made my way back to our benches. Mother unwrapped a heavy dresser mirror she'd swaddled with clothes in her satchel. I felt surprised that she would bother with grooming in our circumstances, but she said something about God and cleanliness. She told me to tidy up so the guards at the interim station would think we were decent human beings and leave us alone. She gave me dried orange peel to freshen my breath. I combed my thick wavy hair with Mother's comb, and dug the sleep from my eyes. I tucked in my shirt but there wasn't much I could do about my stained pants. My beloved *naughty boy* shoes, so named because they withstood the ravages of a rough naughty boy, were normally a source of pride, always spit and polished. Now my mouth felt so dry I could hardly spit, and I'd brought no shoe brush or polishing rag.

As I bent over lamenting the sorry state of my shoes, I glanced at the passengers next to us. They saw me staring at their food and offered a few biscuits to our family. Father asked them where they were from. This type of exchange happened throughout the car. People shared a bit of food, related their stories of escape and communicated plans for new lives in India.

Father told us the train would stop soon in Navaron, and he expected we'd disembark and go through security. I didn't understand why…we'd already been searched in Khulna. He told me we would pass through security in each district station until we crossed the border because different groups were in charge of each place. I instinctively put my hands in my pockets. Father saw me checking for the treasures, and his slight nod filled me with pride.

We pulled into the station, relatively small compared to Khulna. Except for the guards, the platform looked deserted. The armed railway police came aboard each car and instructed everyone to get off. People around us were frightened. No one wanted to be searched or detained, or lose their place on the train. By now, most had heard the rumors of the slaughter and were petrified of retaliation. Some only cooperated in disembarking when shown the rifle.

Passengers spilled out onto the platform, and were ushered into security lines. Along with the other passengers in the car, our family of eight was escorted to an area beyond the small station house. We followed the same routine: Father led the way, holding my niece's hand, with the rest of us grouped close behind. I spotted a wet patch in a dry dusty area, with a water pump standing in the middle of the spot. I'd drunk no water since yesterday. Dry biscuits from this morning stuck to the roof of my mouth. I tugged Father's shirt. "Look, there's water."

He said, "Sh, after we have gone through security, we will all go together to the pump."

I knew better than to make a scene, but wanted water. If we waited until we were searched, the pump might be mobbed, and we may not have an opportunity to get water before our train left. We couldn't miss the train, and I couldn't go without water another day.

Two soldiers began to conduct searches of passengers at the front of the line, while the railway policeman escort stood guard. I watched through the legs of those in front of me, and knew our turn was coming soon. I stood to the side of the line and peered ahead to see more clearly. The soldiers were patting down the men and teenage boys, and with smirks on their faces, the women and adolescent girls. They were confiscating valuables missed at the previous station. But then my heart stopped. They were also frisking children, little boys and girls. Mothers were forced to unwrap the blankets holding their tiny babies still in arms.

The water pump stood on my side of the line, the railway policeman escort on the opposite side of the line. This was my chance to bolt. I let go of Mother's hand, and ran like the wind, daring not to look back.

The handle required all of my strength to pump up and down before a gurgling rush came out of the spout. I tilted my head, put my mouth under the cool water, and drank as much as I could as fast as I could. I stood to catch my breath and mustered the courage to glance around. No one paid attention to me; the escort, the soldiers, no one. I pumped and drank to my heart's content.

By this time, passengers who were finished being searched gathered round me. My family stood closing their satchels and rearranging their clothes. They headed toward the pump. Everyone drank and filled containers until the guards directed us back toward the tracks. I pumped water for everyone until the last moment. I'd taken mental note of our compartment and sprinted toward the track in time to jump on the train before the doors shut.

Mother cried hysterically, repeating her nickname for me, "Monu, monu, monu, you are alive."

My sister admonished me. "Why did you run to the pump? You're not invincible, Ajit." My nephew chimed in, "How stupid. You are lucky the guards didn't see you. You might have gotten shot!"

"Next stop is the border," Father announced when everyone calmed down and the train rolled once again. "Bangaon is a few hours away." He didn't say anything to me about my run to the pump. He put his arms around me, pulling me close to him.

My niece observed us for a moment before speaking. "Ajit, you drank so much water that now you must squeeze your legs together so you don't have to go to that awful bathroom!" Everyone burst into laughter for the first time since leaving Madaripur.

Before long we arrived at the end of the train line, a small border town in East Pakistan. Following another cursory search of the adults, the guards told us to go. A long line of weary refugees, many carrying children or frail parents, with meager belongings on their backs or balanced on their heads, trudged along a dirt road. Father could find no coolies to help us carry our few belongings. We stepped to the side and opened our one trunk. We put clothes over the ones we already wore, and stuffed our small satchels with whatever else would fit. We left the trunk behind, with many half empty abandoned carriers of all kinds. We joined the procession of refugees into West Bengal.

About a quarter mile down the road, the line bunched together. Flying high above the crowds waved an Indian flag. Volunteers with baskets of molasses sweets and rice cake mooris were greeting the refugees. Intimidating but polite soldiers directed people to long registration lines at tables set up in the dirt. On this journey, Father had been forced to stand in lines, something to which he was not accustomed. He looked exhausted, dirty, disheveled. Never before had I viewed him as a human being, simply as my father. I felt sorry for him.

I caught sight of our servants standing across the way. I thought we'd seen the last of them at the train station in Khulna. They told us they'd managed to catch the next train to the border, and were preparing to take a bus to Palta to join relatives. We also spoke with father's legal assistant heading toward the medical tent to get his head cleaned and bandaged. The wound had not been tended to since the rifle butting incident in Khulna.

We made our way to the nearby Bangaon train station, where we boarded the train for Calcutta. Despite the crowded train, we finally felt safe and were able to rest. Father's sister, my older brother, and many cousins were at the Calcutta train station to greet us. Father hugged his sister and then broke down, crying for a long time.

I reached into my pockets and felt the stiff bristles of Father's shaving brush. I'd kept the coins lose in my pocket during most of the escape because I didn't want the guards to notice a rattle in a bulky pocket. After we'd passed through the guards at the train's last stop in East Pakistan, I grabbed Father's shaving brush out of our large trunk. I hid the gold coins inside the canister handle of the brush. Our family would no longer have the glories of the past, but we could survive.

***

A blinding ray of sun that pierced between the mountain peaks of Ethiopia brought me back to the present. I'd been lost in another world for a long time.

My sleeping seatmate's head nodded with each twist of the two-car train around the hairpin curves. Loneliness did not strike me often, but the dawn of the new day shining upon my sleep-deprived body brought with it a nostalgia filled longing. *I wish I had someone with whom to share my journey.*

Chatty Cathy

NINETEEN

PERSEVERANCE

Indiana 2003

My name is Constance.

I am the daughter of Patricia and Mark.

Patricia was the daughter of Clara and Ted.

Ted was the son of Lizzie and Paul. Paul was the son of Verena and Henry.

Henry was the son of Katharina and Gerhard.

In the surreal moments of my grandfather's graveside service, a small herd of cattle from the adjacent farm huddled nearby. They stood on the opposite side of the thin wire fence that separated their pasture from the country cemetery. The cows bowed their heads in solemn silence during the service, paying tribute to a worthy human life. The presence of the mourning animals deepened my sense of incomprehensibility of the meaning of life and death. My solitude felt so profound it seemed to be its own entity.

I looked down the row of gravestones on either side of my grandfather's granite marker, then further up the hill to the old section of the country cemetery. My ancestors lay beneath many of the headstones. They included my three times great grandfather who emigrated from Germany, his son whose first wife died of smallpox, and his grandson who built the old home-place overlooking the river valley. I couldn't help but wonder how I would be remembered by generations to come.

A few weeks before my grandfather dissolved into death late in his ninety-seventh year on earth, I entered a contest. I submitted a poem celebrating my family's diversity in hopes of winning a spa week in the Arizona desert. A pragmatic friend, who loved my poem, but often burst my bubble with the truth, told me I had no chance of winning. My life held nothing to set it apart, nothing marketable.

The remark hurt. I was struck by the fact that the artificial yardstick used by the world to measure a life's worth was misplaced, and often lead to unhappiness. Teenagers evaluated themselves based on beauty. Women measured themselves by how much they got done, in both personal and professional aspects of their lives. Men judged themselves by the career rung achieved. Couples assessed their lives by how much they'd acquired, or what they did for each other.

Deep within myself, I felt my worth in the connection to the cosmos. I'd experienced remarkable things on this mysterious journey of ongoing destiny. Visions of kaleidoscope colors and lovely light-filled blue spaces deep in my center. Synchronicity and illusions. Dreams of ancestors, and premonitions connecting me to the world beyond. Wondrous experiences of life and death that provided perspective and glimpses into the spiritual realm.

Under the open funeral tent, with death so fresh, I wondered how the world would define me upon my passing. My friend may have been correct, my life story was not worthy of winning a contest. The journey of a chubby Hoosier girl in the shadows who became a California dreamer didn't hold much fascination. Society would not recognize what I valued within myself, but may see one thing in my life that set me apart. In future generations, I anticipated being remembered as the one who married a man from India.

As my grandfather's coffin was lowered into the ground, I tried to block out the image of his body in the cold dark earth. I redirected my mind to the legacy of my marriage to an Eastern man. My descendants may wonder what compelled me to enter a mixed race union of two cultures in the 1970's. My answer to the future generations is simple. My marriage to an Indian man simply followed the flow of my life.

***

I was conceived during my parent's honeymoon in January of 1953, the year that marked the end of a one hundred year curse on our family. While in utero, my mother almost lost me in an auto accident on a bridge, but she lay down between the dried stalks in the cornfield to calm herself. In October, I was born in Stork Memorial Hospital, the first child in one hundred years of my lineage, free of the stigma of the curse.

***

My childhood doll, *Chatty Cathy*, had been the one thing on my wish list to Santa in 1960. My parents combed the stores on Christmas Eve, snagging the only Chatty left in our small Indiana town. Chatty was like me…a curly blond with hazel eyes and a button nose. She wore a little blue and white dress that matched her shoes. As a child, I pulled her cord again and again, never tiring of her eleven phrases.

If Chatty said, "Tell me a story," I could talk to her, tell her *my* story, without interruption or skipping embarrassing details. Once I tried to hit my sister because, in my mind, she hadn't done her share of the dishwashing duties. Instead of hitting her, my hand came down on the point of a long knife. Everyone else focused on my sister, but Chatty understood my trauma.

I was a chubby child. My parents' friends kept their pet's food in a bowl on the bottom shelf of the half-circle end cabinet. I snuck some of what looked like chocolate candy, then spit it out. The laughter rang in my ears. Later at home, I reached around Chatty's back between her shoulders and hooked my index finger in the round plastic ring attached to the cord that made her speak. Pulling the string until it would stretch no more, then letting go, Chatty exclaimed, "I'm hungry." I felt less guilty, free to be myself with her.

We both got old, and she won't talk to me anymore. Oh my dear Chatty Cathy, I wish time would rewind and I could sit with you once again under the Christmas tree. I'd mindlessly pull your cord until hearing your innocent and unconditional words of comfort, "I love you."

***

One weekend, we visited my grandparents' white clapboard home in the center of a romantic little town nestled below the monastery on the hill. Early Sunday morning, Grandma took me to her bedroom, reached into her top dresser drawer and handed me a birthday angel. She stood three inches tall, was dressed in a flowing white gown and carried a bouquet of marigolds on long

261

green stems. She wore a halo, gilded slippers and an October banner printed in capital gold letters.

After church, we left my maternal Grandma and Grandpa's house to travel the fifteen miles to my paternal Grandmother's. A meal waited for us on the table in the small house she shared with her single brother. We ate fried chicken, or fried squirrel if my uncles' hunting trips were successful. Side dishes were real mashed potatoes with milk gravy, and homemade canned green beans. To soak up the extra gravy on the plate, we used slices of greasy white bread which had previously layered the bottom of the meat serving dish. We ate soft orange cake with white icing for dessert.

At Christmas, she laid a tiny little wrapped present for each grandchild under a miniature tree on the sewing machine in the corner of her living room. We played six handed euchre at her round oak pedestaled table. Before we left, my father gave me money, and I ran across the street to the country store to buy Grandma a half-gallon of vanilla ice cream. We left Grandma on late Sunday afternoon, contentedly sitting in her rocking chair eating ice cream, with a spittoon on the floor next to her. She watched her black and white TV, above which hung a calendar picture of JFK tacked to the pink wall.

Our family began the drive home from southern Indiana in our '50's Chevy. Two joy riding teenagers rounded the blind curve, heading straight for us. My father swerved into the drainage ditch, avoiding a crash, but perhaps my angel saved us.

***

When my fingers pressed against my eyes after receiving communion, I experienced lovely kaleidoscope colors. As a ten year old child, I felt God in those colors. I begged Him to make me thin. That didn't happen. Then President Kennedy went to Dallas and returned in a box, and my understanding of the universe changed forever.

Women who wore black habits joined my birthday angel in the constant watch over me. At the beginning of sixth grade, I was assigned a beloved lay teacher. When her room became overcrowded, the principal asked me to permanently change to a split class taught by a nun. For the first time in my life I made my voice heard with those in authority. I did not want to give up my wonderful exciting teacher to be the good girl.

The nuns at our Catholic school wanted us to have minimal contact with boys. I actually felt shy and scared around boys in eighth grade, but the restriction prohibiting boys and girls at the same party seemed ridiculous. My parents must have agreed with me, or perhaps I neglected to tell them how the nuns felt. In any case, for my thirteenth birthday in eighth grade, I held the first boy-girl party in my class. How my teacher found out, I'll never know. One nun took me aside the Monday following my weekend party. Miss goodie two shoes, me, received a verbal thrashing. I didn't consider myself a rebel, but when the nun told me I had committed a sin, I inwardly laughed at the stupidity of her judgement. My mother taught me to be nice, so I don't think I told the nun my true feelings, but I might have.

My free thinker status solidified after our habited teacher assigned a paper entitled, "What Christianity Means to Me." My essay did not spout rhetoric. Instead I wrote, "…is the faith of Christianity the true one? or is it Buddhism or the Protestant faith or one of the other hundreds of faiths?" I believed in my haloed angel, but did not buy what the church told me. My beliefs flowed and made perfect sense to me. But they may have been considered radical thinking for a thirteen year old girl from a devout Catholic family in a small Indiana town.

***

In the cool summer evenings following eighth grade, I rode my bike on Hulman Street through a nondescript Midwestern neighborhood to my friend's house. I barely said hi to her parents before we descended the stairs to see what the mysterious Ouija would reveal.

We sat opposite each other, but close enough for our alternating knees to form a table on which we positioned the Ouija board. My fingertips lightly touched one side of the Ouija heart shaped indicator. At times it felt as if electricity connected my hand to the pointer. My friend's fingers spread out on the edge of the opposite side.

"Who am I going to marry?" I asked the Ouija. I'd asked this question previously, but Ouija's answers had been undecipherable.

The pointer darted to the M. My mind scanned a list of boys. Whose name started with M? First name or last name? I didn't have time to answer myself, needing to concentrate on the indicator racing from one letter to another, barely resting on each before whipping across the board. Ouija seemed irritated with my repetitive question. The speed made it difficult for me to be precise, but the answer to my question appeared to be a long unrecognizable word. I wondered if the long crazy name beginning with M belonged to a foreigner.

The next afternoon, I lay in our backyard staring at the heavens. I chose a grassy spot void of bee filled clover and away from the sandbox where my three younger siblings played. White puffy clouds drifted across the blue sky, at times obscuring the sun's rays. I spoke to my soul mate somewhere in the universe. "Whoever you are, and wherever you are in this world, I love you and want to share this life with you. Until that day comes, take care of yourself."

***

My parents were both teachers, and in the summer months, our family ran a small golf course and driving range. I started working in the clubhouse when ten years old, learned to play golf, and eventually gave golf lessons to middle aged ladies who couldn't swing their hips.

During high school, I shook Bobby Kennedy's hand a few months before Sirhan Sirhan murdered him in a hotel kitchen. Blurry films of Martin Luther King getting cut down on the balcony of a cheap motel played over and over on TV. I watched men land on the moon, and sang, *Where have all the Flowers Gone?* along with the footage of hippies at Woodstock.

I listened to Walter Cronkite give the Vietnam War death toll at the end of every nightly news broadcast. I cheered at ball games and danced at sock hops in the gym, but remained seated for the national anthem while those standing looked down on me on from both sides. The war made no sense to me. I supported our boys by wanting them home and not in a box in the ground like my friend's brother. I still startle to my core when I hear *Taps* and a gun salute.

I identified with the song *I can't get no Satisfaction*. One weekend at a party, I sat in my girlfriend's dimly lit converted garage with folding chairs set up around the edges of the room. Paired up couples made out to the Rolling Stones as they belted out their woes over and over again. I was with a guy I never met before, most likely another thirteen year old. I don't remember his face or name, and never saw him again. I have no idea if he got satisfaction or not because we never said a word to each other.

Not long after, my father asked me why I never seemed satisfied with my life. It had nothing to do with the make out session. The turbulent sixties changed anyone who lived through them. But I was not only changed, I was molded by those times. I spent my most impressionable years, from seven through seventeen, undergoing a barrage of external and internal changes including the election of a Catholic president, the threat of nuclear war, the Peace Corps, assassinations of three beloved men, the beginning of civil rights and women's lib, the Vietnam War, the music of Woodstock, hippies, student protests, and a man on the moon. Factor in adolescence and high school. I did not wish my life away, but I certainly grew up with the dissatisfaction of the world.

***

Indiana University exploded my sheltered little world. My first roommate came from New York to IU to become a professional orchestral musician. I'd never met a Jewish girl, let alone someone who played the flute in a symphony. She seemed stuck up to me, but I must have seemed like a country hick to her. I felt alone, and terribly missed my baby brother and family back home.

I listened to Judy Collins and saw Vietnam War protests in the meadow. Smoked pot and walked three blocks to satisfy the craving for Baskin Robbins blueberry cheesecake ice cream. Learned about women's lib and voted in a presidential election. Worked at McDonald's and in the library. Studied speech therapy and psychology and learned to question the semantics guiding my beliefs. Rejected Catholicism and lost my virginity.

Fuck. I'd barely heard the word, let alone said it. My friends seemed determined to liberate me. Upon their dare, I stood at the ninth floor window of my dorm room, and shouted the forbidden gem across the campus.

Since then, in my thirty-five years as a Speech-Language Pathologist working with stroke victims, I've heard many patients yell out expletives. Some patients recognized their words after the utterance, but were unable to stop themselves. Others had no clue they were using foul language. If they wanted to tell me, "I want a piece of toast", they might say, "Shit shit shit shit shit shit," in the melodic intonation characteristic of a perfectly logical sentence. Horrified families often told me they'd never heard cussing cross the lips of their gentle grandmothers. That was probably true, but I wondered if the little old women had often cussed under their breaths.

Following graduation with a master's from Indiana University, I landed my first job as a Speech Pathologist in a tiny little town in Kansas. I worked in a facility for the severely developmentally disabled, at first not having a clue as to what to do. Formerly infamous as an institution for the worst cases, the school reinvented itself into a training center on the cutting edge of treatment. My definition of the human species expanded exponentially, resulting in an acceptance of all people on the basis of their human status, not on what they could do. I read and espoused the philosophy we all do the best we can based on what we know at the time.

***

During my early twenties, I canoed down a flood stage river in the Ozarks. Our party came upon an emergency scene in which two drowned young people lay trapped beneath an overturned canoe caught in a logjam. Emergency crews were waiting for the arrival of a helicopter to lift the canoe in order to remove the bodies. We portaged around the accident and climbed back in our canoe to continue our journey.

Within minutes, our boat capsized, and threw me into the white water rapids. The current carried me through a patch of small jagged rocks breaking the surface of the water, and straight toward a large rock. Although not a strong swimmer, adrenaline kicked in and I swam to the bank, clawing my way onto a small spot of bare solid ground.

Downriver, on the opposite shore, I could see the leader of our group, a curly headed daredevil, waving wildly to me. The canoe and my other friends were near him. The leader yelled and frantically waved his arms to motion me to come to him. *I can't jump in that river. No way.* The bank cut straight into the solid earth, without any semblance of a navigable path hugging the shore on my side. Even if I could make my way through the thick underbrush and rugged forests behind me, country roads were rare in the back woods Ozarks bluffs.

I looked toward the leader with knowledge I had no other choice. I felt a rush of fear, and a surge of power propelling me forward. I jumped back into the raging waters and swam with utter determination across the current of the wide treacherous river. The little white caplets of the fast running river popped up to cheer me on. I neared closer to shore, but missed the branch the leader held out to me. Dodging roots of the trees in symbiosis with the river, he ran along the riverbank extending the limb until I finally grabbed hold.

***

I needed to escape the small Kansas town. At age twenty-four, I accepted a job in Corpus Christi, Texas near a friend. I moved to Ocean Drive by a stone step breakwater fronting the bay. One winter weekend, I walked alone along the concrete bottom step of the breakwater. I slid on the wet moss and almost slipped into the ocean, unnoticed. Later, while walking the warm sands of Padre Island beach, I thought about my life and past loves. I defined my want, someone I could grow with.

One night, I worked late in my office preparing for a state inspection. The research psychologist I'd previously met in staff meetings saw my light and popped in to say hello. He reintroduced himself to me, not as Dr. Mukherjee, but as Ajit. His light brown skin looked as smooth as velvet. His eyes twinkled, and the gap between his front teeth did not distract from the appeal of his laughter.

The universe responded. Synchronicity had been validated. I found where I belonged.

***

Ajit was thirty-eight years old. He was born in India, and had lived in England, Ethiopia, Columbia and Alabama before moving to Texas. After a few dates, his eyes met mine in the top floor restaurant at the La Quinta Hotel. We were a May to December romance, a brown and white romance, an old world bachelor with an independent woman romance. Colleagues seemed surprised and intrigued by our relationship.

From our perspective, we were a good match. Despite my preference for tall blonde men, Ajit's intelligence and sense of humor attracted me. We shared our work and held similar political views. We enjoyed restaurants, movies, sports and travel together. He was raised a Hindu, but attended a westernized Jesuit boarding school in the Himalayas. I considered myself spiritual in the cosmic perspective, but not religious. Spiritually, we were both everything and nothing.

More than the tangibles, I loved the mystery of him. The long intricate Bengali ragas he sang while washing the dishes. The Sanskrit symbol 'om' he wrote with his index finger on the fogged up bathroom window following his long morning shower. The fact that he would not swat at a fly, but let me use the flyswatter instead, risking *my* karma in the process. I did not need to change for him, nor he for me. We felt as if we belonged together.

On one of our first dates, Ajit read my palm, my Line of Destiny, although he didn't share all of the information with me at the time. I moved in to his place, a third floor apartment overlooking the bay waters, keeping my own apartment just in case. But the outcome of our relationship never really stood in doubt. Ajit flew home to India during the winter break. He showed his family a kodachrome square slide of me sitting in a wicker king chair. He told me that his mother, Nanibala, thought I looked like Queen Victoria. She didn't object to the cross cultural issues, or the love marriage. She never again tried to arrange a match for Ajit.

We missed each other during the holidays. Upon his return, we felt solid. During a road trip, Ajit wasted no time in asking me to marry him. I called my Midwestern parents to tell them about Ajit. After hearing of my engagement to an Indian man fourteen years my senior, my parents drove to Texas on spring vacation, the first chance they could get away. I needn't have been concerned; they liked him from the start.

A year later, California beckoned. We hitched a U-Haul to Ajit's silver Cutlass Supreme and moved to the west coast to pursue dreams and adventures. We adored our California lives, snuggled in a private love nest in the beauty of the Napa Valley. On a Friday afternoon in December, we dressed in our best clothes and climbed into my orange Datsun. I drove and sang *Gonna get Married*. Ajit sang a child's Indian folk tune, repeating the joyous chorus many times over.

We married in the Frank Lloyd Wright designed Marin County courthouse in December 1978. Eight friends helped us celebrate with cheesecake and individual bottles of champagne. We smoked pipes, Ajit's filled with cognac flavored tobacco and everyone else's with pot. From our Sausalito suite, we sat enchanted by the twinkling lights of San Francisco across the bay, capped by the stars above. We felt mesmerized by our rare and beautiful love, and promised each other that after this life, we would meet on Orion, where the universe began, to share the next.

***

At the peak of my orgasm, a lotus unfolded in the deepest center of my being. The crimson and purplish flower appeared, without a stem, devoid of background. Muted orange and yellow velvety soft striations blended into the base of each petal. The flower began its unfolding beyond the bud stage, partially open. The time lapsed opening did not come in a burst, nor did it proceed in slow motion, but rather in symphony with my body's release. Visions are not only seen, they are felt. I felt wonder, and bliss.

I told Ajit the next morning during breakfast. "Last night, at the height of my orgasm, something happened that never happened before."

"What's that?"

"In my mind's eye, I saw a lovely lotus unfold."

He stared at the Saturday edition of the San Francisco Chronicle spread out on the table in front of him. He took a sip of coffee, a new flavor we were tasting. Then he looked up at me.

"You saw a lotus unfold while we made love?"

"Yes."

His face looked pale in comparison to its normal rich bronzed tone. His entire body took a deeper breath than he needed to speak the words.

"Connie, you are pregnant."

I was taken aback. There appeared to be no reason to believe him. I teased Ajit about being an Indian guru, but I'd not seen evidence of special powers a mystic would possess. My monthly flow tended to be irregular and I had no symptoms of pregnancy. I carried on my usual routine of life. After forty-five days without a period, I went in for a urine pregnancy test. The results came back negative.

In retrospect, I should have known the reading was false. I have little visual artistic talent, but had taken a few painting courses in local community colleges. For the first and only time in my life, I felt compelled to paint abstract swirly things, somehow sexual yet spiritual in form.

We bought our first home, a little Cotswold Cottage near a park in Sacramento. Ajit and I lifted boxes and couches onto the U-Haul, drove to our new home, and unpacked the truck. We tried the neighborhood Chinese restaurant and I got nauseous after eating the spicy kimchee. I made an appointment with an OB/GYN. The doctor took one look at me splayed in the stirrups, and said "You are three months pregnant." The nurse extended her hand to help me rise up to stare at him.

On the way home, the radio aptly played *The Way we Were*. I dug into the glove box and broke in half a stale pack of cigarettes I'd stashed to smoke at parties. Ajit came home from work, and I told him I was three months pregnant. We looked at each other in shock, trying to absorb the life changing news.

When we first met, my husband told me the mole on my chest, between the axis and my heart in the Sagittarius region, meant good luck. The unfolding lotus was a testament to our love, and the wonder of the universe. We felt awe.

***

Life is impossible to figure out, I don't care who you are, or where you are, or what you are. No one really knows any more about life than anyone else. We enjoy the blue sky above and the ocean shimmering silver in the sun. We flow with our destiny and if we are lucky, find where we belong. We live amazing stories, one life at a time. And we leave those that follow wondering who we really were.

EPILOGUE

Not the End

California 2036
My name is Pria.
I am the daughter of Misha,
and the granddaughter of Constance and Ajit.
I am the great granddaughter of Pat and Mark,
Jitendra and Nanibala, and Motindra and Lily.
I am the 2x great granddaughter of Clara and Ted,
and Kumar and Soudamoni.
I am the 3x great granddaughter of Lizzie and Paul,
and Avoya and Shyamsundari.
I am the 4x great granddaughter of Verena and Henry,
and Durga Charan and Padma.
I am the 5x great granddaughter of Katharina and Gerhard,
and Ram Sundar, Shanti, and Daya.

In the blue cottage by the sea, I positioned my tea cup on its saucer. I opened the thick manuscript to the first story. A pictured heirloom from Grandmother's china cabinet accompanied the chapter. I visited an ancestor from a place and time I'd never known. I spent the day walking on the beach, writing, and watching the orange sun slide behind the horizon, all the while allowing Nanibala's Belief to permeate my very being.

Grandmother's writing became my world. I read her manuscript, one chapter each morning. On the nineteenth day, I prepared to read the last of her stories, Perseverance. A golden note stuck to the top of the page read, *A defining moment is one which is out of your control…you have no real choice.* I promised myself to think more about those words later in the day.

My name is Constance. I was confused. It didn't make sense that Grandmother included her own story. She'd told me the manuscript contained stories about our ancestors, those that came before us, not those living on earth. An ever so slight sensation on the top of my head distracted me. I raised my hand to swish away whatever insect had decided to visit, then continued reading. *I am the...* The barely perceptible pressure on my head reasserted itself, this time as if a hovering hand cupped my crown. In the back of my mind, a whispered but clear voice spoke. "Take care of yourself."

As the words of her chapter slipped across the page, a feeling of peace came over me. I walked outside to sit on the deck steps and watch the waves. The sound of a car engine alerted me someone was approaching the cabin. I peeked around the side of the house in time to see my father drive up and open the door.

"Hi Dad! What a nice surprise!" He didn't say anything nor did he immediately try to get out of the car. Instead he sat in the seat with shoulders slumped forward. He took a breath before he finally looked up at me. His fallen face was marked by puffy eyes.

"It's your grandmother, Pria."

"Oh no, Dad. Don't tell me... please."

"She didn't come out to the patio this morning. I approached the eerily quiet casita and unlocked the door. Your grandmother looked peaceful lying in bed. She had died in her sleep."

Father climbed out of the car, slowly and deliberately, as if he'd aged ten years since the last time we were together. I hugged him as tight as he hugged me, each of us holding the other up to keep from buckling to the ground. We sobbed, our bodies racking with the shock of loss.

Father loosened his hold. "I'm sad she died alone, but it didn't look as if she suffered. Only one thing seemed unusual. She clutched a blue satin ribbon in her hands."

I had questioned why Grandmother wrote about herself when she was still living on this earth. I now knew the answer. At the time I read her story earlier that morning, she had already become an ancestor. A chill ran through me. My grandmother had whispered, "Take care of yourself."

We spread Grandmother's ashes at sea, near the island where Grandfather's remains dissolved into the Pacific waters. I thought about what she'd told me all those years ago. Grandfather's soul's mission had been accomplished, therefore he'd completed his time on earth. During the busy times of my life, her words often hid in the back of my mind, the haze of my fabric. With my grandmother now gone, I wondered what her soul's mission had been...and what mine was.

***

Returning to live in the girlish bedroom of my childhood home did not comfort me. A week after Grandmother's death, my brothers returned to college, my parents to work. Since my first trip to the butterfly grove with my grandmother, I believed the essence of the departed lived on. But that did not prevent me from the deep grief of missing those I loved and lost. They could no longer smile at me or hug me, nor impart words of wisdom.

My upstairs window looked out onto our backyard. The casita in the corner under the shadow of the Dehradun pines had not changed, making it difficult for me to believe my grandmother was really gone. I went downstairs, took the stone path across the yard, and entered the casita. With the exception of the housekeepers, no one had spent much time in the little home since Grandma's passing. The space felt lonely, made even more so by the smell of her baby powder which still permeated the room.

I sat on the side edge of Grandmother's bed feeling close to her, knowing she died in its warmth. I slowly slid open the top drawer of her nightstand, and was gripped by what I found. Wound in a neat little bundle lay the blue satin ribbon that had been tied around the manuscript box. Grandmother held it in her hand the night she died. The housekeepers must have found it while changing the sheets. I intertwined the ribbon through my fingers, laid across the bed and wept before falling into a deep dream-filled sleep.

A young woman faced away from me, long blond tresses flowing down her back. She slipped into a rowboat and magically glided away. Movement of the oars created parallel lines in the silky smooth water. She eased into song, rowing in time with the melody's rhythm.

...Life is just a dream...Life is just a dream...Life is just a dream.

"Where are you going?" I cried.

She didn't answer, nor turn around. Instead she continued slow steady strokes, eventually disappearing into the mist rising off the pond.

Upon waking, the phrase, *Life is just a dream,* echoed through my mind. Reviewing the mental images in my half sleep state, I reached into the drawer to grab a pen and a notepad. I hurried to scribble down my dream recollections before they left me. I tore out the page and replaced the pad of paper in the nightstand drawer. I came across my grandmother's journal.

On the cover, the Indian goddess Lakshmi sat in meditation pose on a lotus. My grandmother liked to collect all things lotus: knick knacks, candles, books. She mysteriously explained the beautiful flower arose from murky waters, much like the human soul. I wanted to look inside Grandmother's journal, to understand her mind and heart, perhaps *her* soul. Yet I didn't want to feel that I was invading her privacy. I decided to compromise. As I often did with books, I opened to a random page in hopes of finding a treasure.

> *High on a green knobbed hill that once belonged to my ancestors, the goldfish flitted in the pond. The tiny town nestled in a mystical valley below, as if a mirage from a fairy tale. There I spent summer nights feeling the breeze through the wide open windows in the upstairs bedroom of my grandparent's home. In the early morn, the abbey bells rang out from the twin spired church, prompting me to linger in bed until the final note rang softly in my ears.*
>
> *I want to give the same feeling of peace to Pria.*

Closing the journal, my tears dropped onto Lakshmi's face. *Life is just a dream* still rang in my ears. I caressed the cover, gently placed the journal back in the nightstand and tried to collect my thoughts. The blue satin ribbon which I'd intertwined through my fingers had slipped off of my hand and onto the bed. I wound it round and round before replacing it in the drawer.

Feeling overwhelmed with surreal emotions, I needed a breath of fresh air. I brushed past the china cabinet, glancing at its unlit treasures. Without touching the switch, its lights mysteriously came on, illuminating the heirlooms. My shoulders leaned back into a deep breath of recognition. Ignoring it any longer was impossible. The ancestors were talking to me.

Trembling with anticipation, I opened the cabinet doors, recognizing the individual keepsakes in Grandmother's stories. I reached for the treasure from the first story. Urbashi, the green clay statue of the dancing girl, evoked the voice of Ram Sundar. I touched the German cup, which called forth Katharina's presence. One after another, the voices of my ancestors spoke through the things they once owned, just as my grandmother told me she'd experienced.

I reached up to turn off the cabinet light switch, and spotted Chatty Cathy on her perch atop the cabinet. She no longer talked when her string was pulled, but I distinctly heard her voice saying, "Tell me a story." I turned off the cabinet lights, lost in another world, and returned to the main house.

***

Early the next morning, I began to reread my Grandmother's stories. When she first shared the manuscript with me, she'd revealed the stories were sparked by my paternal great Grandmother's belief...a pet that comes to you in an unusual way is an ancestor. I asked Grandma which ancestor she thought had been reincarnated into their beloved pet. She said she had some romantic notions who it might be, but of course she didn't know nor did she feel it was important. The significant thing, she said, was that by reading the ancestor's stories, I would learn what I needed to know.

The sticky note attached to the front page of Grandma's story came to mind. *A defining moment is one which is out of your control...you have no real choice.* I realized that although each ancestor possessed their own special virtue, in their defining moment, every one displayed courage to follow the authentic within them.

Ram Sundar found courage to pursue having a son, though he dearly loved his first wife. Katharina displayed courage when she left her homeland and her identity to provide for her family. Durga Charan discovered the courage to save his sister from sati, and Sister Angie in her unwavering belief that God called her. Sophie seized the courage to leave her abusive brother, and Avoya to kill the man eating tiger. Philomena courageously ate soup with her children on her dying day, and Verena mustered the courage to protect her child despite the personal cost. Kumar demonstrated the courage to love a Muslim girl, and Lizzie found the courage to think for herself. Lily summoned the courage to give up her child to a better life and Motindra displayed the courage to fight for his country. Clara showed the courage to return for love. Jitendra mustered the courage to provide for his family and those who needed him, and Nanibala showed the courage to love all forms of life. Patricia demonstrated the courage to endure pain with grace and Mark accepted the courage to recognize his time to die. Ajit developed the courage to carry the coins while fleeing for his life, and Grandmother summoned the courage to keep her heart and spirit open to the universe.

The ancestors spoke to me, as they had my grandmother. No real choice existed but to listen. I drew courage from them to be true to my authentic self, to find where I belonged.

In the following months, I finished my writing degree, then traveled to the Midwest to feel my grandmother's presence in the hills of southern Indiana.

I also began preparations for a December trip to Bangladesh. The country had been the state of Bengal in Northeast India during my grandfather's time. In Grandmother's notes, a blurry photo of an ancient Indian temple was identified as the arched entrance gate to my grandfather's childhood home. I wanted to see the ruins of that sacred place, and imagine Grandfather's voice on the wind, singing classical Indian ragas that soothed the soul.

What brought me the most joy and peace was having my grandmother's manuscript published. After carefully cutting open the box containing the first copy, my tears splattered on the front cover. I flipped the book over and smiled at the sight of my grandmother's picture beaming at me. Opening to the epigraph page, I once again read, *The goal of all life is spiritual wisdom.* —*Bhagavad Gita.*

I hadn't really understood until now.

AFTERWORD

Unfolding

In mid-January of 2004, my son, Misha, burst through the front entrance. "I'm home…and I brought a new friend with me!"

Ajit, my husband, emerged through the double French doors from the master bedroom into the living area. A shiny, black, fifty-pound puppy sprinted toward him, wagging her tail and jumping on the surprised man. She pushed her front paws off Ajit's chest, lifted her nose to sniff the air and bounded through the house with newfound freedom.

The dog darted into the great room toward me. I lay stretched out on the couch following a long day of work. She planted a kiss, a lightning-quick lick, on my lips, causing me to cringe, then giggle. I sat up, wiping the wetness from my mouth. The pup stood by and grinned in satisfaction.

Misha, laughing with delight, entered the room and plopped on the carpet in front of the TV. He gestured and called for his friend to come join him.

"I must admit, she's really cute," Ajit said, settling into his favorite chair.

"What's her name?" I asked.

Our son was generally not one to waste words in small talk. But in the gentle world of petting his new puppy, he began his story.

"The shelter named her Senta. I'm changing her name to Madison…like the Avenue in New York City. I'll call her Maddie for short."

"How did you find her?" I said.

"I visited a couple of shelters this past week and played with one other dog, but didn't feel she was the one. Today I stopped at Walnut Street Rescue, and spotted a cute puppy on my first walk between the cages. Senta's black coat looked so soft and cuddly. She showed white markings on her underside, and one resembled my lucky number seven. When I said, 'Hi, Girl,' she cocked her head first to one side, then the other. Her tail thumped the floor and she whined at me.

A shelter staff member stopped beside me. 'Ah, the German Shepherd whine. You know, they are the only breed that can really talk in that way. Senta must like you.' The worker extended the back of her hand through the bars and Senta slowly licked her fingers. The girl excused herself to return to duties, but she turned back and added, 'In case you haven't noticed, Senta is special. She seems to understand human emotions.'

A male staff member came into the hall from the doorway opposite where the girl exited. He noticed me staring into the cage. He said, 'It's unfortunate not many people want big black hairy dogs. Senta's been here over the limit of six months, but the staff likes and respects her, so we stretched her time. Unfortunately, if no one adopts her in the next few days, we'll have to put her down.'

I led the puppy to the patchy grass in the fenced lot. She didn't ignore me, nor clamor for treats. Instead she sat at my feet and looked into my eyes, just like she is now. I feel a connection with her."

Ajit and I had been staring at Maddie while Misha told his story. Above the dog's big brown eyes, golden spots shaped like apostrophes hugged both inner corners of her brows. The decoy eyes could easily have been mistaken for real eyes if the light were dim. With Misha's words in mind, I thought the evolution of Maddie into a being with two sets of eyes, an awake set and an asleep set, might be more than coincidence.

"The eyes are the windows to the soul," I said.

"All I know, Mom, is in some weird way, I feel like she saved me."

The puppy crouched down on all fours, intently following the stuffed squeaky toy Misha waved high in the air. Madison barked and jumped up toward the toy, then chased her tail in circles before crouching to restart the sequence. Ajit, Misha and I laughed like children…and Madison beamed her own shiny white smile. Our family of three had become a family of four.

***

Misha's identity the previous few years had been tied to law school. But shortly into his first semester in New York City, Misha discovered law school wasn't meant for him. He lost his identity, much like his father when he left

India. Ajit and I moved our only child back home to Indiana over the long Thanksgiving weekend.

One evening after arriving home, the three of us sat in front of the TV. In what seemed like an offhand comment, Misha said, "I've often regretted growing up without a dog."

"We worked, and moved. All the time," I defended. "Besides, the only dogs I ever knew were my father's outside hunting dogs. We never owned an indoor pet, except a goldfish."

Without hesitation, Ajit added, "I would have become too attached."

Misha shifted in his chair, and stared out the window. "When I was ten and we visited our family in India, I saw lots of skinny stray dogs with curled up tails on the streets. Most didn't pay attention to me, but one black pup followed me everywhere. On the morning of our return flight to the U.S., the little dog waited for me at the yard gate to play. I hugged him and told him he couldn't go home with me on the airplane. He needed to stay in India."

Taking a deep breath, Misha continued. "He licked the tears off my face. It broke my heart. Mom, Dad, I've wanted a dog forever. And now I plan to get one."

Ajit and I looked at each other, our objections obliterated.

***

Maddie made each of us more of ourselves. She played with Misha, took walks with Ajit, and snuggled with me. She demonstrated love equally and unconditionally in a way we each needed, yet she brought our family closer together.

The grad program at IU accepted Misha for fall admission. He and Madison moved to a downtown condo near campus for the school year. Three flights of narrow steep stairs led to the cramped apartment. Ajit and I felt sad picturing Maddie peering out of the only window at a brick wall. After I wrapped up my day at the hospital, I'd visit Maddie to take her out for long walks in the park. On weekends and holidays, we'd become a family of four again. Misha finished grad school in May, and moved back into his old room at home.

A few weeks later, he came to us. "Mom and Dad, there are no good jobs around here. Uncle Lou told me I could stay with him in LA while looking for work there."

I tried to keep my emotions in check. "We'll miss you, but you have to live your life."

"What about Maddie?" Misha said.

Ajit didn't hesitate. "We'll take care of her until you get settled."

On a scorching Midwest summer morning, Misha backed out of the driveway, waving to me crying in the garage. The world waited for him, two thousand miles away from us. All the goodbyes leading to this one were just practice. In the study, Ajit stared at the woods behind the house, shedding his tears less visibly, while stroking Maddie to comfort them both.

***

As Ajit himself predicted, he became increasingly attached to Maddie. And to my surprise, so did I. We kept reminding ourselves the puppy belonged to Misha, and soon she would be with him, far away. In September, before the leaves began to turn, or the snow began to fly, we drove Maddie across America. She sat in the rear seat of the Volvo, watching the scenery unfold. She romped with us in the parks of Lawrence and Boulder.

After five days, we finally arrived in LA. We parked at the curb in front of Misha's rented Westside home, specifically chosen for its fenced backyard. When he opened the front door, Maddie's tail launched into a circle wag, and she leapt out of the car running straight for the house. The pup grinned from ear to ear, pink tongue protruding, sporting a hockey smile with a missing lower tooth. She whined, talked, and panted with excitement. For hours, she pranced and played, and licked her savior relentlessly.

We enjoyed exploring the beaches and parks of LA together, but at the house, Maddie seemed constantly on edge, never fully relaxed. One of Misha's roommates owned a big dog that considered the space her own territory. The other roommate called Maddie a bitch. In response, Maddie squatted on the rug in front of him, something she'd previously never done.

Misha, Ajit and I realized the dream of Misha and Maddie together in LA was not to be. Misha's commute and long work hours required he would often be away from the house. At those times, the roommates expected that Maddie be pent up inside Misha's room. We could not bear the thought that she would remain isolated for twelve hours a day, just as she had been at the pound, waiting for someone she loved. Few words were spoken in the most difficult family conversation we ever held. We choked on the emotions of what we knew needed to be done.

Maddie jumped back in the Volvo for the return trip to Indiana, leaving Misha alone and brokenhearted. His dog...and his parents were gone. He remembered the dog in India, only this time Misha stayed behind.

Ajit and I were devastated for our son. We drove to Vegas in heavy silence, cancelled the reservation at a fancy hotel that refused dogs, and stayed in a dingy room at a cheap motel across from the airport. During our first visit to the glitzy city, we drove with Maddie up and down the strip, never getting out of the car, except to run in for takeout at the Chinese express.

We took a long scenic route home through five western national parks. I wondered if Maddie dreamed of Misha as she slept. Her eyes stayed half open, and rolled back until only the whites showed. She gave a muffled bark, her stomach jerked, and legs moved as if running with the wind.

***

Not long after we returned to Indiana from our cross country trip, a wren flew into our home's open door toward the high sunrise window of the vestibule. The bird hit the window, and stunned, fell to the floor. I feared the worst when Maddie sprinted to it. To my astonishment, she whined, cradled the semiconscious bird in her open mouth, and carried the creature out to the middle of the backyard. She released the wren onto the grass, and nudged the bird until it flew away unharmed.

Following dinner, Ajit and I relaxed at the round kitchen table, eating dessert. Our beloved puppy sat on the floor between us, waiting for little tastes of human food.

I said, "Maddie's compassion amazes me. She seems like a wise old soul."

"Maybe she is. My mother, Nanibala, believed that if a pet comes to you in an unusual way, it is an ancestor," Ajit said.

"An ancestor? Do all Hindus believe the same thing?"

"Not necessarily."

"Do you believe it?"

"Maddie acts like a human sometimes."

"Yes, I agree, but do you think she's an ancestor?"

"I'm starting to believe it."

The next evening, I asked Ajit, "Do you think we got Maddie in an unusual way?"

Ajit didn't blink. "It's not uncommon for parents to inherit their children's dogs, but look at Maddie's life. She narrowly escaped death. We drove her across the country to Misha, and brought her all the way back. I think those things are unusual."

"So…" I said, half-seriously, "which ancestor is Maddie? One of yours from India, or mine from Indiana?"

My mind had been opened. From that day forward, Ajit and I often discussed which ancestor Maddie might have been. Our pet gave Ajit the honor of validation of his inherited beliefs. With no fixed belief, Maddie further facilitated my exploration of the infinite. Many mornings, I sat in my pajamas in a zero-gravity chair on the back deck overlooking the woods thinking about Nanibala's belief.

I peeked into Ajit's eastern and my western roots, and attempted to discern the ancestors' true nature through the defining moments of their lives. Their virtues and vices became clear to me. I felt compelled to write the accounts in Misha's old crimson and gold IU notebook. Nanibala's belief threaded together generations of parallel lives on opposite sides of the earth.

***

On a Monday night in early December, my parents and sister were headed to a basketball game. An oncoming car holding three exchange students slid on black ice and T-boned their car. I held my father's hand in the trauma center as he exited this world. My mother broke her neck and both legs, and my sister's pelvis cracked against the steering wheel. In the aftermath of the accident, my attention focused on rebuilding lives…my mother's, my family's, my own. The IU notebook gathered dust under piles of insurance papers.

During the next year, Misha flew home on holidays. After his grandmother and aunt recovered, Misha begged Ajit and me to move to California with Madison. We had toyed with the idea ever since Misha left for Los Angeles.

Ajit's 70th birthday approached. My father had slipped away in one breath. I could not ignore the fact that life is shockingly short.

Ajit and I flew to California, and bought a Ventura County foreclosure on our first and only day of searching. Our Indiana house sold in one day. The move seemed meant to be. We resigned from our jobs, weeded through our material possessions, and wrapped up our Indiana lives. Maddie bounded outside and ran free in the big fenced backyard for the last time. With tears of nostalgia clouding my vision, we settled into the Volvo. We drove cross country once more, this time knowing our family would be living close to each other.

When we reached our new condo, the first thing I unpacked was my old IU notebook. Again, the stories of ancestors began unfolding before my eyes. Nanibala's Belief led me on a wonderful journey, and my sincere hope is that you have enjoyed traveling along with me.

Namaste. May the peace within me honor the peace within you.

Constance

Made in the USA
Lexington, KY
25 May 2015